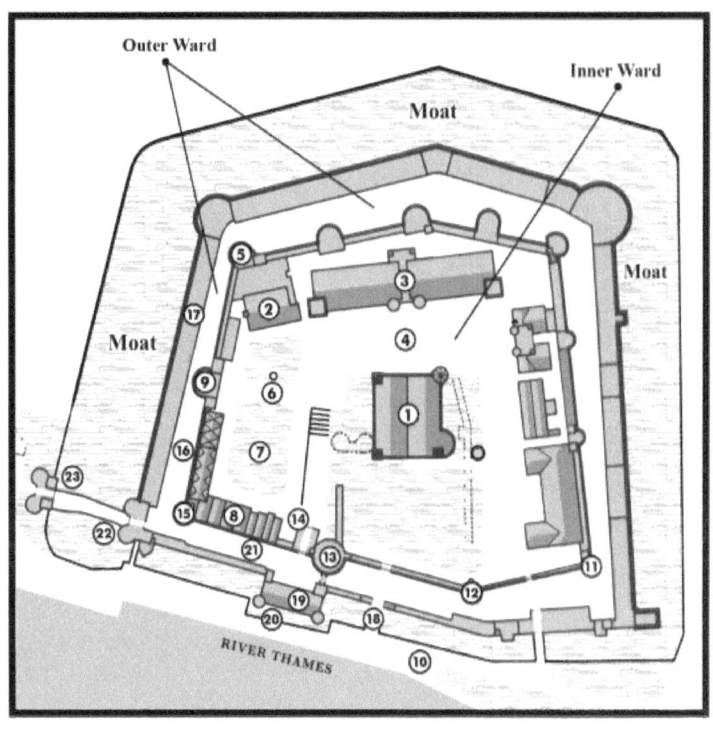

Outer Ward

Inner Ward

Moat

Moat

Moat

RIVER THAMES

1. White Tower
2. Chapel of St. Peter Ad Vincula
3. Waterloo Barracks (jewel vault)
4. Parade Ground
5. Devereux Tower
6. Scaffold site
7. Tower green
8. Queen's house
9. Beauchamp Tower
10. Tower wharf
11. Salt Tower
12. Lanthorn Tower
13. Wakefield Tower
14. Bloody Tower
15. Bell Tower
16. Mint Street
17. Casemates (Yeoman Warder lodgings)
18. Henry III Watergate
19. St. Thomas Tower
20. Traitors Gate
21. Water Lane
22. Byward Tower (entrance)
23. Middle Tower (checkpoint)

Fatal Castle

David Boito

Published by Ideafeast Books, 2025.

FATAL CASTLE

First edition. October 31, 2025.

Written by David Boito.

Dedicated to those who protect and preserve historic relics for future generations.

The Gift

Fall 1850

Queen Victoria peered out the window. A black fog of particulates clouded the London sky. Factory stacks and residential chimneys belched smoke into the cool air. An ornate carriage navigated the haze, passing the Royal Mews and Marble Arch on its way to Buckingham Palace. Flags flew from poles on each side of the carriage: the British Union Jack surrounded by red and white stripes. This was the emblem of the East India Company (EIC). The carriage came to a stop at the palace entrance.

Two officers of the EIC disembarked. They wore red coats, white pantaloons, gold epaulets and shiny boots. They strode to the back of the carriage and pulled out an iron box. It was a cross between a steamer trunk and a safe, the type of container the Wells Fargo stagecoach used to cart gold from bank to bank across the Wild West.

Royal Palace Guards met the carriage and saluted as Lord Dalhousie emerged from the cab. He escorted the officers with the iron box upstairs to the entrance.

The fireplace in the State Room glowed. A strong fire consumed a neatly stacked pile of birch logs. Rich tapestries lined the walls. They added an aesthetic while helping to insulate the space. The Queen returned to her State Throne Chair at the far end of the room. A Scotsman in military uniform entered with the East India officers and the iron box in tow. A royal attendant announced his presence.

"Your majesty, may I present the honorable Lord Dalhousie, Governor-General of India!"

The Queen nodded for him to approach. Dalhousie smiled proudly as he marched across the soft Persian rug. His officers walked behind him in lockstep, one-two, one-two, gracefully carrying their piece of baggage.

Dalhousie radiated as he showed off the diamond. "Your majesty it is my great honor and privilege to present this treasure as a symbol of the conquest of India. It has found its proper resting place in your hands."

The two officers set the iron box down on the floor and proceeded to undo its padlock. The first officer raised a velvet bag out of the strong box. His adjutant gingerly pulled out its contents. It was a large gemstone—a chunk of crystallized carbon millions of years in the making, one of the largest Mother Earth had to offer. The soldiers handed the gem to Victoria with deference.

"Your majesty this priceless jewel was found in the diamond-fields of Golconda in Southern India. It is called Kohinoor, which means mountain of light. It weighs 190 carats. Our geologists at the Royal Academy say it originated from deep in the Earth's core. Perhaps 75 leagues below the planet surface."

Victoria gazed at the gem with awe. "It is ours at last," she replied.

"The young boy prince, Dulep Singh offers it to you as a gift to show his loyalty."

"His generosity is duly acknowledged," replied the monarch. "I shall have the keeper of the jewels set it in a brooch."

The elation of the moment was interrupted as a disheveled British sailor burst into the hall. He dashed across the red carpet on a trajectory for the Queen. Several Royal guards ran after him. He closed to within yards of her Majesty. Her closest sentries stood shoulder to shoulder, bracing for impact. Did he have a knife? A firearm? It was unclear. Before anyone could tackle the intruder he abruptly stopped and kneeled gracefully.

"What is the meaning of this act of impudence?" Victoria asked. The sailor was immediately restrained by her bodyguards.

"Majesty, I am your humble servant. I heard the Kohinoor diamond has been proffered to you. I beg you not to accept it!"

The Royal Guards shook their heads and prepared to escort the man out of the hall. But the Queen raised her hand. "Why would you say that?" she asked the beleaguered sailor.

"It is my ship that sailed the seas from India so that you might hold that very jewel in your hands. I have lost two of my men on that voyage and I am told it is because the diamond is cursed!"

"Two sailors meeting their Maker does not a curse make," replied Victoria.

"It is much more than two sailors, Majesty. Have you heard the long list of possessors of this diamond now deceased? Nadir Shah. His son, Shah Rukh. Shah Zehman, Shah Shuja. A long line of Persian princes all dead."

Dalhousie's face flushed. "These rumors are completely unsubstantiated! This man has consumed too many flagons of drink. Send him away for public flogging!"

Victoria gazed at the gem once more and turned to Dalhousie with an icy stare. "Do you seek to see me hexed?"

Lord Dalhousie put his hands together in a gesture of submission. "Most beneficent majesty, certainly not. The rumor of a curse is untrue. But even if it were, what the sailor did not point out is that those dead possessors of the diamond were all males. The legend says 'Only God or a woman can wear the Kohinoor with impunity.' And she who does will rule the world."

The ring of these words struck a chord with the Queen. Her features softened almost immediately. "Who said this?"

"You will have to forgive me Majesty for I am not a scholar or historian but I am told this is written in an ancient Hindu text from 1306, shortly after the discovery of the diamond in Golconda." Dalhousie was seemingly worried the wrong answer could seal his fate.

The Queen pondered for a moment. She enjoyed the notion that Dalhousie feared for his life and career. Her frown eased into a broad smile. "I like the sound of this prophesy! Take the diamond to the Tower for safekeeping!"

Part I
Castle Amidst Skyscrapers

Chapter One

February 2023

Queen Consort Camilla has declined to wear the Kohinoor diamond at King Charles III's Spring coronation. Rumors suggest she was influenced by the protests of Indian Prime Minister Narendra Modi, who issued a statement saying "the use of the crown jewel Kohinoor brings back painful memories of the colonial past."

The diamond has been a longtime subject of controversy, given that it was the subject of repeated requests from the Indian government to return the gem, the last official request made in 2016. The Indians maintain the Kohinoor, mined in the Golconda region, was not given as a legitimate gift to Queen Victoria by young Prince Duleep Singh. They insist it was surrendered under duress after the fall of the Sikh dynasty to British troops.

Downing Street contends that the diamond was a gift and while the era of British colonialism contained some regrettable incidents, the diamond is better off in its custody.

The Kohinoor will remain at the Tower of London, as the Queen Consort has elected to wear Queen Mary's crown, set with the less controversial Cullinan diamonds, for the coronation ceremony.

Ashley Bellamy was a diamond fan since she was a little girl. Not the Arizona Diamondbacks, not Neil Diamond, she was just a fan of diamonds. If there had been such a thing as diamond cards, as there were baseball cards, she would have every single one. She knew every faceted cut, every mine, every type of stone and the history and legends that went along with them.

She sat at the workbench with relish and inspected the rock through the jeweler's loupe. "I've never seen anything so beautiful in my entire life," she replied.

Bernard, the royal jeweler, leaned over her shoulder as she gazed through the magnifier. "The diamond has gone through changes.

Prince Albert had it re-cut in 1852, reducing its size from 186 carats to about 105. The re-cut resulted in sixty six facets and an absolutely brilliant view."

Ashley took it all in with stars in her eyes. She looked around at her surroundings. Off to the side was a high tech exhibition room, designed for multitudes of tourists to view the precious jewel, but at the same time assuring maximum security. Two inch thick shatter-proof glass separated the jewel from its admirers. This room in the Jewel House gallery was normally filled with tourists but today it was just Ashley and Bernard. They were within the confines of the under-ground vault. Cameras and electronic motion sensors measured their every move.

Ashley noticed an old vintage safe in the corner. It looked to be a hundred years old. "What's that?"

"One of the old safes," he said. "We don't use it anymore. Trying to get it out of here."

"It's too heavy to move?"

"No, we have equipment for that. It's booby trapped. Some of these old safes were designed with a theft deterrent. There are am-poules of a chemical called Chloropicrin strapped inside. If a burglar strikes the dial with enough force or drills through the door, it will break the glass vials inside and release the gas."

"That's been sitting down here all this time?"

"Yes. It was only recently brought to my attention. We need a hazmat team to remove it and they are backlogged lately."

Ashley stepped back a few feet from the antique safe to give it a wide berth.

Bernard smiled. "It's nothing to worry about as long as you're not trying to break into it."

She smiled, not at all relieved by his downplay of the threat.

He poured a splash of gin into a crystal glass.

Ashley shook her head. "I don't drink this early in the morning."

Bernard smiled. "Not for you to drink." He dipped a Q-tip in the gin and offered it. "Would you like to clean it?"

"Clean what?"

"The diamond."

"But if I clean it then I will have to hold it."

The jeweler pointed out the two white gloves Ashley wore on her hands. "That's why I gave you those."

"I thought that was just a general precaution for anyone who works down here."

He placed the diamond in her gloved palm. She felt a frisson of energy go through her. Was this in her head or some kind of actual property of the stone?

Bernard noticed her recoil. "What's wrong?"

"I felt a little shock," she replied.

"That's normal. I felt it too, the first time I held it. It's just your nerves, probably."

She took the Q-tip in her right hand and ran it over the facets of the jewel. "Why gin?"

"Gin is made of ethanol and water. When these two substances combine, they form a weak acid that can break down any grime without leaving streaks."

She swabbed the facets methodically. There were a couple of flecks of dust which she removed with a flick of the cotton-tipped stick. "Okay, done!" She held the rock up to the light and watched it disperse into the colors of the spectrum.

Bernard smiled. "The woman who holds the diamond will rule the world."

"No, thanks. I don't want that job."

"Not even for a day?"

She chortled. "No. Maybe half a day?"

Bernard looked at his watch. "Time's up. I have to get this back on display before opening." He took the diamond from her.

"Thanks for the private viewing!"

"It's just between us."

"Us and whomever else is watching the cameras?"

"The Royal Guards have already vetted you. But don't tell your father! He would have my head if he knew I let you down here!"

He pressed a button and a large metal door opened, allowing Ashley to exit.

***

Ashley walked out of the doorway into the sunshine. She was met by a soldier who stood upright in his red tunic with gold brass buttons. A bearskin helmet adorned his head. He held an intimidating automatic rifle. This was a Jewel House guard, a member of the active military unit in charge of security. "Hey Ashley!" he whisper-shouted, in defiance of his mandate to remain completely taciturn.

She waved cheerfully. "Hi!" How could she not be cheerful? She had just held the most famous diamond in the world in her hands. She looked up and witnessed the London skyline, filled with modern high rise buildings. There was the Shard, which resembled a sharp piece of glass, the Walkie Talkie, that evoked a giant radio handset and the Gherkin, modeled after an upright pickle.

She took her eyes off the skyline and faced forward. She was within the Inner Ward – the innermost circle of the Tower of London, most famous castle in the world. Construction began in 1066 by William the Conqueror, a Norman king who invaded and ruled England with an iron fist. He introduced the Norman concept of a castle fortress as his key to power. The Tower was the result.

Currently not just one tower but a total of 21, high keeps were scattered in and about thick walls that formed the Inner and Outer Ward. This was a typical fortress design. If an invader breached the outer wall you had an additional fortification to fend them off. It made it much harder for an enemy to capture the castle. The jewel exhibit was in the Inner Ward, beneath a converted military barracks named after Waterloo.

Ashley still had diamonds on her mind as she walked across the Tower Green. The Green was a lush green space that formed the center of life in and around the original palace, the White Tower. She walked toward the Bloody Tower, so called because young Prince Edward V and his brother Richard were likely killed there. Beneath the Bloody Tower was a heavy portcullis gate used to seal off the Inner Ward from the Outer. Ashley walked through and turned left down a cobblestone street. A row of Georgian and Tudor style residence buildings were built against the Tower's thick outer wall. The street was called Mint Street as it lead to the former location of Britain's Tower Mint, where the coins of the country were fabricated for over five hundred years.

Ashley walked with purpose down the cobbles because she wanted to get back home. It was not her home per se it was her father's flat. She was from Southern California. She had lived there with her mother for the past ten years. This place was home to her father, who happened to be employed here at His Majesty's Tower of London.

***

Clive Bellamy had a sense of malaise today. He couldn't put his finger on why. It was a generic sense of foreboding. He hadn't slept well and he didn't have much appetite so that certainly was not conducive to a state of well being. He just had the feeling that something was off in the universe. Some people might sleep a day like this off. He did not have that option. He had a job to do and no choice but to face the day.

He stood outside the Byward Tower in his blue "undress" uniform. The blue tunic emblazoned with a red cypher for King Charles did not adequately shield him from the cold wind so he was happy he had worn his thermals this morning. He adjusted the undress flat cloth hat on his head while lamenting that it did not cover his ears on this cold morning. A group of men dressed exactly like Clive filtered out of the employee canteen and gathered. There were several women as well, all dressed in the same uniform. Each one of these individuals had been hand-picked after twenty-two years of experience in the British armed forces. They had all been inducted into the Yeoman Warders, the elite fraternal order responsible for guarding the Tower and guiding its visitors safely throughout the premises.

"Muster!!!!" Clive yelled at the loosely assembled group. He was the Chief Yeoman Warder and as such he was the head of the group of 34 other warders or Beefeaters, as they were frequently called.

The 34 Beefeaters lined up with military precision and stood at attention. "Holograms?" Clive called out. Each Beefeater tapped their official ID tags which contained a unique holographic icon to the Tower.

"Aye!!!!" The Beefeaters replied.

"Very well! Let's open her up!"

At the outermost keep, the Byward Tower, an iron grating was lifted. The Beefeaters on the pulley gave a thumbs-up and the portcullis gate was locked off in the open position. A crowd of tourists looked over expectantly from across the Tower moat, now a dry green space twenty feet below.

Clive addressed the crowd with an Elizabethan accent. "Ladies and gentlemen! Welcome to his Majesty's palace and fortress, the Tower of London! As you pass over the bridge, please take note of the moat below! It was originally dug in 1270 by King Edward I. It is fifty meters wide and used to be full of water and fish, providing a food source for the inhabitants of the castle. During the mid-1800s the Thames' low tides left it still and putrid. The Duke of Wellington ordered it drained. Except for rare flooding, it has been dry ever since. So no need to hold your nose, thank heavens!"

The tourists rushed across the walkway and lined up at tables. Purses and backpacks were searched by security. Clive conjured his loudest voice. "Once you make your way through security please gather around the Beefeater podiums so we can begin your tour!"

As the crowds parted Clive noticed Detective Inspector Emma Winklough, a smiling brunette with a shock of hair dyed platinum blonde in front. She was mid-thirties and wore a white button down shirt and tweed jacket. Something about her posture and demeanor said police. She approached and shook his hand. A fetching young girl, about six years old gripped her other palm. Clive was a big fan of Emma, his go-to local liaison for all things law enforcement.

"Inspector? To what do I owe the pleasure? Is this your daughter?"

"None other. This is Roxanne," she said.

Clive held out his hand for the little girl. "Nice to meet you, Roxanne!" She giggled and grabbed at his hat.

Emma gently scolded her. "He needs his hat, darling."

Clive put his hat back on. "What brings you here, Inspector?"

""I wanted her to see the Tower."

Roxanne jumped up and down. "This is where you chopped people's heads off!"

Emma looked both ways to see if any bystanders overheard. "Roxanne!"

"There's a bit more to the story than that," Clive explained. "Let me show you around."

Emma's cell phone buzzed and she looked down at a text. "We're not staying. Domestic violence situation on the East End."

Roxanne raised her arms in protest. "Mommy I don't want to go!"

"I'm sorry darling but mommy's got to go to work. We'll come back later."

Clive shrugged his shoulders. "Sorry."

Emma patted him on the shoulder. "We'll take you up on the personal tour another time. By the way they moved me to Whitechapel station, CID."

"I see they keep you busy."

"Yeah, maybe I'll have to call on you for backup!"

He laughed.

"You are a constable, aren't you?"

"We are vested with full powers of arrest, but…"

"That's good enough for me!" She took Roxanne's hand. "Come on, sweetheart." Roxanne took her hand and reluctantly walked away. Clive's sense of foreboding came back again. It was a knot in his stomach. Maybe a cup of tea would help?

Several other Yeoman Warders took their places on platforms. The rest dispersed inside the Tower complex to stations and posts.

Clive glanced down Mint Street and spotted Ashley, who strolled across the cobblestones. What's she doing out so early, he thought. She usually sleeps in till at least nine o'clock. Must have gone to get a cup of coffee at the canteen. But she doesn't have a cup of coffee in her hand. He was doing his best to get to know her after so many years apart, but she was unpredictable, this one. Unpredictable and very stubborn. Like him, he supposed. Ashley waved and kept moving. He waved back and turned to the task at hand.

***

Ashley walked to the Northern end of Mint Street. A walk-up beckoned: gray limestone with arched windows. This was an area called the Casemates. In medieval times, a protected enclosure to fire on the enemy, it was now converted to Beefeater lodgings. She briefly checked the dampness of the potted plants on the stoop, then walked inside.

The living room was warm and inviting, though definitely on the masculine palette. Blues and browns dominated. There were antique wood-stained shelves and tables, a brown leather sofa and an uphol-stered blue armchair. Several incandescent lamps threw warm light on the walls. Those were decorated with tributes to the medieval era: an ancient longbow, a lute and several coats of arms. Another wall featured framed landscapes and seascapes by the British painter John Constable.

Ashley threw her keys on a side table and headed to her bed-room. On the wall was a hastily hung *One Direction* handbill. Re-cently purchased poster art leaned against the desk: falling diamonds over black, a vintage De Beers *Diamonds are Forever* advert and a retro Cartier necklace placard. Several gossip and fashion maga-zines adorned the side table. She collapsed on the bed as her phone buzzed.

Why did you leave so early last night?

She picked up the phone and smirked.

I told you I had to be home by midnight!

She went out to a karaoke bar last night with her friend Babs and met someone. Heath was his name. He looked a little like Harry Styles but had a terrible voice. They sang a couple of karaoke songs together. He blurted the Backstreet Boys' "I Want It That Way" com-pletely off key. A couple of mai-tais later they close-danced to "Shape of You" by Ed Sheeran. She then realized what time it was: two past eleven. She had to be back at the Tower by midnight. All residents had to be in by midnight or you were locked out.

Her phone buzzed again.

I didn't realize you were Cinderella!

She did not want to tell him she was staying at the Tower with her dad. She did not tell him she was here because she had broken up with her boyfriend of three years and this was a cleansing trip. Plus she got to see diamonds. She barely knew Heath. She would not just be a hookup. She was also not looking for a *London Boy*. She just went out for a good time, that's all. She wanted to let her hair down. Why the hell did Babs let this happen? It was all her fault.

I am Cinderella. I am currently swabbing floors at the behest of my evil Stepmother.

Smile emoji. I didn't tell you but I'm also a Prince. Not the type of prince that would rescue you though. You would have to do that for yourself. I am into self-rescuing princesses.

Wait a minute. She must have given him her number while under the influence of that second Mai-tai. That was not Babs' fault.

Really? Because I was thinking you're a frog and I do NOT kiss frogs.

She should not have said that. That was mean. She actually thought he was cute.

You do not have to kiss me ever again. But what are you doing this afternoon? We could meet at Camden Market! There's this amazing dim sum place...

Dim sum? Why did he have to mention dim sum? She loved dim sum! Wait a minute. Did I kiss him? She did not remember that.

I never did kiss you! How could I not kiss you again if I never did in the first place?

The phone indicated that he was typing.

LOL you got me there. Glad you were paying attention! Nothing gets by you. How about the dim sum?

She waited. She was not going to reply immediately but he had found her weakness. Dim sum was the key to her heart. Babs was right. She needed to get out of the prison more. Since she had arrived she had stayed within the Tower grounds most of the time. She was a history major after all and doing research for her thesis. I mean, why wouldn't she? She had access to this repository of historical events that virtually no one else in the UCLA history department, much less the world had. She might as well work it.

Okay, text me the deets and I'll be there at two o'clock. Bye! Smiley face emoji.

Chapter Two

Clive stood on a ledge before a gathered crowd of tourists. He still had that knot in his stomach. It was not from nervousness about public speaking. He was accustomed to that. This was a sixth sense he only had experienced a few times in his life. The last time he had this distinct feeling his mother had died. He hoped this was a false alarm, maybe just something he ate that didn't agree with him. Yeah, that had to be it. Come to think of it he did eat some haddock & chips last night. Possibly the fish was a little off though it tasted okay.

The tourists looked at him expectantly, bedazzled by his Victorian uniform, a navy-blue tunic embroidered with royal red rosettes, navy trousers and patent leather shoes.

An impish gentleman pointed to his uniform. "That's not the one I seen you in when I drank me bottle of gin!"

Clive was used to grandstanding attention hounds. They asked insincere questions purely for laughs. .

"You are correct sir!" Clive answered. "Those are our formal red 'dress' uniforms on the gin label. They are only worn on official celebrations of the State. Which is a good thing because you should try getting in and out of those tights in the loo!" More laughs. Clive could deal with hecklers. He had developed it into an art form. Use the energy of the comment to turn things around.

"I hope they pay you extra for that!" the imp replied.

Clive figured it was time to begin. The natives were getting restless. "Thank you all for coming today! More than nine hundred years ago a castle was built, bigger, stronger and more imposing than any seen before in this country. Because of its unyielding secure and strategic position, the royal families lived here for nearly six centuries. The castle provided safekeeping for the treasures of the realm. It housed courts of justice and the nation's armory. It held king's enemies and prisoners of the state. I welcome you to his Majesty's royal palace and fortress, the Tower of London."

Clive could see his breath visible in the cold morning air. He did not have to do these tours. As Chief Yeoman Warder it was not an official duty. But he enjoyed it. So upon accepting the managerial position after ten years of dedicated service he stipulated that he be allowed to give public tours occasionally. The Chief Constable readily agreed.

"My name is Clive Bellamy and I will be your guide on this passage through history. I am a privileged member of the Yeoman Warders, the elite group who has guarded the noble residents and priceless treasures of this very Tower since the 11th Century. We have earned the nickname Beefeaters. Speculation is it may have had something to do with a beef and mutton allotment the king gave to his guards many years ago."

A teenage boy swaggered forward. "Tell us about the battles and the beheadings!"

"In due time. For now let me point out that the Tower has two lines of defense against trespassers." He pointed to the wall that lined the exterior of the Tower where it met the dry moat. "That is the outer wall. It is approximately five meters thick." He pointed to the wall behind him, on the other side of Mint Street. "That is the inner wall, of a similar thickness but taller. If an invader were to pierce the defenses of the outer he would be stuck on this very street. The King's archers would rain longbow and crossbow bolts upon him."

The tourists looked up at the Inner Wall. Were they picturing archers ready to rain projectiles down on them?

John the Ravenmaster approached Clive. He was a stocky man with a winning smile. His previous service was RAF, where he served as an aviation mechanic. Now he worked on a different kind of bird. His uniform had a badge with a raven's head. He was sprinkled with bird droppings and feathers. "Morning Clive. Orders from the Resident Governor. Change into your State Dress. We've got dignitaries incoming."

Clive turned toward John, trying to keep a smile on his face. "Bloody hell. Again?"

John nodded and shrugged. "I'll take over here while you change."

Clive turned to the group of tourists. "Ladies and gentlemen I do apologize. I have been informed of an urgent issue which requires my attention. I will be turning you over to my good friend, John the Ravenmaster, who will escort you."

There was a chorus of sighs and disappointed grunts. They had already bonded with Clive and now John was to be the substitute teacher.

"Now, now!" John sounded off. "Clive is our Chief Yeoman Warder and from time to time his lofty position requires him to attend to other duties. This is one of those times. Now let's start with a wee limerick, shall we? Here's a story from one of the White Tower's chimneys:

> *A flea and a fly in a flue,*
> *Were imprisoned, so what could they do?*
> *Said the fly, 'Let us flee!'*
> *'Let us fly,' said the flea,*
> *And they flew through a flaw in the flue."*

That broke the ice. Everyone laughed.

***

Clive walked swiftly down Mint Street. Several other warders rushed out of their homes in Tudor State Dress with gold brocade, ruffled collars, breeches, black velvet bonnets, stockings and brass hilted swords. Sheila Hansty was one of three female Yeoman Warders at the Tower. She was a "Lady Beefeater" but she didn't look it. She was lean, trim and graceful on her feet. In fact Clive had never seen her eat any beef, only fish and poultry. Sheila shouted as Clive marched across the cobblestones. "Suit up, Clive! We've got a dog and pony!"

"I heard, Sheila!" He kept his pace as he walked.

Clive rounded the corner to the row of walk-ups that were Yeoman Warder berthings. He noted the welcoming sight of ornamental plants on his stoop, courtesy of Ashley. She brought a certain brightness and light to his domicile, something that reminded him of her mother.

He burst into his apartment to find Ashley poring over her computer. "I thought you were giving a tour?"

"John the Ravenmaster took over for me. There's some kind of dignitary coming and I have to put on the dress reds. You were up early."

"I couldn't sleep so I went to get a coffee. Come here. I want you to look at this." She pointed to her computer.

"I'm really in a bit of a rush."

She crinkled her forehead and shrugged, apparently exasperated. "Okay, fine."

His curiosity was now piqued. He took a breath and looked over her shoulder at the computer. She was in some design software and the screen featured a kiosk with an image of a Beefeater on the side. "What is it?"

"I've been seeing how you're quite overworked and I thought this might help..." She pressed play and the Beefeater on the kiosk came to life.

Welcome to his Majesty's palace and fortress, the Tower of London. I am here to help you get the most of your experience at the Tower. I have a list of frequently asked questions here on the right. Press any of them and I will tell you the answer!

"Is that my voice?" Clive asked.

"Yes. I sampled it when you were giving one of your tours the other day."

"You should have asked me."

"I wanted to surprise you! I've been working on this for days! It's still early stages but I think it could help lift a huge workload off you and the average Yeoman..."

"The average warder would get the idea that you're trying to replace us."

"What? No! I'm just trying to help take a load off so you guys can do what you do best! Like tell your stories! Manage the premises!" She clicked on a map of the Tower with various pins on it. "I even mapped out the best location for each of the kiosks based on crowd patterns that I observed."

He stared at the screen like a deer caught in headlights. "You do realize they cut our budget recently?"

"So you don't like it?"

"It's not that I don't like it. It's very impressive, what you have done. But I don't think the Tower is ready for AI."

"It's not AI dad. It's just an informational kiosk! We have them at all the great museums in the US."

"Where did you learn all of this computer stuff anyway? I thought you're a history major? Shouldn't you be working on your term paper?"

"I am, dad. But sometimes I take breaks and noodle on the computer."

"You have so much here to explore! Not many history majors get to live in a world heritage site."

"Did you ever stop to think that the history I came to study was yours?"

"Darling, my life is an open book! Always has been!"

"Yeah well I'm having a hard time reading that book. It leaves early in the morning and comes back late at night."

"I will make it up to you darling, I promise. We can take a trip to the countryside..."

"I'm going home, dad."

"You are home!"

"To the States. Mom needs me."

"For what? She has a new husband and a mansion in Malibu. Besides, you have to finish your thesis."

"I've got writer's block."

"You have to use the limericks. Much of the Tower's history is told in verse. It's the best way to learn. Let's recite, shall we? In the sunlight tis easy to swagger and strut // To push on a door that is carelessly shut..."

"I'm not in the mood. No limericks."

The sound of bagpipes drifted in through the window. Clive rushed to the closet and pulled out his State Dress uniform.

"I have to go. Some politician is coming over for a song and dance."

She laced up her running shoes as he placed his navy blue undress coat in the closet.

"Going for a run?"

"Yes, I am. To meet someone at Camden market."

Clive tried to cover his disdain for her spandex leggings. They revealed every curve of her body. She had a workout crop top too. It gave a glimpse of her bare midriff. "In that?"

"Yes, dad, in this. Sorry but my corset is at the cleaners."

"Okay. You're right. It's none of my business. Peace offering?" He pulled what looked like a tube of lipstick out of his pocket.

"You bought that for me?"

"Yes."

"Thanks." She smiled as she took the cap off the lipstick tube. Inside the cylinder she found no waxy pigmented substance but a vial with a nozzle on it instead. It was a mace spray canister.

"There are some rough neighborhoods outside these walls in the Tower hamlets. Moped purse snatches and knife muggers. You never know."

Ashley shook her head and inserted the lipstick tube of mace into a side pocket.

"I want to talk to you more about this?"

"About the lipstick mace?"

"No. The other stuff. We can have lunch."

"I'm having lunch at Camden Market."

"Oh. Okay afternoon tea then. My phone will be off for this VIP visit but you can page me and I'll call you back."

"You still have that pager?"

"It's an excellent communication device!"

"For the 1990s maybe?"

He shook his head. "They operate on a much lower frequency than cell phones. That means they will work in a crisis situation. ER doctors still carry their pagers because the hospital can get a hold of them if cell phones go down."

"You're not an ER doctor though. Why can't you just commit to a time to meet?"

The bagpipes beckoned. He removed his belt and laid out his State Dress uniform on the bed. "Because of this VIP tour everything is in flux. But I will make time. Please."

"Fine. Whatever." She walked out the door.

Clive wanted to go after her but the bagpiper wailed again. There was no time. He had to be present for the arrival of the dignitary. He removed his trousers and began the ritual of donning his dress reds, putting his knee breeches on one leg at a time.

Chapter Three

Ashley gripped the lipstick/mace spray canister tightly. Not out of any plan to use it but simply out of frustration with her father. She wished he were as interested in getting to know her as he was obsessed with her physical safety. She could take care of herself. She had taken a few classes of Krav Maga in Los Angeles. She didn't need or want a protector and she certainly didn't need a critic of her wardrobe choices. Maybe that was too much to ask. He was old school in everything he did. His choices in music, his choices in art, his choices in literature were all Elizabethan in nature. It was as if he were a method actor, living the part. Except his part wasn't a movie shoot or cosplay that came to an end. It was his whole life.

She walked across Tower Green past the spot where Anne Boleyn was beheaded by the order of Henry VIII. There was a memorial in front of the Tower's church and sepulcher, the Chapel of St. Peter Ad Vincula. Anne was buried within the chapel, along with other British notables such as Catherine Howard, Thomas Cromwell and Lady Jane Grey.

Ashley marched past the White Tower, the original palace. She headed to the Byward Tower exit. On the lawn just within the Inner Wall were a series of aviaries, bird coops that held jet black ravens within. John the Ravenmaster, in full State Dress uniform, was crouched in one of the aviaries. He held a young raven in one hand, a pair of shears in the other. The bird was cawing loudly.

John cooed to the bird. "It's alright little fella."

Ashley sauntered over to the aviary and took in the sight. "I thought you took over dad's tour?"

"The birds had to be prepped for the incoming VIP. I handed them off to Warder Flaherty."

The captive raven cawed again several times, as if asking Ashley to intervene on its behalf. "That's so cruel." She pointed at the shears.

"Oh, no, don't worry. I'm not clipping his wings. Just trimming a couple of feathers. "

She rolled her eyes. "I know, you have to clip their wings because of the legend. If the ravens ever leave, darkness will fall on Britain forever." Ashley looked up at the gloomy sky. "Sometimes I feel like darkness already has fallen on Britain."

"I don't know about that," John said. "You're here."

Ashley blushed at John's compliment. She liked John. She wished her father were more like him.

Another larger raven with a white albino patch on its belly scurried over to Ashley and dropped a piece of raw meat at her feet.

"I think Herman's taken a shine to you," John observed.

Ashley grimaced. She was a little spooked by Herman. "That thing follows me everywhere."

"Perhaps he's watching over you?"

"More like stalking me," she replied and kicked the raw meat away. This thing was like her old cat, who would drag rodents into the house and present them as gifts.

John smirked. "What are you up to today?"

"Meeting a friend at Camden Market," she answered. She had her phone open to an airline ticketing screen.

John noticed. "Going somewhere?"

"Yeah, I gotta get back to the States. Mom misses me."

"What did he do?"

"Who?"

"You know who."

"Dad?"

John nodded.

"Nothing. Nothing other than what he always does. But maybe that's the point. We just have so little in common."

"What did he not do?"

"Last night I asked him to come to the pub and meet a couple of my girlfriends from the States. But he never showed."

"Believe it or not your dad's a bit shy."

"Not buying that. I've seen him on the dais, talking to crowds of tourists."

"That's different. It's not a normal human interaction. All I'm saying is I know he's proud of you."

"Yeah. Maybe." She made her way down the aviary steps. "Gotta run! Don't want to be late."

"Sounds like an important date!" he said.

"It's not a date, John. It's just a quick meet-up!" She swished her hair back over her shoulders and went on her merry way towards the Inner Wall and the entrance to Mint Street.

***

Ashley ran at a good clip through the Tower Hamlets. The Hamlets were the communities surrounding the Tower. Of course most of the medieval vibe was now gone. Breweries, mills, blacksmith forges and modest cottages for tradespeople were replaced by high rise developments such as Canary Wharf, now a financial hub.

Ashley rounded a corner and headed up Cannon Street. She jogged past St. Paul's Cathedral. Tourists queued up to go inside. It had been almost four miles and she was not tiring. She was buoyed by the comfort of her *On Clouds* running shoes and her frustration with Clive. It was no wonder he had no wife, no steady girlfriend. It was almost like he was married to the Tower itself. He was a high priest of His Majesty's Fortress. It showed in his complete lack of interest in spending time with her. Or maybe she was being too hard on him? Her milder inner voice opined that she was. Maybe by understanding the Tower she could understand him better.

She broke a mild sweat as she headed up Eversholt. She thought of Heath. Did she make a mistake by not taking the tube, where she could keep her minimal make-up intact? No it was not a mistake because she didn't want to impress him. This meet-up was just to let him down easily. Besides she always got a healthy glow when she ran.

Camden Market was a large collection of warehouses and buildings along Regent's Canal which housed trendy food stalls and clothing boutiques. Ashley made her way along the canal and up a flight of stairs to the second story. There were tourists everywhere, gawking at hand-painted Doc Martens, whooping at a street contortionist, queuing up for pork belly meat pies.

Across the arcade Ashley spotted Heath. He sat at a table bathed in the pink neon light of a sign which read Pumping Dumplings. He poured tea from a teapot into two porcelain cups. How thoughtful, she thought. She hoped it was Oolong. "Hi!" she announced and proceeded to the counter to order her lunch.

"Oh, no need to do that!" Heath exclaimed. "I already put an order in for both of us."

She strutted over to the table. "That's a bit presumptuous, isn't it? How did you know for sure that I would show up?"

"I didn't," he replied blandly. "But worst case scenario I could have taken extras home for dinner. Except for the soup dumplings of course. Soup dumplings don't reheat well."

At that moment a plate of soup dumplings arrived at their table. She sat down and took a sip of tea. It was Oolong. "My favorite."

"Mine too," he answered, holding his tea cup high as if it were a toast. He put it down and served her a couple of soup dumplings. "Be careful. They're still very hot."

She spooned one almost immediately after he placed it gingerly in her bowl and blew to cool it off. "So? How has your day been so far?" she asked.

"Splendid, now that you're here." There was an air of flirtation in his voice.

"If I'm being honest I want to get one thing out right away. I'm not looking for a relationship. In fact I'm not going to be in the UK for long. So I don't want to give you any false impressions."

"Yeah, you told me that last night right before you ran off to your gilded carriage."

"It was a good time, singing with you and having a few beers but I think we should leave it at that, yeah?"

"Is that all it was because I remember just a tiny bit of snogging happened, at your behest I might add."

"That was just a moment of victory when we bested that other couple on the applause meter."

"Whatever. So where is it you're going back to? Can you tell me that?"

"Los Angeles. Southern California. It's where my mum and I have lived for the last ten years."

"But you were born and raised here. I can tell because you've got a slight accent. It is certainly no Cali girl cadence."

"You're right. I was born here, Mr. Holmes. My father was in the British military. I'm a bit of an army brat. Spent my first twelve years on bases, from Alanbrooke Barracks in North Yorkshire to Horne Barracks in Wiltshire, to Berengaria Village in Cyprus."

"What's your dad do now?"

"I don't want to talk about it. Tell me about you. What do you do?"

"I work for BT."

She bit down on her soup dumpling and squeezed delicious chicken broth into her mouth. "BT. You mean, bacon-tomato as in the sandwich?"

"No! British Telecom."

"Oh! Of course. You sell cell phones."

"No. I am a lineman. Spend a lot of time underground in the tunnels laying cable."

"Oh, how interesting!"

"It is, actually. You would be surprised how much of old London I've seen. We use the old tube tunnels for a lot of stuff."

"Why are cables needed when everyone has a cell phone?"

"We install the cables so your mobile will work while you're in the tube! It's called the Telecommunications Connectivity Project. We hook up transmitters so you don't lose signal. Haven't you ever been sending a text or an email and racing to get it sent right before the train leaves the station? You won't have to do that anymore! You will have 5G connectivity everywhere you go!"

She giggled, impressed with his fervor. "You're quite passionate about this project, aren't you?"

"You would be too if you knew what went into it."

"I'm sorry. I did not show the proper amount of interest, did I? "

"It's not like that. You have the right to be impressed or unimpressed as the case may be."

"I'm a history major. I find the old tube system tunnels quite interesting. Tell me."

"There's quite a few. Some of them are haunted."

"No."

"Oh, yeah. You can hear voices and moaning and whatnot."

"Moaning? For what?"

"I have no idea. I'm not a ghost."

"I don't believe it. Do you have video evidence?"

"No. But I can do better than that. I can show you."

"Bollocks."

"The old Mark Lane station under Tower Hill is the best."

Now he had piqued her interest with his mention of the Tower. "You've been down there?"

"Of course I have! Plenty of ghosts in what's left of it."

"Take me."

"What?"

"I want to see it."

"Now?"

"Why not? Are you afraid to put your money where your mouth is?"

Heath seemed a bit stunned by her suggestion. His Adam's apple twitched. "No. Of course not. I'm just not allowed to bring civilians down there."

"Pish posh," she said. "I'm a history major, not a civilian. I'm here doing my thesis project on the Tower of London and this is an aspect that I've never learned about."

"Alright. As long as you agree to wear a hard hat."

"Done." She did a happy dance to celebrate.

***

Clive burst out of his apartment in royal red State Dress. His sixth sense was proving to be valid. Thoughts raced through his head. Was this the bad juju he was in for? What kind of VIP showed up without any advance notice? Is it a security thing where they can't publish their schedule in advance? He did not like these impromptu displays. Pomp and circumstance is meant to be planned, not delivered at the drop of a hat! He dashed down the stoop in his shiny dress slippers with large rosettes across the instep. They were too narrow for his wide feet.

He headed towards his office in the Outer Ward and passed the Raven's Roost aviaries. John tidied the cages. "You shouldn't be cleaning the cages in your royal red, John!"

"Just a little window dressing, Clive, in case your VIPs come over this way. Can't have the place looking like a street pigeon's nest, can we?"

"I suppose not," Clive replied.

"Did they tell you who it is?"

"No, they did not."

"Possibly one of the royals?"

"Highly doubtful. They don't usually pop in for a visit."

"I suppose we shall see, then, shan't we?"

Their colloquy was broken by the sound of shouting from outside the Outer Wall. Clive rushed towards the sound of the commotion. He climbed a ladder to one of the parapets. Below he spied a small group of picketers and protesters carrying placards. They read things like:

British Empire hordes stolen artifacts!
Return the Kohinoor!
The Time of Empire Is Over! Return Ancient Relics!
Elgin Marbles to Greece! Kohinoor to India!

Clive shook his head. The scene only added to his malaise. That sixth sense was still twisting coils in his gut.

John caught up to him, a little breathless. "What's this?"

Clive sighed. "Same old song and dance, different day."

***

Ashley followed Heath down Vine Lane. She gripped her phone and wiped off the camera lens. She wanted to get some good pictures of this purported catacomb that led underneath the river to the Tower. It was an esoteric piece of history that she could include in her thesis paper. She took another look at Heath who walked at a brisk pace. She was slightly intrigued by him. He was sort of attractive in a British techie-nerd way. Last night a lot of the other guys had that posh club-goer swagger. He did not.

The little voice in her head sounded off. Did she really ask him to take her down into the old subway tunnels? What girl in her right mind would ask a guy she barely knew to do that? But somehow she felt comfortable with him. His unassuming warmth put her at ease.

Heath put his head on a swivel. He looked to see if any other city workers on the street recognized him. "You know I could get fired for this!"

She patted him on the shoulder. "No one will ever know. I can't imagine there's any cameras in the ghost tunnels."

"No, no cameras, except for the ones up here." He pointed out one at the corner of Vine and Tooley.

"Not a problem." She hunched over so her face pointed to the ground. "Go on. The facial recognition will not register."

"Where'd you learn all this stuff?"

"What stuff?"

"About security cameras and so forth. It's not typical Cali girl topics of conversation."

"Oh? Have you been conversing with many Cali girls?"

"No, no...I didn't mean like that. I just, it's not what you would expect that's all."

"You need to get over your stereotypes. You would be surprised how much I know about security and various London technicalities most people are not privy to."

"Who did you say your dad was again?"

"I can't tell you that."

Heath shrugged and led her to the Unicorn Theatre, a modern concrete and glass building where children's plays were staged. "This building was built on the site of the entrance to the Tower subway. Picture yourself in 1870 and you would see a queue of Londoners ready to pay one pence for a ticket across. The cars only held twelve people."

Ashley let her imagination run wild. She could picture Dickensian characters in their Sunday best waiting for access to the subway and a trip to the Tower.

He led her to the back of the theatre where a storage shed stood. It was surrounded by a locked fence. He unlocked it and they stepped inside. Then he opened the shed door.

Within the confines of the shed was a hatch. Heath opened it and Ashley peered down a tube lined with an iron stepladder. She stared at the long descent. "How far down is that?"

"It's about fifty feet. Feel free to back out. I won't hold it against you."

"Oh, hell no. We're going down there."

"Suit yourself." He put on his helmet lamp. "You have to wear a high-viz vest. No exceptions."

"But I don't have one."

He stepped inside the iron door and pulled a bright yellow and orange reflective jacket off a hook. He proffered it to Ashley. "Here you go."

She put her arms through the holes and cinched the Velcro strap around her waist. "It's exactly my size!" The vest hung down her waist almost to her knees.

Heath led the way down the ladder.

Ashley followed. She was very happy she had worn cross training gear. It was perfect for the excursion.

"You sure you're okay?" Heath asked as they neared the bottom.

"Yes, fine," She took another cautious step down. She did not love heights but this was an opportunity she would not miss.

Heath reached bottom. "Back in 1860 they had a brand new invention for cutting out tunnels. It's still used today. It's called the Barlow-Greathead shield and it's a circular cast-iron shaft that pushes through the earth little by little while protecting the workers within. They used that thing to push this tunnel 410 meters."

The guy was nerding out on subway tunnel cutters. Wow. The more she talked to him the more attractive he became. But she was not looking for a relationship. She was leaving town. She told him that so it was not like she was leading him on. She stepped off the ladder and joined him. She looked through the tunnel. It was lit by a row of dim lights as far as the eye could see and undulated like a throbbing artery. You could hear the water of the Thames washing over. Drips penetrated here and there. It was a bit unnerving, like stepping into the mouth of a sea monster or something.

"Where are the train tracks?" she asked.

"Long gone," Heath replied. "The train only lasted a couple of years. It held just twelve people per car. Not very profitable. So they ripped the tracks out and put in a pedestrian walkway. They dropped the price of crossing down to ½ pence. It was much more successful especially with the poor East Enders. But then Tower Bridge opened in 1894 and that was free so they no longer came. The pedestrian walkway closed in 1898."

"You're just a wealth of information!" she noted, with a touch of sarcasm. She would never tell him this but he reminded her of Clive. He too nerded out on historical details. It was a little bit creepy, comparing the two. She shoved the thought out of her head. Heath assumed she wanted to hear these dates and milestones. Right now she didn't need the play by play. She wanted to soak in the space on her own.

He pointed out a poster featuring a family wearing coats like Sherlock Holmes might wear. It read: *Mandleberg Waterproofs*. "These were the Victorian raincoats of the day. The old adverts are pretty well preserved."

Another faded placard featured a small baby fed something called "gripe water." It promoted this concoction to prevent baby flatulence, teething pain, diarrhea and skin rashes.

She chuckled. "Wow, this is quite a time capsule."

"Yeah, there's a lot of stuff down here like that."

Ashley noted the tunnel was lined with wires. "So you install the cables through here?"

"I help maintain them. These fiber-optics were installed in the 1970s. Prior to that the tunnel was used for hydraulic pressure pipes. They were used to be used to power a lot of London back in the day."

Ashley was impressed with his appreciation of the surroundings. Perhaps she had underestimated him. There was some substance there, and his karaoke voice was not that bad. He could sort of carry a tune. But then again, she was leaving and did not want to create any sort of attachment. Her ponderings were brought to a sudden halt by a loud explosion above them.

Chapter Four

The subway tunnel rattled and shook as the Thames sloshed overhead. It felt like they were in the belly of a whale. The tube reverberated with overwhelming force. Ashley's skull pulsed with the brutal sound. It must be collapsing, she thought. We have precious seconds to live. So she did that which most anyone would do under similar circumstances. She reached for the closest human contact she could find: Heath.

"It's okay, it's okay," he told her. He did not seem fazed in the least.

"It's okay? What the hell was that explosion?"

"It's the seven gun salute off the Tower Wharf. They're almost right above us."

"The cannons?"

"Yeah. We're perfectly fine."

"You've been down here before when that's happened?"

"Oh, sure. A number of times."

"Did you know they were going to do that?"

"No of course not. Normally we have advance warning."

"Do you think something's wrong?"

"Oh, no. They are ceremonial guns."

Another loud bang shook the tube violently again.

"I think I'd like to leave now."

"Sure. Of course."

The sound echoed throughout the tunnel. She gripped his hand and they walked back as fast as they could.

Another blast resounded. The place shook like it was the core of a volcano. She felt a claustrophobic, sinking feeling.

She could see the end of the tunnel now. The ladder was still intact. It gave her hope. They reached it and he helped her up the gangway. She climbed as fast as she could. Then another explosion. The access chamber shook. She hung on for dear life and glanced below. Heath was right behind her. She kept going. Step after step. Her ears rang. Her head throbbed. Her nerves were shaken like a martini. The sound exploded again. She started to see spots.

"It's okay! You can do it," he said. "We're almost there."

She placed her right foot on the first rung of the ladder and unclenched her hand from around his to place both hands on the sides of the ladder. "I'm sorry," she said. She felt like she had let him down.

"Nothing to be sorry about. I would never have taken you down if I had known they would be firing the cannon."

She climbed up. One foot after the other. Breathe. You can do this. Another blast. The ladder shook. She froze.

"I think that's the last. Not sure though if it's the 21 gun salute or the seven...depends on the reason for the..."

Another blast. Her knuckles were white from gripping the ladder.

"I guess it's the 21 then. Sorry. Keep going. We're almost up."

She planted one foot after the other and ascended the final few steps. The hatch was still wide open. She poked her head up and into the utility building behind the Unicorn Theatre. Then she clambered out. Heath popped up behind her. Then another blast of sound.

"It's alright. Come on. You need fresh air." He opened the door to the shed and held it for her. She walked out. The sky was blue. The sun poked through the clouds. Then one more round. She clutched him again, tightly.

He unlatched the fence gate and led her towards the river bank. She shivered. He showed her the Tower across the Thames. It was still there in all its glory. He pointed out the four howitzer guns on the edge of Tower Wharf.

She looked over and saw the guns, manned by the members of the Honourable Artillery Company. The world was not ending. The sky was not falling. They were not under terrorist attack. She looked at Heath. He smiled and shrugged apologetically. In that moment his visage was enchanting. Maybe not the countenance of a knight in shining armor but one of a reliable, kind man. He smelled like soap and cherry throat lozenges, not at all a displeasing combination. The relief came over her in a giant wave. Her blood pressure eased and in an impulsive moment she kissed Heath for the second time in two days.

***

Clive fiddled with his earplugs as he stood on Tower Wharf. He remained a safe distance away from the guns. His sixth sense was still lurking. The Honourable Artillery Company, so named by Queen Victoria as the oldest regiment of the British Army assigned to fire royal salutes, stood at attention in their blue and gold uniforms. They triggered the 25 pounder guns (so called because each shell weighs 25 pounds) to wrap the gun salute.

John the Ravenmaster emerged from the water gate.

Clive turned to him. "Who ordered the red carpet treatment?"

"No idea," John replied. He scratched at his neck where the ruffled collar touched his skin.

Clive shook his head. "We're just window dressing now. There's no honor in being a warder anymore."

John adjusted his tights. "I wouldn't say that."

Clive pointed out a billboard on the side of a ferry making its way up the Thames. It was a photo of a sexy young woman in the same uniform they were wearing. The billboard read:

Beefeater Gin. It's not just your daddy's gin anymore.

"Don't let it get you down, Clive."

Clive's dismay was broken by the buzzing of his phone. He picked it up. It was the Resident Governor. "Proceed to the Byward Tower. They're pulling in."

Clive and John hoofed across Tower Wharf towards the Byward Tower entrance. A host of Warders in State Dress stood at attention. Several Met police cordoned off an area free of pedestrian and vehicular traffic. A BMW SUV with diplomatic plates pulled up. An attaché from the Ministry of Tourism hopped out. She was amped up with coffee and exuberant energy. "Okay he's coming! Let's give him a warm welcome!"

Clive forced a smile as a limousine pulled in. He expected a prime minister or ambassador of some repute to exit. But the vehicle door opened and an unshaven man in a Hugo Boss sweat suit alighted. He wore gold chains around his neck and a Christian Dior durag on his head. Beckford, his assistant, followed along with a photographer.

The man did not take note of the dignitary level reception. He moved immediately to the edge of the Tower moat and looked down at the lawn which covered the basin. He pointed at his assistant, who dutifully took notes on his iPad. "Our moat will be a combination swimming pool and we'll have a bridge over it like this one built exactly to scale."

The assistant jotted the note on his tablet.

The Ministry of Tourism attaché shuffled over, taking care not to fall off her high heels. "Mr. Slater, welcome to His majesty's Tower of London. May I introduce Chief Yeoman Warder Clive Bellamy. He is in charge here at the Tower."

Clive reached out for a handshake . "Welcome to his Majesty's palace and fortress, the Tower of London, Mr. Slater." Slater left his hand hanging.

Slater pointed out Clive's State Dress uniform to Beckford. "We'll dress our doorman exactly the same way." Beckford jotted down the note.

Clive caught the slighting reference but ignored it. He had to main a sense of decorum given his role as a representative of his

Majesty. "Shall we come this way? Let's get started on your tour. This place was built by William the Conqueror, beginning in 1066. It's known as a royal palace, a prison, a treasury, a place of execution and perhaps most famously, as the repository for the Crown Jewels."

Slater paid no attention. He was buried in his phone. Clive paused for a moment. A Las Vegas developer? This was the VIP the Home Office rolled out the red carpet for? He did not care how much money this guy was throwing around or whom he was friends with. This was an absolute disgrace. A sacrilegious waste of resources and time. To what purpose?

"Right this way! You are currently in the Outer Ward of the Tower. It has two concentric circles inside the moat. The Inner Wall is higher than the Outer Wall, allowing bowmen and archers to rain bolts, stone projectiles and even chamber pots on the invaders. There was only one time this defense system did not work for the Tower. It was in 1381 and it was known as the Peasants' Revolt. The kings' subjects were just barely recovering from the Black Plague when the king hit them with higher taxes. 400 men led a siege against the fortress in protest..."

"Can we move on now?" Slater asked, looking up from his phone.

Clive swallowed his pride and strode down Water Lane towards the gateway to the Inner Ward. His phone slipped out of his pocket and the screen lit up with a photo of Ashley.

Slater picked it up. He noticed the photo of the attractive young woman on the screen saver. "That your girlfriend? She's pretty hot for an old fart like you."

Clive cringed and took the phone back. "That's my daughter." He wanted to lay out this disrespectful creep. But he couldn't. He had to finish the tour. This was his job. Hecklers were hecklers no matter rich or poor or VIP. He would ignore the noise and continue. He would not let this guy get to him.

Clive pointed to a medieval catapult on the Outer Wall. "You will also notice above a trebuchet, used to shoot projectile rocks long distances. It is a giant slingshot, if you will. You may have also heard it referred to as a *siege engine*." Several men dressed in medieval garb stood next to the trebuchet and practiced high falls from the castle wall on to an air bag below. "These stunt men are practicing for a public exhibition scheduled later today!"

Slater hammered the screen of his phone. Judging by the frantic keystrokes, it was an animated conversation. Beckford and the photographer appeared to be interested in Clive's color commentary so he continued. He led the group through an archway with a heavy iron grating suspended above.

"This is the Bloody Tower, so named for the alleged murder of two young princes, Prince Edward and his younger brother, Richard by their uncle, Richard III. More on that later."

They stepped on to plush green lawns of Tower Green. Clive gestured as they passed items of note. "On the right is the large and imposing White Tower, the King's original palace. On the left is the home Henry VIII built for second wife Anne Boleyn. Speaking of Anne you will notice a commemorative sculpture. This marks the spot of her execution scaffold. It was considered more dignified for nobility to have their heads removed without spectators and Anne was afforded this luxury."

Slater finished his text-a-thon and looked up from his phone. He motioned to his assistant.

Clive continued his narration. "In addition to Anne Boleyn, Henry VIII's fifth wife, Catherine Howard, lost her head on this scaffold."

Slater turned again to Beckford. "Our signature drink will have to be the Bloody Mary. But we'll have an Anne Boleyn cocktail and we will advertise that *it will make you lose your head*. Are you getting all this?"

Beckford jotted it down on the digital pad. "Got it!"

Slater leaned in. "We'll get miniature axes as cocktail stirrers..."

Clive cut him off with more commentary. "On this very green the King sponsored knight's tournaments!"

Slater dove back into his phone.

Clive pointed out a wooden contraption. It was two posts with thick beams across: a hole for a head and two smaller holes for the hands. "If you were a drunken spectator who disrupted the festivities you might be placed in the stocks." He had a momentary thought of where he would like to place Slater. "Or they might simply hog-tie you and drag you out on a tumbrel." Clive pointed out a medieval wheelbarrow.

Slater kept tapping on his phone.

Clive directed attention to the Northeast corner of the green where a majestic stone church stood. "That is the Tower's own place of worship, the Chapel of St. Peter Ad Vincula."

Slater took in the architecture of the Chapel. He waved Beckford over. "This is what I want the entrance to the casino to look like!"

Seeing some semblance of interest Clive opened the door to the chapel and motioned the group inside. "Please come in," Clive asked. He noted Slater's durag. "As this is a sacred place of worship, I will have to ask that you remove any headgear. Additionally no photography allowed within the chapel," Clive announced the rules generally, so as not to embarrass anyone in particular. He also pointed to a sign which had the regulations clearly stated.

They entered the chapel and walked towards the nave. The stained glass windows gave the pews a tinted glow. The cusped arches afforded a glowing natural light. "The bones of Queen Anne Boleyn, Sir Thomas More and other notable Tower guests are interred beneath," Clive related. He noticed Slater still wore his hat.

Slater nudged Beckford. "I want tables designed like pews. We'll have cocktail waitresses dressed in low cut monk's robes. Are you getting this?"

Beckford dutifully keyed the instructions into his iPad. "Got it," he said. He raised the iPad to take photos. Clive intervened, placing his hand over the lens. "As I said, there are no photographs allowed." He turned to Slater. "Additionally I will have to ask you to remove your hat."

"This is not a hat," replied Slater.

"Regardless, sir, it is head-gear and expressly not allowed within the chapel," Clive replied with as much equanimity as he could muster.

Slater rolled his eyes and ripped off the skull cap. "I am feeling a bit of an inhospitable vibe here. I will share my concerns with the Home Secretary when I see him."

"All due respect, Mr. Slater, you will have to go higher than that," Clive replied as he pointed to a crucifix at the altar. "This is a working church and sacred burial site and He is ultimately in charge."

Clive turned to John, who seemingly forced down an urge to laugh but coughed loudly instead.

***

Ashley sat next to Heath on a bench at Queen's Walk. They were on the south bank of the Thames, viewing the Tower on the other side of the river. They were shoulder to shoulder and she felt awkward. Why had she kissed him? It was entirely the wrong message she wanted to send. Yes, he was cute and disarming and maybe he had grown on her a bit since she had re-examined him this morning with sober eyes. But she was not looking for anything serious.

"You sure you're okay?" Heath asked.

"Yeah, I'm fine now. It was all just a bit much under there."

"I wouldn't have brought you down if I had known. Usually we get some warning. The guns are usually for holidays, or the coronation or something."

"My dad didn't say anything about it either." She remembered though that Clive had told her there was some dog and pony show and he was getting dressed in his royal reds.

"What do you mean?" Heath asked.

She still did not want to mention where she lived. "I meant...my dad is usually listening to the news and he tells me if there's something special happening."

"Wait. So your dad lives in London?"

"Yeah. He does. That's why I'm here."

"That's great! So you will be coming back then."

She was impressed with his enthusiasm. "I suppose I will, yeah."

"What does your dad do?"

She just really didn't want to go into it. "He's semi-retired." That was a bit of a lie. He had retired from twenty-five years in the armed services, that part was true. But he definitely was not retired in any sense of the word.

"I see. Cool."

Ashley's eyes scanned the banks of the river. The Honourable Artillery squad rolled the ceremonial guns back inside the fortress. "I guess I better be going."

"Can I walk you back to your flat? Or your hotel?"

"No need. I'll be fine. I want to thank you for showing me this spot. I do love history and despite the surprise it was quite interesting."

"Yeah. No worries. When are you leaving?"

"Not sure yet. Probably next week."

"Can we meet again before?"

"I'll ring you." She felt awkward so best to leave.

She jogged off towards Tower Bridge. As she took in the elegant overpass she understood why the Tower underground had gone out of business. The tunnel experience was too nerve-racking for the average commuter seeking to cross the river. Bridge and tunnel battled it out in the marketplace and bridge definitely won.

***

Clive led Slater and his entourage across the quad to the Waterloo Barracks, the largest building in the Tower complex. He wanted more than anything to wrap up this tour quickly and get this Las Vegas stooge off the grounds. He thought of his hero, the Duke of Wellington who defeated Napoleon at the Battle of Waterloo, the building's namesake. He was sure Wellington would not suffer a fool like this easily. But he also had an awareness of politics and chain of command. Maybe he could bore the guy to death. Maybe that would make him leave faster.

He conjured up a monotone voice and lectured slowly. "The Duke of Wellington built these barracks in a neo-medieval style during the year 1845, at the height of military presence within the fortress. The stone structure housed over eight hundred soldiers. In the mid 1990s it was re-fitted as a jewel repository, wherein you now stand."

A long line of visitors queued up for a visit to the jewel vault, the star attraction for many people. Clive led Slater and his assistants past the velvet rope and inside the building, much to the chagrin of the jewel fans. Slater walked and texted at the same time. Clive hoped the brash developer would slam into a wall. But no such luck. Slater navigated the corridor without incident.

Clive swiped his key card and nodded to the guards as they entered the Treasury Room, where the Crown Jewels were displayed. Slater looked up from his phone. The first of several jewels was separated from the viewing public by thick bulletproof glass. "This is possibly our most famous jewel, the Koh-I-Noor, or Mountain of Light. It is the world's largest cut diamond. It is what's known as a superdeep diamond, meaning it gestated not far from the Earth's core, a distance of about 750 kilometers below your feet."

Slater took in the surroundings and turned to Beckford. "We'll have the shopping mall built to look like this. Let's reach out to Cartier. I'm sure they will lease a shop." Beckford made a note of it.

"The diamond was a gift to Queen Victoria in 1849, although many debate whether or not it was given under coercion. This gives rise to demands that the diamond be repatriated to India."

Slater took a very unsympathetic tone. "I saw your protesters out front there. Seems like you got a bit of a PR problem."

Clive smiled weakly. "As a symbol of the seat of power in the U.K. we are no stranger to protests of many kinds and we respect the right of people to peacefully assemble in the name of free speech."

Slater pressed his face to the bulletproof glass, leaving a fresh smudge on the otherwise crystal-clear pane.

"Please refrain from placing hands or faces on the glass as we proceed through the rest of the vault. Thank you," Clive instructed.

Slater took a look at the placard pinned to Clive's chest and read his name. "Clivey-boy, in case you didn't notice, I am not your average visitor. It is very likely this very diamond will display in my castle soon enough. So you can dispense with the petty schoolmarm scoldings. We're all adults here."

Clive was at wit's end with this guy. He remembered the phrase *kill them with kindness*. He would do the same with Mr. Robert Slater. Figuratively, not literally. "Of course, Mr. Slater, no scolding intended, simply wanted to make sure you stay safe as these panes of glass are known to harbor bacteria and we just had a group of sneezy school kids pass through here."

Slater backed away from the glass immediately. He whipped out a small bottle of hand-sanitizer from his pocket and sprayed it on his hands.

Yeoman Warder Kincaid, a salt and peppered stocky Beefeater, popped in to check if the coast was clear to release a group of public visitors into the exhibit. He blanched when he saw Clive. "Apologies for the intrusion, sir!" Kincaid skulked back out of the room. Clive saw an out.

"No intrusion at all!" He turned to Slater who was back in his phone. "May I introduce Yeoman Warder Bruce Kincaid, who will escort you through the next leg of the jewel vaults while I attend to an urgent matter." He did not wait for anyone to accept his excuse, he simply darted out the nearest exit and rushed up the stairs.

On the military parade ground several Scots Guard soldiers marched the bi-hourly changing of the guard. Clive rushed to the office of the Resident Governor. Groups of tourists parted to let him through. He reached the door of the Georgian brownstone and swiped his keycard.

The Resident Governor greeted him. "Clive? I thought you were on tour with our VIPs."

"I am. I was. Kincaid is guiding the tour for the moment. Sir do you realize this special tour is holding up the queues to the jewel vault and this supposed VIP is not a VIP at all but simply a hotelier from America? Permission to call off the red carpet treatment? I have no idea who ordered this.

The Governor wore a simple suit today, it gave him the look of a typical bureaucrat. "Public Relations Office, Ministry of Cultural Affairs."

"All due respect, sir, but since when do we give 21 gun salutes to civilians?"

"It's really not up to me, Clive, but I will tell you that he is a billionaire – made his money in crypto currency – and he wants to license the rights to the Tower name for a castle hotel in Las Vegas. It represents quite a bit of revenue that would allow us to do some upgrades here."

"Upgrades? Why would any Yanks come here when they can see a cheap knock-off in Las Vegas?"

"As I said, Clive, this is not up to me..."

"The gun salute is only for heads of state! We are not running some circus show over here! I don't care how many billions of dollars he's vowed to line some MPs pockets with!"

"Take a moment, Clive," the Resident Governor replied with a slightly threatening tone.

Clive breathed deeply. "I'm sorry Resident Governor. This has all caught me a bit by surprise and this chap is quite unseemly if you ask me." Clive turned around and walked out back on to the Green.

He walked briskly across the grass, glancing up at the Beauchamp Tower which loomed above the west Inner Wall. It was known for housing high ranking prisoners who scribbled graffiti on its walls before they met the headsman. For this moment he felt like one of those prisoners. Although he would not meet his fate on the scaffold, he could meet a fate with HR if he lost his head in the presence of the crypto-billionaire.

In his haste he did not see Sheila Hansty. She tapped him on the shoulder and he spun around. The State Dress complemented her. She had butterscotch highlights in her hair and the red of her tunic set it off nicely. He had always liked Sheila. She was a veteran of the Adjutant General's Corps Staff & Personnel Support Branch. She led a team of auditors in the payroll department for the duration of her armed services career. She was a whiz with bookkeeping and helped him on several occasions with reports of cost overruns.

"Clive? Are you alright?"

"Fine, yeah," he replied.

"Where is your VIP party?"

"I had to take a break from it."

"Why?"

"Because the VIP is an arrogant prick. He's going to license the trademarks of the Tower to build a hotel replica in Lost Wages."

"Where?"

"Las Vegas."

"Oh, I get it. I'm sure you can talk some sense into the Home Office, can't you?"

"This is above my head. They're kowtowing to his every want and need."

Sheila smiled. "Well, it isn't over till the Fat Lady sings, you know."

"I know HRP needs his money but this is ridiculous. It's completely undignified to license the Tower's imagery!"

"It's all pie in the sky for now."

"That's not the way the Resident Governor puts it."

"We used to having a saying at the MOD Head Office in Whitehall. Worrying is as effective as cheating at cards without a marked deck. The real troubles in your life will be things that never crossed your mind."

Clive liked Sheila. He didn't quite understand the quote, but it was obviously accountant humor. "You have a point," he said. "Well I had better get back to the Jewel House."

"How's Ashley? I haven't seen her this morning."

"She went on a run. We had a bit of a row."

"Over what?"

"She wants to go back to her mother."

"You haven't made firm plans with her to see the countryside yet, have you?"

"No," Clive admitted. "It's not that I don't want to, but one thing after another has come up."

"Clive this fortress has been here almost a thousand years. It will be okay if you leave for a day or two. You must show Ashley that you value her by spending time with her."

"I spent plenty of time showing her around here."

"That's not the same. This place can be gloomy day in and day out without a break. Especially for a young girl."

"I'll speak to her. I don't suppose you would want to go with us?"

He figured it would be good to have Sheila there to smooth any arguments over between he and Ashley. There was a tension between them ever since she arrived. He felt nothing he did was good enough for her. He was also never sure how much her mother had slandered him. Did she poison pill Ashley's opinion of him? He certainly didn't want to ask.

Besides, he enjoyed Sheila's company. Malcolm, her husband wouldn't mind. He didn't even live at the Tower, but rather spent all his time at their vacation home in the south of Spain. During one of his brief visits he explained how the warm weather was imperative for his health.

"It's not about me, Clive. It's about the two of you. The last thing I would want is to be a third wheel."

"Right. Point taken." She was right as usual. He shared things with her that he would not with anyone else. She was one of the "guys" but at the same time she was not. There was a softness beneath her tough exterior. He had a feeling she revealed it only to him and perhaps Malcolm. He found himself staring at her flaxen hair. It was braided in a Celtic knot. "I should go," he said. "Can't keep the VIPs waiting."

"Who's babysitting now?"

"Kincaid."

"He's a good one. I'm sure he's handling it."

"Thanks. I'll give you the full report later. Fancy a pint at *The Keys* after the ceremony?" The Keys was the private Yeoman Warder's pub at the Tower for one hundred and fifty years. Its location within the fortress was kept secret from the general public.

The ceremony he referred to was the Ceremony of the Keys. Each night at 9:52PM it was Clive's duty to preside over the ritual of closing the Tower of London and locking its gates. He was accompanied by a precision military regiment of Foot Guards. They usually allowed thirty or forty lucky ticket holders to witness, a tradition performed every night for seven hundred years.

"You know me better than to think I would join you for a *pint*," Sheila replied. "But I will consider a hot chocolate with marshmallows on top." She winked and walked off.

"That's what I meant!" Clive shouted. "A wee slip of the tongue." He caught another glimpse of her Celtic knot. It poked out primly beneath her red Tudor bonnet.

Yeoman Warder Sprowley, approached Clive from behind. "Sir?"

Clive spun around, startled. "Yes, Sprowley? What is it?"

"Your presence is urgently needed in the command center. We have a situation."

Clive nodded and followed Sprowley across the Green.

Chapter Five

The day was not getting any better. Clive's malaise continued. He kept thinking of Ashley. He had to talk her out of leaving. She just got here! What was it so far? Twelve days? They barely were able to catch up. He was doing his best to make time for her but something always came up. She obviously didn't understand the pressure he was under. He wanted to take her fishing at Beech Hill Lake, take her behind the scenes at the British Museum, he had a list of things for them to do. He had to convince her not to give up on him.

The Tower Operations Center was an ultra modern surveillance center and situation room within a medieval edifice. Banks of closed circuit camera feeds lined one wall, giving it the appearance of a television station. The console was manned by several Scots Guard soldiers and a red-bearded Yeoman Warder who kept alert watch over the various angles covering the nooks and crannies of the fortress. Clive and Sprowley entered the room, passing a conference table that was not quite round, but intended for conclaves of the modern day knights of the Tower of London.

Clive put his eyes on the camera monitor that covered the entrance to the White Tower where the suspicious abandoned bag had been found. "What is it?"

"White Tower camera three. Take a look," Sprowley answered.

The Scots Guard selected a hi-def monitor and zoomed in on the item in question.

Clive noticed what looked like an unattended diaper bag on the steps. No visitors paid any attention to it. "Must be a mother left it."

Red beard clicked on nearby cameras for alternate angles on the scene. They looked for pausing mothers of small infants, anyone in search of a missing item. Clive scanned for strollers, perambulators, anything that might give a clue to the owner of the diaper bag. "No one searching," he indicated to the Scots Guard.

The Scots Guard zoomed in on the image of the diaper bag. "We got something that looks like a wire protruding."

Clive studied the image. "Could be headphone cables."

Scots Guard disagreed. "They look electrical, not audio."

Clive picked up the radio. "Warders Mason and Kirby report to White Tower entrance. Investigate the unattended bag on the steps. Exercise all precaution."

Mason and Kirby briefly went off camera until the next CCTV lens picked them up. They neared the White Tower. The main palace was whitewashed in the year 1240 during a trend to paint prestigious buildings white. It was no longer completely white per se, it was back to its natural ragstone and limestone colors. It was a square stronghold, with a watch tower at each corner. This was the site of the Tower armory, where large quantities of gunpowder were stored. The White Tower also contained an armory museum displaying many ancient weapons for the public. Crossbows, longbows, blunderbusses, muskets, swords and staffs were all prominently exhibited there in chronological order of their invention and use.

Mason and Kirby scanned the crowd. Several tourists taken with their State Dress uniforms asked to pose for selfies. They gracefully declined.

Yeoman Warder Kirby approached the diaper bag cautiously. Mason waved at several bystanders to step back. It was a Burberry designer tote. It did not look like the typical accoutrement of a young mother. The camera zoomed in and Clive studied the cluster of wires. Were they connected to a battery perhaps? He noticed a young mother nearby with a pram, rocking it back and forth. Of course! This had to be her bag. It was all much ado about nothing.

"Ask that mother if it's her bag," Clive prompted via radio.

Kirby did so, pointing out the tote.

The mother seemed a bit testy. She shook her head.

Clive felt the stomach knot again. He spotted a young father, carrying a two-year old in his arms. The toddler was crying. "Ask him if it's his."

Mason asked, feigning an air of joviality. The young father shook his head no. There was no one claiming the bag, nor was anyone looking for it.

Clive could not take the chance. "We've got a code blue. This is not a drill. Exercise all protocols."

"Roger," replied Yeoman Warder Kirby. He pulled some police tape from his pocket and cordoned off the area.

Clive turned to Sprowley. "Call Met Expo Squad."

"They're already on their way. They said to proceed with evacuation protocols."

Clive looked at the cameras. He could see Kirby, Mason and several other Warders clearing the public out of the area. "Let's keep all public back at least 100 meters," he instructed. "Any public inside the White Tower should exit from the other side."

"Copy that, sir. Sprowley answered.

Clive picked up the radio. "This is Clive. No radio or cell phone usage within one hundred meters of the suspicious item, copy?" There was always a concern that a radio or cell phone signal could trigger an incendiary device.

The Resident Governor turned to Clive. "Perhaps we should have Met take down the local cell phone towers?"

"Let the Expo team decide when they arrive. I'm going to the Water Lane entrance to see them inside."

"There's already a couple here," Sprowley mentioned. "They were in the area on a training exercise so I took the liberty of consulting them. Jainsley let them in."

"The more the merrier, I suppose," Clive intoned as he left.

***

Clive walked with a fast gait down the cobblestone steps towards the Water Lane entrance. An IRV, or Incident Response Vehicle, approached from St. Katherine's Way. As they drew closer Clive waved and put his key into a control box. The hydraulic bollards lowered into the ground and Clive walked up alongside.

At the wheel was Richard Bindar, a square-jawed man of Indian descent. Clive recognized Bindar. If he recalled correctly Bindar had been on a personal leave for months from the Met expo squad. It was not uncommon. Life on the bomb squad took its toll on the psyche and frequently people needed time for self-care.

Clive greeted him cordially. They were not friends, simply on-the-job acquaintances. "Richard, how are you?" He decided to ignore the fact that Bindar had been out for awhile.

"I'm back on duty," Bindar answered. "Wish I were visiting under better circumstances."

Clive noticed three men and one woman in the back of the van. They all wore the uniform of Met explosives and ordnance disposal (EOD) officers.

"Welcome. We've got a stray bag on the Green. Spotted some wires protruding. We've cleared an area of 100 meters around the bag. All personnel are out of line of sight and off radio comms within the clear zone."

"Cordons are up?" Bindar asked.

"Affirmative," Clive answered. He glanced at Bindar's hand. He was gripping a rabbit's foot.

"Got your good luck charm, I see," Clive noted, in a jovial tone. It was not the first time he noticed Bindar's affinity for talismans. He recalled a silver ankh around his neck on several occasions. It was definitely outside of Met uniform guidelines.

Bindar placed the rabbit's foot in his pocket. "Don't tell me you're one of those PETA do-gooders."

"No," Clive answered, a bit shocked by the backflash.

Bindar stayed on the defensive. "The feet are harvested after the rabbits are already dead, okay?"

"Sure, sure, no problem."

"I have had one of these for years. My luck has never failed me defusing bombs. So you can keep your opinion to yourself."

Clive sought to lighten up the mood. "You might as well have some sort of protection given the stories of all curses in this place."

Bindar nodded. "That's right."

"Did you hear about the rabbit fossils found in Northern India?" Clive asked.

"No I did not."

"They carbon dated them. Fifty three million years old. The rabbit is a survivor. Not only that, they live and lived in deep burrows underground. They're in touch with the gods and spirits of the underworld."

"Like you said, I need all the help I can get. Now let's get on with it." Clive felt relieved he had lightened the mood. But there was definitely something off about Bindar today. He hadn't seen the guy in at least six months, of course. Getting to know your local bomb disposal tech was sort of like getting to know your car mechanic. If you knew him too well that meant your car was a lemon, or in the case of bomb disposal you were a sitting duck for terrorists.

The van pulled across the bridge that traversed the moat and went through a tunnel into the Outer Ward. Clive followed, clearing a path for the vehicle through a throng of exiting tourists.

"Oh, one more thing," Clive added, sidling up to the driver's side of the van. "A couple of your Expo Officers beat you to the punch."

"My Expo Officers?" Bindar replied with forced equanimity.

"Maybe not yours. I think they're from Central South command, Brixton. They were in the area doing some training so they're already on scene."

Bindar turned to his second-in-command, a pale Irishman with ginger hair. "Sedgewick! Take the wheel, I'm going up there." He stopped the van and Sedgewick slipped over to the driver's seat.

Bindar hopped out and followed Clive towards the White Tower as Yeoman Warder Kincaid emerged from the jewel exhibit with Slater and his entourage. The VIP tour had mingled with another group of tourists, three women and a young girl plus a couple of men who looked distinctly American. Kincaid led them to the Wakefield Tower, site of the *Torture at the Tower* exhibit. Slater proudly posed for a photo at the entrance sign before they headed underground.

They seemed completely unaware of any disturbance. Clive waved at Kincaid but he did not see him.

Bindar beelined for the two expo officers from Central South. They hovered over a bag in the distance. Clive followed.

"Hopefully your mates from Central South have some intel by now," Clive said.

Bindar ignored the comment and marched up to the cordon the Yeoman Warders had placed. He ducked and passed under it. "You stay here," he ordered Clive. "Make sure you and your men use these ear protectors!" He threw Clive a box of foam ear plugs.

Clive accepted the box. He turned to Yeoman Warder Kirby who stood on guard at the cordon, waving people off. He was doing his best not to alarm them. "Don't worry folks, the White Tower will re-open again soon. We have a little bit of maintenance to do."

Several people nervously backpedalled and headed across the Green.

Clive handed Kirby a pair of ear plugs. "Take these as a precaution," he ordered.

"Thank you, sir," Kirby replied. He was a man who had been in the military since he was seventeen, so the word sir was ingrained in his vernacular. Many of the yeoman warders were like that. Kirby placed the ear plugs in.

Clive walked over to Yeoman Warder Mason and offered him ear protectors as well.

The sound of jackhammers at the construction site next door echoed throughout the Tower grounds. But Clive did not bother to put in his own ear plugs. He watched as Bindar conferred with the two Central South EOD guys. There was a tall one and a shorter, stocky one. They wore helmets and Kevlar protective vests. They shrugged and laughed as they pointed at the bag. Given the levity, Clive figured it must be a false alarm. Maybe a prank. But Bindar did not seem convinced.

He put his arm around the short bomb tech and led him behind a wall out of sight. A moment passed and Bindar emerged alone. He waved the lanky expo officer over. Lanky approached and they both disappeared behind the wall. What were they looking at? Some kind of a transmitter? Clive was not sure. The jackhammers rattled.

Bindar materialized alone and walked back to Clive. "I want a full evac. That includes you, your staff, all non-EOD personnel. You've got ten minutes," he ordered.

"What is it?" Clive asked.

"Potentially a dirty bomb. No one, I repeat, no one is to go beyond this cordon except for me and the members of my team. I'm going to need plans of the entire facility. We will need to do a sweep and make sure there are not others."

"Got it."

"I also want the Tower and its environs evacuated. Radioactive protocol."

"Copy that."

Bindar's voice expressed frustration. He pointed out two of his men who set up a signal jammer on a tripod. It was near the location of the bag with the dirty bomb. "We have a local jammer here on scene to prevent radio trigger signals but for the broader area we are going to need to take down all cell phone towers within this zone."

"We'll get the phone company right on that," Clive replied.

"Let the police know comms may be down awhile. They should hang back outside the evac zone until further notice and stay off radio frequency devices."

Clive nodded. "Do you require any back-up?"

Bindar waved him off. "I have all the team I need, thank you."

Clive nodded and returned to the Tower command center to enact the evacuation plan. It was the same plan they used to close the Tower each day. He watched CCTV monitors. A team of Warders began with the Outer Ward, closing off entry points and herding visitors towards the exits.

In this situation the Warders were under strict orders to tell people that the Tower was closing due to a broken water main. They deeply apologized for the inconvenience and asked people to hurry along.

Once the Outer Ward was given the all clear, another team entered Tower Green and ushered people off. These people could see the cordon around the steps to the White Tower. They were not so sure this was a plumbing problem but they left anyway. Several visitors asked about a refund. Clive instructed the Warders to notify tourists to hold on to their tickets, a refund would be issued the next day.

Gradually parents escorted disappointed children to the Outer Ward and the designated exit points. Tourists and sightseers grumbled and filed out. The crowds thinned dramatically.

Clive ordered the two other Warders on duty at the command center to leave. He took a seat at the console and watched the monitors himself. The Bell Tower camera showed Sheila approaching. It was her turn to ring the Curfew Bell. Ordinarily she would pull the sally (woolen grip of the bell rope) at closing time: 545pm. But today was obviously different. She pulled several times and loud clangs ensued, announcing the early closure.

Several more teams of Warders proceeded methodically into the Inner Ward. Kirby and Mason worked to clear the Green itself. Another team evacuated the White Tower. There were still many buildings to clear with hidden stairwells, underground exhibits, parapets and other places where tourists could get stuck or locked inside. Each of these had to be given the all-clear.

Part II
Siege

Chapter Six

Ashley came off Tower Bridge and strode towards Tower wharf. Throngs of people headed her way, leaving the exits at a clip. Could there be something wrong? She had never seen such an exodus at mid-day. She sped up her gait but she was a salmon going upstream. A pleasant middle-aged woman in a Spice Girls t-shirt careened out of nowhere and bumped right into her. "I'm sorry," the Spice Girls fan offered.

"What's going on?" Ashley asked.

"You haven't heard? They say it's a plumbing problem but I heard it's really a bomb scare," Spice Girls answered.

Ashley had never ever heard of the Tower shut down for plumbing repair. According to her dad, it was a rare occurrence for the Tower ever to shut down at all, except for Christmas or a pandemic.

She quickened her pace and put more energy into parting the crowd. "Excuse me! Coming through! Pardon me!" She pushed her way to the Wharf. She saw someone she recognized in the distance. It was Yeoman Warder Sheila, dad's friend.

Sheila stood at the gate to Tower Wharf, ushering people out. "Sorry for the disturbance folks but the city of London demands we shut down due to the water main leakage. We appreciate your understanding!"

Ashley popped up on her radar, the only person heading inside. "Excuse me! Pardon me! You cannot enter at this time, madam," she cried out.

Ashley stopped right in front of her. "Sheila, it's me!"

A look of recognition came across her face. "Ashley! What are you doing? You can't come back in, love."

"Why not?"

Sheila looked around at the general public. She did not want to give anything away so she whispered in Ashley's ear. "We're all being evacuated! I can't give you details but there is a hazard."

Ashley knew immediately the rumor she heard was true. Of course Sheila did not want to elaborate.

"Where is he?" Ashley asked.

"Your dad is managing the situation at the moment. Best if you wait for him outside."

"Outside where?"

Sheila pulled some money out of her pocket. "There's a good little pizza place just outside Camden Market called Vittorio's. Lunch is on me. I'll tell your dad you're there."

"I just came from Camden Market!"

"I'm sorry, love. It's where your father would want you to be."

Ashley had no idea what that meant but she was going to find out. Why would her father want her so far away? If he did that meant there was something dreadfully wrong. She shifted her ground and darted through the gate out of Sheila's reach.

Sheila waved at her. "Where are you going? You can't go back in!"

"I'm not leaving without him!" Ashley ran back through the Tower Wharf and headed for the water gate entrance.

***

Clive's office was the epitome of neatness. He had a computer in the center of his desk that he used as little as possible—only for email dispatches. Otherwise it was an analog space. He had a row of fountain pens neatly laid out on a desk blotter. He had a notepad of parchment paper. Several large file cabinets contained printed files of information he might need. He didn't trust the internet and he didn't trust the reliability of a computer to hold all of his informa-

tion for him. A potted fern was in the windowsill. It was a gift from
Ashley.

He spoke on the landline phone to Emma at the local Met police
incident response post. There were no pleasantries exchanged this
time. "Close Tower Bridge to all traffic except emergency personnel.
Close all streets on the outskirts of the Outer Wall. Close the Tower
Hill tube stop. Let's clear all those areas for emergency use only."

Emma responded cool and collected. "Will do, Clive."

"Also get a hold of the phone company. We need to take down
cell service within a one kilometer radius, in case they are using a cell
phone trigger."

"Copy that."

Clive grabbed some keys out of the center drawer of his desk
and walked into an anteroom which contained several cabinets with
wide, short drawers. He walked to the cabinet in the corner, placed a
key in its lock and twisted. He opened the third drawer from the top.
Inside were several blueprints – scaled drawings of the various parts
of the Tower. Each individual tower structure was represented along
with all ingress and egress points. It had notations for where electrical lines, catacombs and other points of interest were located. Clive
had insisted on these paper blueprints. The historical architects had
all of this on CAD programs but these were backups.

He rolled the plans up and placed them in a tube. He returned to
the command center. A quick perusal of the monitors revealed Kincaid and the tour group with Robert Slater at the *Torture at the Tower* exhibit. Slater hovered over the Scavenger's Daughter device, designed to compress a person's body to the point of death. He posed
next to it for a picture. In the presence of these instruments of death
and mayhem was the most animated Clive had seen him. Kincaid
and the rest of the tour group had no idea an evacuation was called.
Radios didn't work down there. Clive had to alert them to leave as
soon as possible.

He glanced back at another exterior monitor. The Inner Ward was almost clear of tourists. Only Bindar and his team remained. Clive rushed toward the Wakefield Tower entrance.

He passed the raven aviary. John the Ravenmaster employed rituals to entice the ravens back to the aviary. He put a favorite treat, mice, into their respective cages. Raven Wally, Crater, Jackabee, Lori, June and Harcourt beelined back to quarters to feast on their morsels. One bird did not take the bait: Herman, the alpha with the albino patch on his belly, stayed in position at the top parapets of the Waterloo Barracks. It was as if he were watching over the place.

"Come on now Herman! You must come down. We are taking a little trip," John called.

Clive had ordered the birds to Hampton Court. They could not risk losing them in a catastrophic incident.

John closed the doors of the mobile cages and placed each in the back of a van. He called again to Herman but the raven remained on his perch, stubbornly refusing to budge.

John turned to Clive with defeat in his voice. "I don't think he will leave."

Clive could see the bird was in no mood to follow orders. "Leave him here then. We don't have time to dither."

John shrugged. "Herman considers himself the prime protector of this place."

"Well then, he'll take his own chances."

John grabbed June's cage and placed it beside Wally's. He made short order of loading the rest. That totaled seven. There were the six duty ravens and one of the backups. In this case the spare was not Harry of Windsor but Josie. The ravens did not protest the manhandling as they were in food comas from digesting their large mice.

Sheila Hansty approached. Clive bristled. "What are you doing here?"

"Have you seen..."

John cut her off. "Herman? Yes we've seen him and he refuses to leave."

Sheila nodded.

Clive softened his tone. "Is everything okay?"

Sheila had a nervous demeanor. "Sure, yes, fine." Was there something she didn't want to tell him?

"I want you both out of here as soon as possible."

Sheila looked him in the eye. "What about you?"

"I have to alert Kincaid and our illustrious guest down in the torture exhibit. They did not hear the call to evac."

"I'll do that," Sheila replied. "You go wrap up the sweeps. I know you won't leave until everyone is accounted for."

Clive nodded and took another look at Herman, who broke his circling pattern above and descended towards something that apparently posed an interest to him.

***

Mint Street was normally vibrant with Beefeater's kids playing on their bikes, wives sharing the *Daily Mail* gossip pages on medieval stoops and Beefeaters themselves taking snack breaks. Right now it was tumbleweeds, a ghost town obviously left very quickly. Ashley ran up the cobblestone path. She held her phone to her ear. She rang her dad but it went straight to voicemail.

"Dad? Where are you? I'm here at the Tower looking for you. I know you haven't left because you would never do that but you need to! This is not a sinking ship and you are not the captain! Call me." She hung up.

She rushed to her father's flat and ran inside.

"Dad? You there?"

The place was empty. She ran back out. Police sirens echoed off the stone walls. Herman the Raven spiraled above. Ashley yelled loudly. "What do you want?"

Herman flapped his wings. "Caw, caw, caw!" He perched himself on the parapets of Broad Arrow Tower, a defensive fortification of the Inner Wall. It had arrow slits in its semi-circular projection, allowing archers to position themselves with a view of London city.

Wait a minute, was Herman trying to tell her something? No that couldn't be. He's just a raven! She decided to skip it. She had more important things to do than worry about a thick billed crow.

She dashed off down the cobbles towards an entrance to the Salt Tower, the place where the king had stored his most valuable food preservative back in the day. Salt was prized in an age with no refrigeration, hence this turret was named after the precious commodity. She slipped through the entrance and entered the Inner Ward. She arrived next to the workshop building, a modest structure built in Victorian style.

There was activity near the White Tower. Two Met cops pushed a droid-like contraption towards an abandoned satchel. Two others fiddled with a small satellite dish. What the heck was going on?

***

Clive returned to find Tower Green almost clear of tourists. Two of Bindar's men unloaded the "wheelbarrow," their bomb bot. Clive noticed the female EOD officer in the van writing something down. He had not seen this team before today. Perhaps they were a new crew? This was not the time for training greenhorns.

Clive handed Bindar the tube with the blueprints for the facility.

Bindar took the container. "Thank you. Now it's time for the rest of you to leave as well. You don't want to put any of your team in harm's way."

Clive nodded his assent. "We're just about cleared the place out. But we still have to evacuate the jewels."

"There's no time. Just lock them down."

"We can't leave them without a guard."

"The jewels will survive radiation. It actually might make them bluer. Ever hear of irradiated diamonds? The guard won't like the radiation. You all have to leave."

"Okay but I plan to stay."

"You can't do that, Clive. You must leave with the others. Hopefully we'll get this sorted soon enough."

"I can be of some help in deciphering the blueprints. I know this place like the back of my hand."

"No need, Clive. You know the policy. This is EOD jurisdiction. If something happens to you, it's on me. Sven? Please escort Clive to one of the exits."

Sven, a sinewy man with Danish features, rushed over and stood behind Clive.

Clive felt like a captain being escorted off his own ship. He had done nothing wrong. He was doing his duty.

Chapter Seven

The Tower Green, epicenter of the fortress that was the Tower of London, had seen many dramas unfold during its tenure as a village square for the royals. Those historical dramas had occurred mostly hundreds and hundreds of years ago, prior to its current incarnation as a tourist destination. Today's drama was distinctly different. The Green was empty except for a gaggle of Met cops who hovered around a package on the steps of the White Tower. They had some kind of large device that looked like a satellite dish.

Ashley viewed the unfolding situation from behind an abutment at the base of the Inner Wall. She watched her father escort a Met officer off the Green. She thought about approaching him but did not want to reveal herself for fear of getting kicked out. She would leave when he left and not before. Two men ran a cable to the satellite dish. Another man looked over architectural blueprints. He looked like the commander of the unit as he pointed things out and gave commands she could not hear. A uniformed woman stood by his side. Another officer pulled a kit case out of the van. He pulled out what looked like a large gun. A small missile launcher? She was not an expert in firearms but that thing was no ordinary gun.

Where was Clive going? She had to tell him she was here. Sure he would be mad but she wanted him to leave and remove himself from the danger zone. If everyone had to evacuate then he did too. He was not a cop. He was no longer a front line warrior. He was her father and this was a civilian position he occupied. He needed to be with her.

She picked up her phone and rang his number again.

***

Clive walked briskly towards the exit, escorted by Sven. At this point he was very concerned. Why had Bindar insisted that he leave? That didn't make sense. If he wanted to risk his own life that was his call, not Bindar's. He could be of help in deciphering the blueprints and making sure the area was cleared. Was Bindar covering something? What? He had known him for at least five years and always found him to be a capable, dedicated public servant. But then he had not been well of late.

His phone vibrated in his tunic pocket. He was able to slip it out without Sven knowing. It was Ashley. Thank heavens she had gone to lunch at Camden Market. She probably was calling to make sure he was okay. He ignored the call and slipped the phone back in his pocket.

"Is that a phone?" Sven asked.

The phone vibrated again. Clive didn't answer. It made a slight sound as it brushed against the fabric of his tunic.

"You should pick it up. We don't want to worry anyone."

Clive picked up. "Hey?"

Usually he said *Hi Ashley* but today it was just, *Hey.* He wanted to send her a signal that he could not talk, that something was wrong, without saying so. The longer he stayed on the phone the more likelihood he might give something away to Sven, whom he didn't trust. He had learned this in the military – you don't give away personal details to potential unfriendlies. They could use these as bargaining chips against you.

"Dad? Where are you?"

His neck muscles tightened. "Where are you?" He hated answering questions with questions but he was trying to pretend he was speaking with someone he didn't care for.

"I'm here!"

"At the restaurant?"

"No I'm here at the Tower. Looking for you. I'm near the Innermost Wall."

Clive looked over to see if Sven had overheard. He kept marching forward, staring at the parapets above. Obviously he had not.

"Dad?"

"You need to leave right away. No questions."

"I'm not leaving without you, dad. Where are you? We'll leave together."

"No. I can't talk right now. Just leave, okay?"

"I'm not leaving! Just tell me where you are and I'll come to you!"

He hung up. He could not risk any further conversation without knowing Sven's intentions. Ashley was inside the fortress? What had possessed her to come back when she was safely away? His heart sunk. Would she heed his order to leave? He doubted it. She was too stubborn this one. He was not planning to leave the Tower but now that Ashley was inside these walls he knew he had to get her out at all costs.

Suddenly a loud explosion shook the stone walls. Clive recognized that sound. It was a rocket propelled grenade. He had seen and heard his fair share in Afghanistan. He hit the ground, breathing heavily, expecting more rocket fire. None came. Sven flinched at the sound and ducked.

Clive quickly regained his feet, smelling smoke. He looked towards Cloister Walk. There was a cell phone tower on fire. It was obliterated. They had taken out the cell tower with an RPG?

Sven smiled.

Clive scowled. "Couldn't wait for the phone company to turn them off?"

"No we could not, mate. Any microwave transmissions could be the death of us."

I am not your mate, Clive thought to himself.

They walked down Water Lane towards the Byward Tower. On the right side of the lane there was an exhibit where the former Lion's Tower (long since demolished) had been. The Lion's Tower was the location of the King's menagerie, the zoo at the Tower which had once housed over 300 different animal specimens. At the moment there were cages with metal wire sculptures to represent the animals formerly on display.

"I didn't realize you guys had such firepower?" Clive pointed toward the smoke plume from the RPG hit.

"Oh yeah. Sometimes you have to fight fire with fire."

Sven's radio crackled. Bindar's voice came through. "Is he off-site yet?"

Clive gestured at the radio. "Shouldn't you guys be off radio comms?"

Sven's expression turned sour. "You let us worry about that."

"You know, come to think of it, I've known a lot of expos in the Met bomb squad but I never heard your name. Sven is it?"

"That's right."

"Not very British."

"Yeah, my mum was British and my dad was Danish."

"Yeah but that doesn't answer why I never heard of you."

Sven said nothing. He walked in step with Clive, close enough to grab him if the need arose.

They reached the entrance to the zoo exhibit. The door to an animal cage was left open. A padlock on the hasp hung unlocked. Sven paused. "You want to stay here?"

"Of course I do," Clive replied. "I can be of assistance to you and your team."

Sven glowered. "Be my guest." He grabbed Clive by the collar and shoved him in the cage.

Clive landed between a lion and polar bear sculpture. He looked up to see Sven close the door and padlock it.

"Hey!" Clive barked. "This is not what I meant!"

Sven turned the other way and headed back to the Tower Green. He did not look back.

Clive pulled his phone out of his pocket. He had no bars in the upper left corner of the screen. There was no signal, a result of the RPG hit to the neighboring cell phone tower. He was stuck.

***

Ashley rushed up the walkway towards the Bloody Tower portcullis entrance. The portcullis was open, she presumed so bomb squad personnel could come and go. She walked through the portal to the Outer Ward. Clive was nowhere to be seen. She passed the Wakefield Tower. The *Torture at the Tower* exhibit was underground. A slender Beefeater rushed to the entry of the turret. Was that Sheila? Ashley drew back out of sight behind a kiosk. She did not want Sheila to see her. She had disobeyed an evac order.

As the slender Beefeater disappeared through the Wakefield entrance Ashley thought she heard clanging and banging. She hovered near the door and listened.

A deep voice resonated from the stairwell. "Help us! We're locked in! What's going on?"

Ashley prepared to descend the stairs when she heard Sheila. She spoke with aggressive kindness. "Kincaid, it's Sheila. The Tower's been evacuated. You must have missed the warning."

Ashley turned back. If Sheila was there these people didn't need her help. She remembered Kincaid. He was one of her father's colleagues. "I didn't hear anything on the radio!"

"Sheila's voice was calming. We are off radio comms. Orders of the bomb squad."

"Oh bollocks. How bad is it?"

"We don't know yet. Expos are here but they're worried it's a dirty bomb so all visitors and staff are ordered off premises. I'm going to go get the key to let you out, okay?"

"Many thanks. I've got a VIP down here along with some regular tourists."

"I heard about the VIP, he's with you?"

"Yup. Diplomatic Office won't like that, will they?"

Sheila lowered her voice. "I'll be right back. Keep everyone calm."

"No worries, Sheila. Thank you. If you hadn't come along who knows how long we would have been here."

Sheila rushed back up the stone steps. Ashley ducked into an alcove as she passed. She felt pangs of guilt for not helping but she knew Sheila would insist that she left and she wanted to avoid any further confrontation.

***

Clive looked up from his perch in the lion's cage. He watched four men dressed like Met counter-terrorism tactical police summit the four corners of the Outer Wall. Where had they come from? One manned the parapets of the Develin Tower on the southeast, another the Byward Tower at the southwest, another took Legge's Mount on the northwest and Brass Mount on the northeast. It was as if they were fortifying the castle against an invasion. Who would be invading? It made zero sense.

Only one thought loomed in his mind. This operation was not what he thought it was. Bindar was quite possibly using the incident for his own agenda. Clive was familiar with false flag operations from his time in the military. They were acts committed to disguise the source of responsibility for an incident, to misdirect blame to another party. So far the events of today had all the earmarks of such an operation. Perhaps Bindar was not back on the Met EOD force. Perhaps he was still on leave, unstable, consumed with PTSD, a drug addict or worse. Perhaps he was using his former post in this case to carry out a personal mission. The question was what.

The thought that Ashley was on site disquieted him. She should never have come back. He would feel slightly better if this were a cut and dry bomb scare but given the implications this was something much worse. She had no idea of the puddle she had stepped in by returning.

He rattled the cage door. It did not budge.

***

Ashley walked back to the Tower command center. Her father had to be there, monitoring the situation. She entered the operations room and viewed the banks of CCTV surveillance monitors. This would allow her to find him. She carefully studied each monitor. There were a lot!

The Tower Green was covered from several angles. She could see members of the bomb squad hovered around the abandoned bag but no sign of her dad. She looked at several cameras broadcasting the Outer Ward, specifically Mint Street and Water Lane. The streets were empty although she saw several more bomb squad types patrolling. Patrolling for what? Maybe they thought the bomber would come back to the scene of the crime? That made no sense. Again no images of her father.

Camera ten showed an angle on Wakefield Tower. Sheila was returning to the *Torture at the Tower* entrance with a ring of keys. The lead bomb tech looked up from his post and clocked her. He darted across the Green in her direction. She was in such a hurry she did not notice. She rushed into the castle keep and descended the stairs.

Ashley had to stay focused on finding her father. She continued perusing the cameras but could find no sign of him. She reached into her pocket for her phone. She had bars so there must be service. But when she called Clive's number it would not even ring. It was just dead air. She decided to roam the Tower more to see if she could find him. Then the phone rang. She picked up immediately.

"Dad?"

"No, it's Heath. Did I catch you at a bad time?"

"Yeah, actually you did, Heath."

"Is your dad okay?"

"I don't know because I can't reach him!"

"I just thought I'd call to make sure you're okay. Since I left you near Tower Bridge there's been a mass evacuation of the Tower."

"Yes, I know all about it! Thank you."

"Well, alright then," Heath replied. He sounded disappointed she wasn't happier to hear from him.

"I'm sorry. I'm just under a little stress right now. Hey! You know about phones and telecommunications, right?"

"Yes, of course. As I told you, it's my job."

"If you were talking to someone and the phone got cut off and then you called them back and it just didn't even ring what does that mean?"

"Means that there's some service break."

"But wouldn't that affect my phone too?"

"Depends if your mobile service is a different carrier with a different repeater. It might have to do with that thing at the Tower. There's rumors that the bomb squad is out there. They sometimes jam the phone frequencies in the area because they can be used to trigger a bomb detonator."

"Oh my Lord." It was all starting to come together now. The Met cops on the Green surrounding the package, the satellite dish, it all made sense.

"You alright?"

"My dad works at the Tower of London."

"What? Okay. I'm sure he's out of there. Everyone's been evacuated."

"No, he's not."

"You say you couldn't reach him on his mobile?"

"No. But my mobile is working so I don't understand it."

"Yeah but you're not there..."

"Yes, I am, Heath."

"You're in the Tower right now?"

"Yes. That's where my dad lives. I came back to get him."

"Oh, that's not good. You have to get out. You're in danger."

"I'm not leaving without my dad. Thanks for calling. That's really sweet of you. I'll be in touch." She hung up. Something on the bank of CCTV monitors caught her attention.

It was Sheila, now inside the *Torture at the Tower* exhibit. She was with Yeoman Warder Kincaid and his group of tourists. There was some kind of confrontation happening. Sheila, Kincaid and the tourists were queued up to leave but the doorway was blocked by what looked like the Met bomb squad captain. He was a man of Indian descent and he kept shaking his head, as if saying no.

Sheila and Kincaid seemed to be imploring him to let the group leave and the captain was standing in the doorway blocking their exit. Then he slammed the door in their face. They banged on the door and pushed against it but it was apparently locked from the outside. The group consisted of several adult males, a middle-aged woman, a twentysomething woman and a young girl of about nine. Why wouldn't the bomb squad let these people leave? Maybe an explosion was imminent and he figured it was safer to have them underground rather than outside?

Her mind raced. None of this added up. She had to speak to her father and let him know what was going on.

***

Clive paced back and forth in the menagerie. The sculptures of the lion and polar bear stared at him, stoically. He could not stop thinking about Ashley. She was inside the fortress? What had possessed her to come back when she was safely away? His heart sunk. Would she heed his order to leave? He doubted it. She was too stubborn this one. He was not planning to leave but now that Ashley was inside he knew he had to get her out at any cost.

He regretted inviting her to visit. If he hadn't she would be home in California, out of harm's way. But that was beside the point now, he had to figure out what was going on. There were two scenarios, either this was a legitimate bomb threat and Bindar and his expo guys were taking out the cell phones to prevent a remote detonation or...Bindar had gone rogue and the bomb was just a cover for another plot. He didn't recognize any of these expo officers that Bindar brought. Except the first two that arrived before him. Where did they disappear to? Also no legit bomb tech would incarcerate him. He was a member of His Majesty's Royal Bodyguard and as such was entitled to respect. All of the Met police knew this. No, Bindar was hiding something. That's what scared him more than the potential of a bomb going off. But either way he had to get Ashley out of there to safety as soon as possible.

He reached in his pocket and found a paperclip. He pulled it out and bent each side so it broke in the middle, giving him two L shaped pieces of metal. The slightly longer wire would be his torsion wrench. He forced it into the lower part of the keyway, below the pins. He inserted it hard and bent the side so it would not come out. Then he took the other side to use as his pick. He held the lock firmly in one hand and jiggled up and down.

Back and forth he jiggled, adjusting the wires each time. Nothing. The lock held firm. He removed the paper clip and bent it again at a narrower angle. He reinserted it into the lock. He jiggled again.

Finally he felt something click and the padlock released. He gingerly popped the top of the lock and emerged from the menagerie cage.

He tried his cell phone again. It was still down. He needed to call out. Maybe get some intel on what the hell was going on. He would have to use a land line. He hugged the Inner Wall so as not to be seen and walked back up Water Lane towards the Tower Operations Center and his office.

Chapter Eight

Ashley sprinted up Mint Street toward Clive's lodgings in the Casemates. She had remembered something. The pager. That stupid old pager that Clive could not part with for some reason. She might be able to reach him on that. There was just one problem: she had lost the number. In order to reach him, she had to call it and send an alphanumeric message. She thought she had the number in her purse because Clive had insisted she keep it. But her purse was at home. Did she say home? She meant Clive's house.

She reached the front door and fumbled for her key, then noticed the door was unlocked. There was really no need to lock one's deadbolt within a fortress: it was protected by a regular patrol of guards and stone walls twenty-six feet thick.

She opened the door and rushed through the living room to her bedroom. On the desk was her purse. She rummaged through it, putting lipstick, wallet, keys, chewing gum aside until she found papers at the bottom. She pulled each paper out, one by one. The first was a ticket to the London Eye. The second was an advertisement for a nail salon and the third one had a phone number. It said merely "Dad pager" next to the digits.

She picked up the landline and dialed. A recorded message picked up. You have reached Standard Paging Systems, please dial in your message. She typed in with the alpha-numeric keyboard the following:

Meet Ashley at Bell

She typed the # sign and the recorded voice confirmed it was sending the message. She grabbed her purse and rushed out of the flat, this time locking the door behind her.

Outside on Mint Street she was met again by the piercing eyes of Herman, who perched next to the Broad Arrow Tower. He occupied one of the east-facing battlements. She gestured at him silently to move on. She thought of the trite Edgar Allen Poe verse about a man bereaved who talks to a bird. "Quoth the raven, nevermore." She disliked the poem. Wasn't a big fan of that Alfred Hitchcock movie, *The Birds*, either. Herman did not budge. She rushed down the street towards the Bell Tower.

***

Clive re-entered the Tower Operations Center. There were half-drunk cups of coffee at desks, steam still rising. He looked at the wall of monitors. Most of the cameras had no people in view. The only angles that showed the presence of humans were the White Tower entrance, where Bindar and his team still congregated around the Jewel House entrance. They carried equipment towards the front door. That's odd, he thought. He picked up the landline phone to call out. It was dead. No dial tone, nothing.

Clive heard voices coming down the hallway. He glanced back at the monitors and saw the commandos manning the Outer Wall parapets. They were armed with high powered rifles and looked like Specialist Operations Dept 15 (SO15) counter-terrorism police. But again this was strange. Why would the expo squad need sharpshooters on the Outer Wall when the immediate area in and around the Tower had been evacuated? The bomb squad did frequently travel with SO15 to secure incident locations but they usually had their own vehicles. Clive only remembered seeing the one IRV.

The voices down the hall were closer now. Clive slipped out the door and tiptoed away. He stopped at his office and noticed the ceremonial partisan hanging on the wall. This was the polearm that the Chief Yeoman Warder used since the 16th century. It featured a long wooden handle with spikes protruding to help with parrying sword thrusts, along with a sharp axe blade on the end. Lacking any other quickly available weapon he grabbed it off the wall.

Clive's pager buzzed. But he did not feel it vibrate. It was deep inside one of his tunic pockets, away from his skin. He carried his polearm and skulked out the back entrance on to Water Lane.

He headed towards Tower Green, hugging the Inner Wall. When he reached the Bloody Tower he quickly skated under the portcullis and again hugged the wall to stay out of sight. He wanted to see what Bindar was up to. Surely he and his team had employed the bot by now to ascertain the danger of the IED.

He walked the long way around the White Tower to remain unseen. It took him past the old Roman wall, behind which Bindar had taken the two first responders. What was that all about and where had they gone?

The answer lay in front of him. The two men were face down in the manicured grass. What were they doing? Digging a trench? Defusing another IED? He approached them from behind. He did not want to reveal himself with the risk of getting forcibly removed again. Neither of the men moved. This was odd. They were absolutely still, faces planted on the ground. He stepped on a twig which broke, making a sound. Certainly they would turn around to see who it was but they did not react. This did not make sense. He crouched immediately above them. Not a single twitch from either. Normally in this weather you would see some breath mist coming out of a person's mouth but nothing.

He kneeled down. That's when he saw bullet holes in the back of each of their heads. These men were both killed execution style. Bindar had obviously done it. But why? Perhaps they were not part of his plan? They were a random happenstance he had not predicted? Men not in on his operation? They saw the bomb was no threat. He had no choice but to eliminate them as fast as possible, because he needed that threat. That threat kept the police away. It kept the Tower empty of all personnel except he and his cadre.

Clive realized he was also a random happenstance that needed to be eliminated. So far he had eluded execution, unlike these men. But if he were taken into custody again he was sure to meet the same fate. A bullet to the brain. Bindar was a bent cop. A rogue who knew the routines and inner workings of the police department and could use it to his advantage. Clive shuddered at the fact that he obviously would stop at nothing to achieve his aims. What were they? Clive had suspicions but he could not be sure yet. He poked his head over the Roman wall and got a glimpse of the abandoned valise with the wires. The bot sat right next to it, sitting idle.

He looked to the opposite side of the Green, near the scaffold exhibit. That's when he got a glimpse of Bindar. He circled the execution scaffold and gleefully shot some selfies on it, as if he were a tourist. Something had happened to this guy. This was not the Bindar Clive once knew from emergency response and crisis drills. Meanwhile the rest of the expo crew headed into the Waterloo Barracks.

Clive ducked beneath the wall and ran back under the portcullis to the Outer Ward. He headed up Water Lane. With the electronic channels of communication cut off he had to go old school. His answer was at the end of the lane.

A turret rose sixty feet into the air from a foundation that was solid stone. The Bell Tower loomed. Its heavy ledge and brace door were made of hewn poplar timbers. Clive took out his key and placed it in the lock. The door creaked open. He marched up the spiral stone staircase, past lodgings where Sir Thomas More had been imprisoned by Henry VIII. He went up another flight into the Upper Bell Tower, past the cell where Catholic martyr John Fisher was locked up for refusing to renounce fealty to the Pope. Later, Elizabeth I had been imprisoned here as well by her rival and half sister, Queen Mary I. This Tower was the scene of considerable drama and martyrdom. Up and up he went, till finally he reached a door that led to the rooftop parapets.

Clive emerged on to the rooftop and saw the belfry where the eponymous bell was located. His heart raced. He looked across the Thames. He could see Potters Fields Park, just next to Tower Bridge. He loved that place. Home to markets, bazaars and festivals. It had the most amazing view of the Tower and surrounding skyline which included the iconoclastic architecture of buildings such as the Gherkin and Walkie Talkie.

Why hadn't he taken Ashley there on a picnic since she had arrived? Potters Field had seen much history during its day. In the 1600s internationally renowned Delftware pottery was manufactured there. It had seen an era when traders located cotton, ivory, tallow, grain and sugar inventories in warehouses. It had seen the Great Fire of 1861 destroy many of these warehouses. It had seen the Industrial Revolution rejuvenate its wharf, with leather suddenly the object of trade. It had seen the Blitz with many bombs dropping across its surface.

Today it was empty. The one kilometer radius evacuation protocol was likely the reason. He was sure the police and evacuees were holding back beyond Tooley Street, on the other side of the park. He had told the Beefeaters to congregate there at the site of the old Lalit Hotel.

Clive looked at the bell. Without radio or cell phone comms this was the only way. It would give his position away to Bindar and crew but he had no choice. He would defend his position. He took the rope pull and began to gong very loudly. It was not the typical curfew "all clear" ring. He rang three long times, then three quick times, then three long times again. Just as he rang the bell a ship blasted its fog horn.

He waited patiently until the ship silenced itself. Then he rang again. Three long chimes, then three quick, then three long. Old time nautical SOS in Morse code. Surely someone would hear it and investigate? He looked across the river. No one had appeared to view. Perhaps they were all out of earshot?

He rang the bell again.

Surely he would see some movement forward on the part of the police to investigate? They were sure to have heard it from their command post outside the evac zone. Perhaps one of the Yeoman Warders had heard it and would alert Inspector Emma Winklough? Emma would do something. She had just been here this morning.

But there was no one on the other side of the Thames.

He heard footsteps in the Outer Ward and looked down to see two men rushing down Water Lane in his direction. He readied his partizan and hugged the parapets. Then he heard another set of footsteps coming from within the spiral staircase of the tower keep. How could they have gotten in so easily? He had locked the entry door. The footsteps in the stairwell became louder. He tensed up, bracing for the inevitable. The axe of the long partizan was used by infantrymen to fight off horse attacks. Its spikes had the additional purpose of trapping an opponent's sword if they had one. He would swing hard and low to take out the legs of the incoming marauder.

The footsteps were louder now. They were right outside the belfry. He emerged and lifted the partizan back like a golf club. He cocked his wrist, ready to lash out with force. Then he got a glimpse of familiar ginger locks. It was Ashley! He stopped the blade inches from her neck. They stared at each other in dismay.

"What are you doing here?"

"Didn't you get my page?"

Clive pulled his pager from deep in his pocket. "No." He looked at the screen. The LCD readout showed her message.

"You were raving about this great old technology?"

"I normally wear it on my belt but in the State Dress it has to be hidden so I put it in my pocket. It was not close enough to register the vibration."

"Well I'm glad this all worked out anyway."

"How did you get inside here?"

"I got the key out of the command center."

"You never should have come back. You knew no one was allowed inside due to the bomb threat."

"If I recall correctly, all Beefeaters were supposed to evacuate as well yet you did not."

"This is my job."

"And I am your daughter. I'm not leaving without you."

"You were leaving as of this morning."

"That's different. I'm not leaving while your life is in jeopardy."

"I can take care of myself."

The roaring sound of a large diesel engine echoed through the core of the turret. Clive peeked over the crenellations to see Sven start up a scissor lift. It was normally used for maintenance on high windows. Sven drove it down Water Lane towards the keep. Another of Bindar's men picked up a ladder and carried it towards the Bell Tower. They had obviously heard the bell chimes and realized someone was trying to get a message out. But had anyone on the outside gotten that message? Otherwise it was all for naught.

Clive shook his wrists out in a gesture of frustration. "I don't think you understand."

"Oh I understand. You're perfectly willing to be killed in a bomb blast that will leave me fatherless."

"This is no bomb threat. The bomb is a ruse," he replied. He grabbed her hand and led her to the battlement. He pointed out Sven, piloting the scissor lift towards the keep. The merc with the ladder was not far behind. It was Bindar's second in command whom he had introduced as Sedgewick. None of this crew seemed at all preoccupied with defusing a radioactive bomb.

"These guys are not the bomb squad," Ashley replied.

"No. They're here for some other reason."

Ashley's expression turned to one of dread.

Clive took another peek below and noticed that Sven was now ascending the side of the turret via the scissor lift.

"What are we going to do?" Ashley asked.

"We are going to prevent the escalade," Clive replied. He crouched down and headed for the rooftop hatch that led to the spiral staircase.

"Escalade? You mean that Cadillac car?" she asked.

"No. An escalade is the first stage of any siege. The enemy attempts to climb the castle wall." He pointed at Sven.

She followed him inside the roof hatch. They walked down the steps towards an old oak door. The sign above it said: Buttery. "This is where they made butter?" she asked.

"Did you not read the glossary of castle architecture that I gave you?"

"Not yet," she said.

"The buttery was a room used to store drinks, especially wine, beer and ale." Clive put a key in the door and it opened.

The chamber was now set up as a coffee break room with all of the modern amenities. There was a microwave oven, a hot-plate, a toaster and an electric tea kettle. Clive grabbed the tea kettle and filled it up. Then he placed it on its base. "Don't tell me you're making yourself a cup of tea," Ashley said.

"I'm not daft," Clive said. He opened a cupboard and she noticed it was full of liquor bottles. He picked up a bottle of bourbon.

"A cocktail?!"

Clive handed her the bottle. "I am not drinking with you!" she protested.

"It's not for you to drink," he replied. He grabbed a bottle of cognac. "We need chevaux de frise." He placed his bottle over the sink and emptied it. He then placed it over a trash can and smashed it on the side. The glass shattered into shards which plummeted into the bottom. "Go ahead. Do yours," he said, pointing to her bottle of bourbon.

"I have no idea what you're talking about," she said.

"I thought you knew your medieval history! Chevaux de frise! It literally means a horse of Friesland."

"Friesland. The historic region in North Holland? Didn't they live on man-made mounds that rose above the flood basins?"

"Very good! The Frisians used this tactic against invaders." He grabbed another bottle of liquor and emptied it, then broke it into the trash can. He waved at her to join him.

Ashley did the same with her bottle.

Clive grabbed another bottle, emptied and smashed it. Ashley did the same. They rinsed and repeated again. Pretty soon the bottom of the trash can was filled with broken glass.

"I have no idea what we are doing or what this has to do with horses!"

Clive heard the sound of the scissor lift outside. He grabbed his ceremonial partizan and headed back out on to the roof. "Bring the trash can," he instructed.

Chapter Nine

Clive dragged the trash can full of glass shards out on to the battlements. He looked down through the crenels and noticed the other merc climbing his extension ladder, creeping ever closer to the top. The scissor lift rose on the other side of the turret. Sven was almost to their level. Clive pulled a glove out of his pocket and proceeded to pull glass shards out of the trash can and spread them on the top of the battlements.

Ashley crept up behind him. "So this is what the Frisians did?" she asked.

"That's right," Clive answered.

The other merc reached the top of his ladder and placed his hand on one of the merlons. A shard of glass sliced his finger. "Ahhhh!" He pulled back his hand in bloody agony and lost his footing.

Clive wasted no time and pushed the ladder away from the turret, completely destabilizing the invader. He grabbed hold of a crenel and managed a foothold on the stone wall. The ladder fell to the ground. The merc clung to the side of the turret.

Clive turned to Ashley. "Bring me the teapot."

She adopted a snide grin. "Earl Grey?"

"Just boiling water will do."

"Milk and sugar?"

"Just bring it! We don't have much time."

***

Ashley went back to the buttery. The kettle indeed was hot. She grabbed an oven mitt to pick it up. She rushed up the steps back to Clive. He leaned over a wood platform that was built between two crenels in the battlement. What the hell was he up to? Obviously there was some method to his madness. There was a gap in the center of this platform.

Clive leaned over it. "Have you heard of a murder hole?"

She handed him the kettle. "No, I have not."

"This is it. The Outer Wall has many of them."

"It's called a murder hole because?"

Clive poured the contents of the hot kettle into the hole. Almost immediately they heard an agonizing scream as the ladder-climber was covered in scalding water. He let go of his handhold and fell thirty feet to the ground. Ashley peered over the ledge to see him hit with a thud.

She looked away from the gruesome sight. It made her nauseous. She had never been a part of this level of violence before. She started to feel sympathy for the man sprawled on the ground but wondered if he would feel the same for her if the roles were reversed. He had wanted to kill her, she was sure of that.

"I'm sorry you had to see that," Clive offered. "I wish you weren't here."

Sven looked down at his compatriot's body from the scissor lift. Broken limbs were twisted in gruesome positions. Sven appeared to get a surge of adrenalin, perhaps from a desire for vengeance. The scissor lift continued its ascent. He was almost in line with one of the crenels of the battlements, affording him entrance to the roof of the tower. And he was armed.

Clive retreated to the belfry and rang the bell again. Ashley followed. He gave it three short rings. Stop. Three long rings. Stop. Two short rings. Stop. He handed the bell rope to Ashley. "Continue to repeat my pattern. Exactly."

She took the rope and did so. It felt good to be doing something. She was still in shock from the sight of that man's death. Her father did not seem fazed by it at all. She had never thought too much about what he did in the army for all of those years. But it was obvious they had made him a stone cold killer. She continued to ring the bell. Maybe he was fazed by it but he didn't let it show. Maybe his position at the Tower was a way to deal with all of the violence he had seen for all of his years in service.

She rang the patter again. She was getting used to it now. Someone on the outside had to hear their call for help. Someone on the outside had to recognize the Morse code in medieval bell form.

***

The Bell Tower, built in the late 12th century, was the second oldest tower after the White Tower palace at the center of the fortress. The actual bell itself dated to around 1651 and had been doing its duty as a curfew warning for almost four hundred years. Clive was grateful for its chimes as he peeked over the parapets to see Sven atop the scissor lift. He was ascending to the rooftop, now close enough so he could hear the two way radio.

Bindar's voice blurted over the radio. "What the hell is going on - over?" He obviously was not obeying his own ban on wireless communications, another tell there was no bomb threat.

Sven sounded hoarse. "We're taking casualties. Anders is dead – over."

Clive could see Anders' crumpled body at the base of the keep below.

The radio crackled with Bindar's voice. He did not betray an ounce of empathy.

"And that goddamned bell is still ringing!"

"It's that Beefeater."

"You should have killed him!"

"I'll do it now – over."

"You had better! Or I will get the RPG and go do it myself!"

Clive ducked down behind the battlements. He certainly was making himself a fly in their ointment, for what it was worth. He did not understand what Bindar's plan was, however. Between the merlons he could see the scissor lift sway in the light wind. It continued to rise towards him.

Sven readied himself to hurdle the parapets and mount the Bell Tower keep.

***

In the belfry, Ashley looked at the timber framework that held the bell in place. She wondered if at one time there had been more than one bell hanging from it. There was a gas oil lantern hanging that evoked Victorian times. Her arm was tired. She kept ringing the same Morse pattern. The activity distracted her from the picture etched in her mind of that man falling to his death.

Clive suddenly motioned for her to get out of sight. She got down on the ground behind a merlon.

The merc they called Sven climbed over the turrets.

"Beefeater! You should give up. The police are not coming. They're scared as shite of the radiation. There is no way out for you. Come back down with the others. We won't hurt you."

Clive did not reply. He wielded his partizan, swinging it like a stick-fighter in a martial arts movie. Sven whipped out his sidearm.

Ashley's heart lurched. These bomb-squad imposters were willing to kill.

Clive grabbed a hydraulic line hanging from the scissor lift. He raised his partizan axe and sliced it, spraying high pressure hydraulic fluid. He wielded the hose toward Sven. He attempted to aim his gun but missed.

Clive pointed the hose at Sven's face. He reeled as the oily fluid got in his eyes and mouth. He dropped his pistol and radio to the floor.

The hydraulic fluid sputtered. It was no longer a stream as the hose lost pressure. Sven regained his footing and moved towards Clive. Clive dropped the hose and swung his partizan again, pushing the rogue backward towards the parapets.

Sven lunged, grabbing the handle of Clive's ceremonial axe. They struggled.

Sven pushed Clive to the edge of the battlements. He tottered, only air at his back. Nothing would cushion his fall to ninety feet below. Ashley had to do something.

Sven pushed Clive as hard as he could. He inched closer to the edge. Ashley burst out of the belfry with the detached rope pull. She came up behind Sven and wrapped it around his neck. She pulled hard. He immediately choked, caught by surprise.

Clive regained his footing and swung Sven like a Lindy partner. Ashley let go of the rope. The sudden slack made Sven stumble backwards. Clive pushed him off the battlement.

Clive turned and mouthed a thank you.

Now she had one upped herself. Not only had she witnessed a death—she had participated in killing a person. She noted he would have killed her and her father if given the opportunity. She was reminded of a philosophy class where they talked about the difference between killing and murder. Murder was planning the death of a human being with malice aforethought. She had not done that. Killing was simply ending a life. It was legally justified in certain circumstances, such as self-defense. She had helped to kill this man, she had not murdered him. The thought didn't really console her.

She saw Clive reach down and grab the merc's oily radio and gun. He wiped them off with a handkerchief .

She wished she had never come back here. Why had she? It was because she knew her father too well. She knew that in a potentially volatile situation like this he would be quick to sacrifice himself for the greater good. So if she were here with him, he would not be as in-

clined to play the noble hero and give his life away. She was not prepared for that. She was much too young to be fatherless.

Her thoughts went back to death. The only other time she had
seen it was when her grandmother passed away. Grandma had not
responded to their texts so she and mom went over to her cottage
to check on her. They found her with her head down on the kitchen
table, unresponsive. She was in that pose when you were in grammar
school and the teacher allowed you to take a nap at your desk. Except
this wasn't a nap. The sight and cold touch of her skin had disturbed
Ashley but not too much as it was a peaceful exit. It was not precipi-
tated by any violent action.

There was the time when her dog had killed a baby bird that
had fallen out of its nest on the eaves outside the base housing. That
had honestly disturbed her more than the death of her grandmother.
There were blood and feathers everywhere.

Clive keyed the merc's radio. He switched the channel back and
forth. There was no static, no sound coming out of it. "Battery lost
its charge," he explained.

"Oh, no," she said.

He took her by the hand and pointed toward the staircase. The
scent of burning embers permeated the air. Smoke rose through the
turret shaft. "They are trying' to smoke us out. Follow me."

They rushed down and found the entry door aflame. Embers and
fragments dropped away from the iron straps that held the timbers
together. Someone smacked away at the remaining wood with an
axe. Whomever was out there was highly determined to get in after
them. Just like the man on the scissor lift. Clive directed her to keep
going down.

"Where are we going?" she asked.

Clive pointed to a trap door, partially obscured by a layer of
straw. There was a ladder beneath and it went down into a dark,
danky basement. "You have your phone, right?" he asked.

"Yes," she said. "But it doesn't work. No signal."

"Tap the torch app, will you?"

"Excuse me?"

He grabbed her phone from her and tapped it on flashlight mode. "The *torch app*," he repeated in explanation.

"Oh. I always thought of that as a flashlight."

"Come along now," he said, motioning for her to follow.

"I don't do well in tight spaces."

"Keep calm and carry on," he replied.

She set her foot on the next rung of the ladder and followed him down. She could hear the sounds of the axe breaking through the entry door above them. It gave with a crash and she heard the footsteps of two men entering. They had now breached the keep. She remained frozen so as not to make a sound. She could hear the men's footsteps go up the spiral staircase, toward the belfry.

Chapter Ten

Clive looked at the cylinder of the Bell Tower and thought it looked like an upright cigarette. The heavy timber entry door was aflame and hot air and smoke rose to the top where it escaped through the belfry. Clive and Ashley remained safely below the flames, fumbling through the dark in a narrow tunnel that led underground. Clive lit their path with Ashley's cell phone. He had never been down here before. He had only read about it in the Yeoman Warder Journals of 1948. He perused them for pleasure, in what little spare time he had lately.

There were two metal rails on the ground ahead of them, leading into the darkness. Ashley pointed at what looked like train tracks. "Were they mining something down here?"

Clive shook his head. "No, this was an ancient system for shuttling ammunition: cannonballs, arrow shafts and barrels of gunpowder, from the outer wall to the White Tower."

"Why would they do that?"

"1461, the White Tower was designated a magazine, a repository for barrels of gunpowder. By 1657 the entire building, apart from the chapel, was refitted for this purpose."

"So you know where we're going?"

"Somewhat."

"You never have been down here, have you?"

"No. Just read about it."

Ashley started breathing heavily.

"Are you okay?"

"Trying to avoid a panic attack. I'm not good in enclosed spaces!"

"Your mother never was either. I once took her spelunking and she nearly lost it."

"Spelunking?"

"Yeah. Cave hiking? I took her to the City of Caves in Nottingham. Made her sick to her stomach. Then she saw a rat and she was done for."

"She never told me about that!"

"Didn't she? We used to laugh about it all the time."

"I wish I had seen that."

"Seen what?"

"You two laughing."

"We did all the time. You were just too young to remember. Ready?"

She nodded.

Clive smiled and held up his phone as they pushed forward, stepping over the remaining tracks from the old ammunition shuttle. As he stepped on one of the iron rails he felt a vibration in the metal. It was a high frequency oscillation. He took his foot off the rail and put it on again. It was definitely some sort of pulsation. From where? He could not be sure. These tracks extended underneath the entire Inner Ward of the fortress. But it was odd to say the least. A vibration like that was most likely from some kind of device, perhaps a drill.

***

Ashley shivered and thought of the last tunnel she had seen, with Heath, not that long ago. How embarrassing was that? She had jumped on him like a scared puppy. But she remembered the moment fondly. Why the hell was she thinking of Heath now, in the wake of all that had happened? Maybe because it presented the comfort of some sense of normalcy while she was running for her life? Enough of that. She focused on the mining cart tracks in front of her. Clive quickened his pace. He must have seen something ahead. She hustled to stay on his heels but he was off and away, two, three, four paces ahead of her now. And then he stopped. A cement wall sealed the tunnel ahead of them.

"What is it?" she asked.

"A wall," he answered drily.

"I can see that! What does the writing say?"

There was an inscription. Medieval graffiti if you will. It read:

Her love is sweet
Her love is fair
When we're together
She wears only her hair

"You have got to be kidding me," Ashley said.

Clive took his partizan axe to the wall and made a direct hit. Bricks and mortar shattered and went flying loose. He hacked at it again. And again. There was a sufficient opening in the wall now to get his hand behind it and he pulled back and forth at the bricks. Another clump of three or four came down. Ashley joined in. They swayed the remaining blocks back and forth until it doubled over and collapsed completely.

Behind this wall there was another wall. Ashley's cell phone battery lost its charge. They were in darkness.

"So this is it? This is how it ends? Mom gets your UK pension and I get a fricking funeral way before my time?"

"No, you get my pension."

"Not if I'm buried alive down here with you!"

"Either way your mother does not get my pension. I will not have my money in the hands of that crazy tech investor guy she married. He'd likely invest it in some evil AI that overrides people's brains or something."

"What are we going to do dad?"

"I don't think you've called me that since fifth grade."

Suddenly above them there was the sound of flapping wings. Ashley shivered at the sound.

"What is that? A bat?"

Clive walked a little further toward the sound, down a tunnel that was obviously a dead end.

"Don't go closer to it!" she warned him.

"It must have gotten in here from somewhere."

A shaft of light suddenly flickered and Clive looked up.

"It's Herman the Raven," he said.

"That creepy crow?"

"He's not a crow, he's a raven."

She walked over to where Clive stood and peered up toward the source of the light. Herman was perched at the top of a shaft lined by iron footholds. A ladder of sorts. He flapped his wings as if he were waving to mark the way out.

"You first," Clive said, pointing for her to put her feet on the first rung of the ladder. She gripped the sides. One foot up, then another she ascended up the chute toward her raven nemesis. Or was it raven messiah?

Clive followed her toward the sun.

Chapter Eleven

The ancient Romans revered the raven. A ravens' presence was thought to provide good luck in battle and beyond. As the Tower of London was built right on the remains of the ancient Roman city of Londinium, the ravens were the Roman colonists' legacy. The Raven's Roost at the Tower, aka the aviary, was home to the birds. Wire mesh cages lined the pathway inside the Inner Wall, not far from the ruins of the Roman wall that kept out early invaders.

Clive emerged carefully from an escape shaft behind the aviary. It was shielded from view. He had never noticed this hatch before. Was it some sort of escape route for the ravenmaster of yore? He did not know. But he was happy to step out into the daylight. Ashley took his hand to help him up. He did not need the assistance—he was too proud for that—but the feel of her palm in his brought back a time when she was a little girl and they were inseparable.

Herman roosted on top of his empty cage, caw-cawing. Ashley leered at him. "He gives me the creeps."

"You might be a little bit gracious, he just saved your life."

They both sighed with relief and breathed the fresh air.

Clive felt for the walkie-talkie in his pocket. It was still oily from the hydraulic fluid he sprayed. He had to get it charged so they could call out. There were charging stations in the command center. He would get the radio charged and call the Met. Surely the police would be monitoring channel 16 for emergency communications.

He led Ashley along the back of Raven's Roost, at the footing of the Inner Wall. He turned to see the Wakefield Tower turret ahead. There was a large rain downspout running up the side of the keep. He placed his feet on either side of the brackets that bolted it to the Inner Wall.

Ashley looked at the rickety gutter. It looked like it had been there since the Tudor times. "Dad. You can't climb that. It's too precarious!"

He ascended above her in direct defiance. "You stay there!" he whisper-shouted. "Stay behind the aviary!"

"If anyone should be climbing that thing it should be me!"

Clive did not respond. He was already halfway up the side. He reached the parapets and climbed over. This was a small bridge over Water Street to St. Thomas' Tower on the Outer Wall. Here he had a view of the Thames and Tower Bridge. They were completely deserted. It reminded him of a post-apocalyptic film.

He looked back to see Ashley climb over the parapets. She put her hand on his shoulder and hopped down.

"What are you doing?"

"I told you I'm not leaving you."

"You climbed the downspout?"

"Don't you remember I used to be a gymnast?"

"Yes. I was always very proud of you."

"You never came to any of my meets."

"It was hard to get away at the time."

"Like it's so much easier for you to get away now. So what are we doing?"

Clive walked quietly down the walk with Ashley in tow. The entrance to the command center was at the end on the right. He listened intently to see if he could hear anyone. There was complete silence. He put out his hand indicating that Ashley should hold back in the alcove just behind them. He investigated to see if the coast was clear.

He tiptoed softly down the hallway towards the door of the command center. The door was closed. He dug deep into one of his tunic pockets and pulled out a tactical pen, made of aircraft aluminum, it was designed as both a ballpoint on one end and a personal self defense weapon on the other. He gripped it with the self-defense end exposed, ready to strike if needed. He knocked on the door and stepped aside. In case someone burst out he could swing his arm and strike. But there was no answer. He took his key card and swiped. The door opened. The room was empty. He waved Ashley inside.

The CCTV cameras were still on. He scanned the banks of monitors quickly. Cameras seventeen and twenty two showed the *Torture at the Tower* exhibit. The tour group was inside: Warders Hansty and Kincaid, Slater, the American VIP and his entourage plus a young girl, a couple of women and two men who looked American. This was not good. They were definitely hostages.

Clive looked over to an alcove where there was a line of walkie chargers. He placed the oily radio in the cradle. They were quick charge devices.

A raspy voice startled him. "Hold it."

Clive spun around to see a beefy merc in body armor pointing a Glock at him. Ashley quietly backed out of the room. The merc had apparently not seen her.

Clive studied the man in the EOD uniform. "Busy defusing the bomb, I see."

The merc wheezed as he exhaled. "You're going to have to come with me."

"Certainly. Let me just leave a note here for the others so they know where I am..." Clive pulled out his pen.

The merc shook his head. "That won't be necessary."

Clive gestured toward a pad on the console. "It would be rude of me otherwise. You see they're expecting me at a rendezvous and they'll be wondering where I am." He scribbled something on the pad. "Is that legible?" He showed off the writing.

The merc glanced at it. It read: PISS OFF.

The merc raised his weapon with finger on the trigger. He placed his back to the door just as Ashley slammed it open into him. He toppled forward and Clive slashed up with his tactical pen at the man's exposed wrist.

The merc dropped the weapon and gripped his arm, crumpling with the pain. Clive grabbed him by the scruff of the neck and slammed his face into the table. The man went limp.

Ashley blanched at the sight.

Clive dragged the man to the door. "Lock the door behind me. I'll be right back."

"What are you going to do?"

"Send a message."

He pulled the man into the hallway. He slid him downstairs. At the entrance he looked both ways across Water Lane. The coast was clear. He hauled the man towards the Bloody Tower entrance. There was a timber-hewn oak frame which had three holes: one for the neck and two for the hands. This medieval instrument of torture and public humiliation was known as the stocks.

Clive walked over to the pillory with his captive. He pulled off the top beam and carefully placed the man's head and hands in the block.

Then he lowered the top timber, locking the man into the device.

***

Ashley sat at the CCTV console. The monitors lit up the room with a blue tint. She stared at one monitor in particular. It prominently displayed the merc that Clive had remanded to the stocks. He was out cold. Or worse. A knock came at the door and she reacted with a start.

Clive's voice carried through the door. "It's me."

She dislodged the chair that braced the knob and undid the deadbolt. Clive entered.

"Is he dead?"

"Do you really want to know?"

"You wouldn't leave him to come back and fight another day."

"He would certainly have a renewed vengeance."

"No. I don't want to know."

"I know this is not easy for you. I never wanted you to be here to witness this."

She knew he was right. She had brought herself into this impromptu gladiator's arena. She had no one else to blame. She needed to confront that this is who her father was. He probably had not planned to revisit his old self. He had adopted a new identity as a tour guide and caretaker of one of the world's oldest historical sites. But he was given no choice in this situation. In the eternal question of does one fight or flee cutthroat adversaries he was a fighter. The violence was indeed wretched. She was getting a view of her father that not many, including her mother had seen.

Clive looked over her shoulder. She turned to see what he was looking at. It was the charging station. His walkie-talkie had a green light indicating its quick charge was over. He moved over to the table and picked it up.

He opened the door and checked the corridor, drawing the pistol he had scavenged off the dead merc.

He waved at her to come and she followed him down the corridor and up a flight of stairs to the roof. They emerged into the daylight and climbed another spiral of stairs to ascend the turret. He keyed the walkie talkie.

"Mayday mayday mayday Met CTC come in. This is Clive Bellamy at the Tower of London. The tower is under siege by a rogue bomb squad. They have hostages. I repeat they have hostages and have already executed two personnel in cold blood. Repeat. I am declaring emergency we are in distress and need support—over!"

Ashley looked out across the Thames. There was no one in sight across the river or anywhere for that matter. They were sheltering in place, she supposed.

A voice on the other end of the radio came back. "Caller this is Met Police you are ordered to get off and stay off this channel! We are under orders of radio silence - over!"

Clive instantly replied. "No you don't understand! That is a ruse! The bomb squad are impersonators, using the threat of a bomb to gain access to the Tower! This is Clive Bellamy, Chief Yeoman–over."

The Met officer called back. "Caller I am ordering you to get off this channel and maintain radio silence – over!"

"Please patch me through to Inspector Emma Winklough – over."

Ashley listened intently for the reply. The only thing that came back was a strong pattern of static and random, distorted noise.

Clive keyed the radio again. "Come in Met CTC. This is Clive Bellamy, Chief Yeoman Warder at the Tower."

Nothing. Just more noise and static.

Clive turned to Ashley. "It's no use. They're jamming the radio spectrum. We have to go."

Ashley noticed something in the distance. It was a reflection of the sun off Byward Tower. A bright focused spot as if coming off a magnifying glass.

; "Get down!" he yelled.

She spun around. "What is it?"

The reflection wavered. It flashed on to the parapet and then back to her chest.

Clive dove, placing his body in front of hers like a shield, as the clack of a rifle shot was heard. They both hit the roof together, landing behind the protection of the battlements. But Clive was hit. A hole pierced his tunic.

"Oh my God, dad? Dad!"

Clive gasped.

"Dad!" Tears streamed to her eyes. This could not be happening. She took his hand in hers. "Dad, you're going to be okay. I'm going to get you out of here. I'll be right back."

She scrambled toward the bridge. But he grabbed her leg. "Don't go."

"I have to go."

"What are you going to do? Bargain with them?"

"Yes, if you must know! I'm going to give myself up as long as they agree to let you get medical care. Don't try to talk me out of it, dad. The point is non-negotiable!"

"I don't need medical care."

"What do you mean? A bullet hit you in the chest!"

He ripped some of his tattered tunic away revealing a ceramic ballistics plate.

"I didn't know you had to wear body armor as part of your uniform!"

"We don't *have* to wear it. But some of us do."

She kneeled down to look for any damage to his chest. The bullet had not penetrated. He breathed weakly.

"Are you sure you're okay?"

"The force of the impact may have fractured one of my ribs." He wheezed.

Ashley kneeled down and embraced him. "You threw yourself in front of that bullet for me?"

"Of course."

"I'm sorry..."

"Why are *you* sorry?"

"Because I was stupid. You wouldn't have had to do that if I hadn't popped my head up above the parapets."

"It's not exactly a normal life situation. You were trying to help. Can you take off my cummerbund?"

"Your what?"

"The side straps that hold the ballistics plate on."

"They call that a cummerbund?"

"Yeah."

"A cummerbund is for a goddamned tuxedo not a bulletproof vest!" She gently helped him remove the side straps so he could get the plate off. The Velcro released and she pulled the plate off. It was not pierced but there was a small indentation in it. He inspected his chest. There was no blood. She placed her finger on his sternum. "Do you feel that?"

"No," he replied.

She placed a finger on his lower rib. "How about that?"

"Owww!" he replied. "Yes, I feel that."

She saw a black and blue mark on his skin.

***

The St. Thomas Tower linked to the Wakefield Tower via a small covered bridge that spanned Water Lane , the cobblestoned street that ran parallel to the Thames behind the outer wall. Clive and Ashley crossed this bridge to retreat back the way they came. They passed the king's private chapel, just off his former quarters. Sunlight streamed through its stained glass windows, painting pretty patterns on the floor. Clive's knees ached but he pushed on. They emerged on the inner wall walk and descended the downspout to Raven's Roost.

Once safely on the ground they hugged the wall to the rear entrance of the Bloody Tower. Bindar and his fake bomb squad were nowhere to be seen. The package with the "bomb" was unattended. They made their way underneath the portcullis. This brought them back to Water Lane, the cobblestoned road that paralleled the Thames. Clive again motioned for Ashley to hug the Outer Wall as they made their way around the corner.

She conjured a whisper. "Where are we going?"

Clive pointed out an oak plank door fifty feet ahead. A sign on the door read: *New Armouries*. Clive had to secure weapons for both he and Ashley. If he were to allow her to stay here with him (and he was not at all sure he would do that) he had to arm her. The warders had an ample supply of firearms and ammunition for situations just like this. He pulled a key off his ring and inserted it into the door.

"I don't know how to use a gun," she replied.

"You're going to learn," he answered. "These guys mean business."

"Wow. Go visit your father, mom said. See how he lives. Maybe you'll understand why I left him."

"Do you?"

"Do I what?"

"Understand why she left me?"

"I'm not your ex-wife whisperer, okay?"

"What's a whisperer?"

"Never mind! Show me the guns!"

He pushed on the door and it opened into a room with floor to ceiling gun racks. They were all empty.

Bindar and his crew had taken the firearms. This meant that all bets were off. The mercenaries were extremely dangerous and armed to the teeth. Clive felt an impending sense of doom. Even if he wanted to escort Ashley off the grounds it was difficult with sharpshooters perched on the outer wall. He had to get weapons for them to survive.

Ashley seemed oddly relieved at the lack of weapons. "So much for our gunfight at the OK corral. Now what?"

"We have other options," he answered as he walked out of the room. "We have to go to the White Tower."

She followed him out the door.

Clive thought about Bindar. What was his end game? Why would he do this? Was it PTSD? Did he have an axe to grind? He had a stellar record of public service. But he remembered something

Bindar mentioned at one of their crisis preparedness meetings. His brother, Arun Bindar, was arrested on charges of murder in Austin, Texas while on a trip to visit a tech company. There was a bar fight and the state of Texas tried and convicted Arun of murder in the first degree. Bindar claimed he was innocent and it was a sham of a trial. They gave Arun the death penalty. Bindar pursued every diplomatic channel he could to save his brother. But the UK government looked the other way.

It was shortly after this that Bindar went on medical leave.

Chapter Twelve

The Lanthorn Tower, at the Southwest corner of the Inner Wall of the Tower of London was one of the taller towers. It was designed as a lookout post for the Thames and its water traffic. Named after a lantern hung in its upper window to assist nighttime navigation of boats and barges, the Queen consort located her private apartment there for a time. It was next door to the Wakefield Tower where King Henry III located his own apartment. The room provided convenience for conjugal visits.

Ashley pondered this as she followed her father. He had described the love lives of many of the royals. It was completely unromanticized. Not your fairy tale prince and princess endings. In some ways she thought of them as prisoners in gilded cages.

Clive walked briskly. Via this sheltered route they would breach the Inner Wall. He was determined to reach the Green unseen by Bindar's sentries. They descended a circular staircase from the upper reaches of the Lanthorn and popped out behind the White Tower. The ancient edifice stood in her majestic glory, silhouetted against the cloudy London sky.

"This way," Clive whispered. He darted across the grass towards the staircase where the "bomb" had been found. It still sat there, unattended.

They climbed the wooden staircase to the White Tower entrance. Ashley had only been in this building once since she arrived. It gave her the spooks. A lot of people lived and died in this place.

"Where are we going?"

Clive pointed as he climbed the stairs. They reached the second floor and she noted a sign that read:

Line of Kings

An exhibit featured weapons and armor made in England during the centuries. Knights were mounted on a row of wooden horses.

Clive walked up to an exhibit that read "Harquebusier's Armour of King James II, 1686." It included a breastplate, a back plate, a long gauntlet and a pot helmet along with an ornate face guard. Clive broke open the cabinet and disassembled the suit.

"What are you doing?"

"I need a cuirass," Clive replied.

"A what?" Ashley asked.

Clive held up the breastplate. "It's called a cuirass." He stuck it beneath his torn tunic, where the ceramic plate for his bullet proof vest had been previously.

"That belonged to the King!" Ashley exclaimed.

"Still does," Clive replied. "I don't think he'll mind, given the circumstances." Ashley studied the polished silver protecting his sternum.

"Not sure that will stop a bullet."

"This was called Harquebusier's armor. The Harquebusiers were the first armed cavalry."

"You're saying the armor was designed to stop a bullet?"

Clive nodded.

He strapped the armor tight to his chest. "It's better than nothing."

She took a picture of him with her camera. "A real-life knight, aren't you?"

"I want you to wear one too." He stood in front of a display of smaller armor obviously for a child. He opened the glass cabinet and separated the helmet and visor from the breast plate.

"I'm not wearing that."

"You are the one that insisted on staying here, right?"

Ashley took in the chest plate. It was her size. "A child wore that?"

"Of course he did. The children took to the lists for the games."

She pictured children jousting with lethal weapons. Just another day in medieval England. He helped her strap the chest plate on. It fit like a corset.

He waved her on, deeper into the exhibit. They walked down an aisle lined with display cases. They contained lances, mace, bows, arrows, crossbows, longbows and even some primitive blunderbusses and muskets. He disappeared into a door that read:

Authorized Personnel Only

and re-emerged with a handcart. He walked amongst the rows of primitive weaponry and loaded up several longbows.

He pointed out a couple of crossbows across the aisle. "Grab those."

She gingerly picked up a crossbow.

"You're going to need some ammo too." He darted across the aisle to a quill of crossbow bolts and placed that on the cart.

"Bow and arrow?"

"We put you in that summer camp where you learned archery," he reminded.

"That was twenty years ago! And we didn't use crossbows!"

Clive's face broadened into a grin. "Easier than the longbow."

He continued loading lances, a mace, some more longbows, a blunderbuss and several muskets along with their primitive ammo.

"You honestly think we have a chance of defeating them with these weapons?"

"Yes, I do."

"They have automatic rifles and explosives!"

"But they don't know this place like I do." He pushed the cart along the aisle. "There are places which will give us the upper hand." He pointed out a crossbow. "The Tower was designed to utilize weapons like these. We can win."

Ashley did not know what to say. She was not sure she believed him. But she was here of her own volition and he had been right so far. She found the resentment she held for him all these years gradually dissipating. Each new moment in this escapade gave her a new look and a new context for the man who had been out of her life for so long.

***

The White Tower loomed large on the knoll upon which it was built, overlooking the Thames. It was originally intended to secure control over the city of London. Judging from the impressive skyline of the current metropolis, it had done its job. Clive peeked his head out from behind the south wall. The coast was clear. He waved at Ashley, who pushed the cart of medieval weapons toward him. They stealthily moved toward the west wall.

"Where are we going now?"

Clive pointed to the high tower above the King's House. "Beauchamp Tower."

"The one where they kept the high profile prisoners?"

"Yes, Queen Catherine Howard stayed here prior to her death, as did Lady Jane Grey. Its roof parapets are the most fortified place for archers and it has the perfect vantage point over the Tower Green."

They heard a commotion from the square just north of them. It was at the spot which marked the scaffold where Anne Boleyn was executed. Clive peered over the wall at the northern section of the Green to see Bindar and his lieutenant (Sedgewick was it?) place a chopping block on the spot which marked the scaffold. He recognized that block. It was the executioner's block and axe from the display in the White Tower. The one used to execute Lord Simon Fraser in 1747 for his role in supporting the exiled King James II. Cut from the center of an oak log, it had deep indentations carved to accommodate the head and upper chest of a kneeling victim. Two parallel axe cuts on the narrow neck section attested to its previous use. Bindar had obviously taken it from the museum.

"What is it?" Ashley asked.

"They're loitering around the Boleyn memorial," he told her. It was a half-truth, but he did not want to go where his mind was taking him. "We can't cross the Green this way."

He led her back to the White Tower. They entered and made their way downstairs. "There was a man named Father John Gerard..."

"I heard of him. He was a Catholic priest imprisoned and tortured here."

"Who later escaped. He spoke of the Yeoman Warders leading him through a secret passage between the White Tower and the King's House, accessed by a trap door. I never believed it to be true so I never checked but it's always stuck in my mind."

With that he followed the staircase to the depths of the White Tower. At the bottom he knelt and looked for any possible seams in the floor. Ashley got on her knees and did the same.

"There's nothing. It's all completely smooth."

"It's got to be here."

"I have to use the ladies room. Where is it?"

"There's nothing close by. But you can use the garderobe. Upstairs to third floor then on the right."

"Excuse me?"

"The garderobe. You know, the privy? Also called the draught? The neccessarium? Golden Tower?"

"You want me to use the medieval latrine that protrudes from the exterior wall?"

"Darling, if it's fit for kings and queens surely it's fit for you."

"Never mind. I'll hold it."

She looked down. Clive found a warped wood floor plank. It was bowed into a concave shape. He got his fingers underneath the end of the plank and pulled. It gave way revealing a stone floor below. The stone floor was slightly eroded and the mortar had cracked. He dug at the broken concrete with his hands, a dog digging for its bone. And then he found something. It was wood with a small knob on it. A trap door.

"God bless that Father Gerard! May he rest in peace!"

Ashley joined in. They pulled back the rest of the wooden planks and broken bits of mortar.

***

Clive packed up the cart with their cache of medieval weapons and prepared to travel underneath the Tower Green once again. This was the only way to access the Beauchamp Tower unseen. The Beauchamp would give him a height advantage, so none of Bindar's marksmen could take potshots at them. He could use longbow or crossbow and fire down upon them from many arrow loops and embrasures, openings in the thick brick wall to allow cover for an archer.

Ashley pushed the cart. They approached a section of the shaft that was particularly damp. It smelled of mildew and urine. Ashley displayed a sour look on her face. "This place is just full of tunnels, isn't it?"

"The masons liked to build secret passages."

Ashley nodded. "There's an old subway tunnel down here too. Goes under the Thames."

"How did you know that?"

"I have a friend who works for British Telecom and he showed me. He services fiber optic cables."

"Who is this *friend* and why haven't I met him?"

"His name is Heath. You could have met him if you had come out last night."

"What did you do down in the subway tunnel?"

"We made mad, hysterical love!'

Clive raised his eyebrow.

"Stupid questions get stupid answers."

"Well I'd like to meet him."

"Maybe. If I see him again."

"We're going to get out of here, trust me."

"I don't mean it like that. I mean if I decide to see him again."

"Sounds like he was trying to impress you."

"Yeah, I guess he was."

"So he likes you."

"I suppose he does."

"So what's wrong with that? He's not too bad looking I assume?"

"No, dad, it's just I don't know how long I'm staying here, re-member?"

There was an awkward silence. He pushed the cart forward. There was a vaulted doorway ahead. The solid oak looked to be of the Tudor period with hand-forged hardware. It had some kind of spiritual symbolism, with a carving of two hands outstretched as if reaching for Heaven.

"This must be it," Clive said.

Clive put his hand on the handle to the oak door and turned. It would not give.

"It must be locked," Ashley observed.

"I don't think so. You can hear the latch disengage. The moisture makes the wood expand in the door frame." He put his weight into the door this time and pushed as he turned the latch. The door still did not budge.

He took the tactical pen out of his pocket and wedged it between the door and jamb. He grabbed a blunderbuss and wielded the stock like a hammer against the steel pen. The door gave way with a thud. It opened to a wine cellar with hundreds of bottles of wine. The wine rack shook precariously, tottering from the pounding on the door. Clive stepped in front of the shelf.

Bottles began to drop. He caught the first one or two and set them down on the floor even as three or four more began to fall. He looked like a juggler in a game with too many balls as he did his best to save the inventory.

Ashley rushed over to help. She pushed against the rack to bring it back to its upward position. But more bottles dropped. Smash! A green bottle broke and spewed red wine all over the floor. Then another. "Stand clear!" Clive ordered and she hopped out of the way. Clive let go of the rack and it fell to the floor.

Ashley looked at the pond of wine on the floor. "I almost had a grip on it! We could have saved it!"

"The Resident Governor drinks too much wine anyway."

"Is that who lives here?"

"Yes, he lives in the King's House."

"He's not here of course."

"No, he was one of the first to evacuate."

"That must be nice," she replied with more than a hint of sarcasm.

"His role is mainly ceremonial. Like the Chancellor of a university. You don't put your leaders in harm's way."

Ashley stepped carefully through the shards of glass and puddles of red wine over to the staircase. "I suppose not."

"Will you please take some of the weapons?"

She begrudgingly stomped back down the stairs and grabbed a longbow and a blunderbuss."

Clive took a couple of crossbows and climbed a flight of stairs towards two metal storm cellar doors. He unlatched them and quietly popped them up, leaning them back so they did not slam. He poked his head out of the opening and surveyed the area for the presence of unfriendlies. He kept the crossbow at his chest. The coast was clear. He waved to Ashley and she followed him up the stairs.

Clive grabbed more muskets and arrows. She grabbed three crossbows. Once they had their weapons cache in the cart at ground level they made a beeline for the Beauchamp Tower. They passed a concession on the Green. It read: *King's Burger Palace.* Clive stopped. He took a handful of arrows and entered the establishment.

"I'm not that hungry. Really. It's alright. I'll be okay."

"Shhhh," he scolded as he darted inside the door of the concession. "Come on then!"

She stepped inside the door and he closed it. They went back into the kitchen and found a vat of French fry oil in a fryer.

Clive handed her a few arrows. "Follow my lead," he said. He dipped the tips of the arrows in the French fry grease.

Ashley stood there, her mouth agape.

"Go on! Dip the tips!"

"Why are we doing this?"

He smiled. "Ammunition."

She dipped her arrows in the grease too.

Chapter Thirteen

The Beauchamp Tower stood in all its glory, famous for its role as a last port-of-call before execution. Such historic notables as Lady Jane Grey, Robert Dudley, Thomas Abel, (Chaplain who denied Henry VIII the right to divorce) spent their last hours imprisoned in this tall keep. Clive and Ashley made several trips up the spiral staircase carrying the tranche of weapons he handpicked.

On the roof, Clive looked down from his position. It offered a strategic vantage point of both Inner and Outer Wards. He could see Bindar's sharpshooters, each positioned at one corner of the Outer Wall. They could not see him. He was above them so they had no shot. If they had truly understood castle warfare they would have perched themselves at the highest point available.

Clive led Ashley over to a cross shaped opening in the battlements. "This is called an embrasure."

He placed a crossbow inside it, revealing a perfect fit not only for the crossbow, but for him. There was even a thin horizontal peekaboo hole to see where he was aiming.

He turned to Ashley. "You are completely protected here." He demonstrated by panning the crossbow back and forth and up and down to the ground below. He moved to another embrasure and did the same. "The men below are sitting ducks. That's why they call the area below the killing floor." He pointed down at the upper portion of Mint Street, between the Outer and Inner Walls. "If someone were trapped down there, they would be not be able to hide from archers' bolts."

He handed her a crossbow. She placed it inside the arrow loop. Aimed and fired. The kickback knocked her off balance and she fell on her butt.

"Okay." He placed another bolt in the crossbow channel and latched it. "Fire away."

She aimed the crossbow. "What do you want me to hit?"

"That park bench there? Put the arrow in the middle of the seat."

She aimed and fired. The bolt traveled straight. It lodged into the wood bench exactly centered. "Okay I can see the benefits."

Suddenly the wall shook. "Did you feel that?" he asked.

"Yes, reminds me of LA," she said.

"That was no earthquake. It was an explosion underground, somewhere nearby."

"For what?"

"To penetrate the treasury vault. I think that's why they're here."

"For the jewels?"

Clive nodded and placed longbows and crossbows alongside each embrasure and arrow loop at the top.

Herman circled high above.

He dug a biscuit out of his pocket and Herman swooped down toward him. It was not a normal biscuit. Its dough was soaked blood red. Herman headed straight for it. He landed on Clive's outstretched hand and began eating it.

Ashley was intrigued. "Since when are you the Ravenmaster?"

"I trained as an apprentice when I first came on. I know a few of their tricks.

Herman was thoroughly enjoying the treat. Ashley inspected it. "What is that?"

"It's a biscuit."

"I've never seen a biscuit like that." She pointed out its red hue.

"Ah. Yes. It's soaked in blood,"

"What kind of blood?"

"Probably chicken or rat blood. Those are their favorite items on the menu."

Ashley cringed at the thought. Herman finished his blood biscuit and Clive took out a scrap of paper. He scribbled something with his tactical pen and rolled up the paper. He attached it to Herman's left foot.

"I didn't know he was a carrier pigeon."

"He's not but I figure it's worth a try." He showed her the message. It read: S.O.S.

Clive readied to launch Herman into the air.

Ashley held up her hand. "Wait!" She held up her GPS luggage locator.

"What's that?" Clive asked.

"It's a GPS locator for my purse. I was thinking maybe there is some way we could use it for them to find us."

"How would they do that?"

"There's an app. It's on my cell phone."

"Herman can't lift your cell phone," Clive replied.

"I know that! But maybe they can do a search!"

"Who?"

"I don't know! MI5! Whomever James Bond works for!"

"That's MI6."

"Okay, whatever! It's worth a shot. Can't you put something in your note about that?"

Clive reached to grab Herman but he was already airborne with the message.

"Come back!" Ashley whispered.

Herman dive-bombed toward her. It rattled her, this big bird about to land on her head. She put her hands out to shield herself. She still held the Air Tag. Herman landed on her arm. "Ewwww! Get him off me, dad."

Before Clive could do anything Herman nibbled on the luggage locator chip. After all it was blood red, just like the biscuits Clive gave him.

The chip slipped out of her fingers. Herman had a firm grasp of it in his beak.

He must think it's another biscuit." Clive tried to snatch the gadget away but Herman swallowed the locator whole. The raven burst into the air.

"He did not do that. He did not do what I think he just did."

"Yes, I think he did," Clive observed.

"It's a piece of plastic not a biscuit! He ate plastic!"

"It's small enough he should be able to poop it out. I think he'll be okay. "

"I'm not worried about him. I'm worried about us! We need that thing for them to find us!"

Herman ascended to an altitude hundreds of feet above.

"Where is he going to go?"

"Maybe he'll find John if we're lucky. It's a longshot but you never know. He's very, very smart."

"He ate a luggage locator. That's stupid."

"Now that you fed him he'll be loyal to you for life if he wasn't already. I think he took a shine to you the first time he saw you."

"Puhleeze." They watched Herman fade into the distance.

Clive moved to the next embrasure. There was a wrought iron statue of a life-sized knight. It gave visitors a sense of what the medieval castle garrison looked like. Clive dragged the sculpture behind a merlon. He bent down behind the arrow loop and checked the line of sight on the crossbow.

His eye was caught by activity on the Green below: Bindar and his men once again gathered around the fake bomb near the White Tower. What was this? They knew the bomb was no threat. That could only mean one thing: they were putting on a show. Then he saw the reason why: a camera drone hovered over the Tower Green, weaving back and forth in the air.

Clive had seen drones like this before. It was not your average consumer grade model, used for taking pictures of real estate or spying on your neighbors. This was military issue. It appeared that his mayday had not been in vain after all! Perhaps his message had reached Inspector Winklough. The police were checking out the scene without putting lives at risk.

Bindar appeared to be busy at work defusing the fake bomb. He waved away the drone and pointed at the bomb, indicating the proximity was a threat. The drone suddenly pulled back. Clive's heart sank. The cops were going to be fooled again by this guy? They were still buying his bogus story? Did they not see the bodies of the two legit bomb techs Bindar executed? Evidently not. Their bodies were hidden behind the wall somewhere. He looked toward the village stocks. Someone had released the merc's body he had placed there.

Clive wanted to wave at the drone but he could not. It would give away his and Ashley's position. The drone continued to retreat. Then he saw something that astonished him. A German Shepherd dog wandered into the Inner Ward. It had its nose to the ground and approached Bindar's conclave.

Bindar caught a glimpse of the animal and a look of dread came over his face. His men pulled their weapons.

"He's not an attack dog!" Clive thought he heard Bindar say.

It was a sniffer dog! The cops had sent in a bomb detecting K9 to see if there was an actual bomb. The dog sniffed around at the abandoned bag that was supposedly the item. Normally if the K9 found an explosive scent it was trained to sit next to the find and wait for its handler. Clive figured the handler must be nearby and out of sight. After thoroughly sniffing out the satchel and the area around it the dog did not sit. He trotted out as if called by a dog whistle. Meanwhile the drone in the sky monitored this from above.

Several of Bindar's men pointed weapons at the dog. Clive heard him yell: "Do not shoot the dog!" He likely knew that most K9s were trained to immediately turn and attack a suspect at the sound of gunfire. If they missed he would be triggered.

The dog headed toward the portcullis of the Bloody Tower. Clive figured the handler must be outside the Outer Wall. There were several drainage pipes the dog could slip through.

Bindar waved at his men to stay put.

Clive picked up his radio and keyed the mic. "Met Police come in. I am a Yeoman Warder inside the Tower, over."

A friendly female voice came over the channel. "Clive is that you?" He knew immediately it was Emma.

"Inspector! Yes it's me. Did you receive my message?"

"Yes, Clive, of course."

"Inspector the bomb squad is not real. EOD officer Richard Bindar has gone rogue and is leading a squad of imposters. They have taken over the Tower. Do you copy?"

"Yes, I copy, Clive."

"He's got about ten to twelve men. I have already eliminated three of them already. But we have casualties. Two EOD techs who arrived on scene from Bishopsgate North station were not part of the plot. They were shot in cold blood. Bindar and his team are armed to the teeth. They have complete run of the Tower. Do you copy, Inspector?"

"Yes, Clive. Good copy."

"He has hostages. Eight or nine people including the VIP guest sent over here by Ministry of Tourism this morning. They were down in the dungeon exhibit of Wakefield Tower and did not hear calls to evacuate."

"Roger that, Clive. The cavalry is here. We are moving back in now. I have ordered boots on the ground, firearms teams with scaling equipment for the walls..."

"No, no, Inspector. This is a fortress, you must think in terms of castle warfare. The corner tower keeps are each manned by sharpshooters. They will rain fire down on anyone attempting an escalade. They have RPGs capable of taking down a helicopter."

"So what do you suggest, Clive?"

"This is an open line, Inspector so I can't say much. But there is a man named Heath, who works for BT as a cabler. You should consult him and he can lead you."

"Heath from BT?"

"Affirmative," Clive replied.

Ashley rolled her eyes. "What are you doing?"

"Your friend knows the old subway tube. That's the best way for the police to get in."

"You can't involve him! It's too dangerous!"

"Don't you think he'll want to help us?"

"Yes but it puts me in an awkward position!"

"We're already in an awkward position don't you think?"

"Fine. Yes."

The radio crackled again. "Clive. Come in?"

Clive keyed the radio. "Yes, Inspector. I'm here. You should reach out to Heath who can lead you the best way in."

"I'm on it, Clive."

"Copy, Inspector. Over and out."

A wave of relief washed over Clive. The Met would get this sorted. If they came in under stealth they could overwhelm Bindar and his mercs and free the hostages. He looked at Ashley.

"Didn't you say you had to use the loo?"

Ashley nodded.

"Come on, then."

He led her back down the spiral staircase into the core of the Beauchamp Tower.

***

Ashley washed her hands and marveled at the luxurious King's House lavatory. The walls were clad in expensive Italian tile and the knobs were ornate gold hardware. She placed an Egyptian cotton towel on the rack just so and emerged into the hallway. Clive stood in the foyer, waiting.

"Was the facility to your satisfaction?" he asked.

"Better than the garderobe," she replied.

"Are you hungry?"

"That's quite solicitous of you."

"I am your father."

"Yes, I suppose I am a bit famished."

"Come on then," Clive said.

He led her into the well appointed kitchen. The highest quality appliances, marble counters and beautiful oak cabinetry. He opened the Sub-Zero.

"This is all such a waste," Clive said. "He doesn't even cook in this beautiful kitchen. Goes out to dinner most nights with the glitterati."

She looked inside the fridge. There were several jars of high end Russian caviar, some bottles of vodka and some finger sandwiches from Harrods's Food Hall.

Clive took out the jars of caviar and the finger sandwiches and placed them in a bag.

"Caviar?" Ashley asked.

"That's mostly all the bloke eats when he's home. Washes it down with the vodka. I told him it would be the death of him. Come on, let's go."

He opened the kitchen door and scanned the Green for unfriendlies. It was empty. They scurried back to the storm cellar entrance. Where had Bindar and his men gone? Likely back into the Waterloo Barracks, she figured. It made sense if they were indeed trying to get at the jewels.

They descended the cellar steps back towards the tunnel from which they came.

"Where are we going?" she asked.

"To your boyfriend's subway tunnel to meet the police."

"He's not my boyfriend, dad."

"Sorry, didn't mean to put a label on it." He closed the storm cellar doors behind them.

They walked through the broken glass and soggy carpets of the wine cellar, back into the tunnel once again.

Chapter Fourteen

At the north end of the old subway tunnel (now a telecommunications portal) there were about 96 steps where the Victorian-era commuters would exit to ground level. Clive and Ashley waited at the bottom of that staircase where the subway tube plunged beneath the waters of the Thames. It was cold down there. Clive paced and Ashley shuffled her feet as she munched on a bite of Beluga caviar and crackers. It was divine but she figured that might have more to do with the fact that she needed the salt, since she had perspired a bit during all of the morning's insanity. This morning, when she had been on the south end of this tunnel with Heath, seemed a lifetime ago.

Clive kept looking through the tunnel for the cavalry aka the Met to arrive. No one came. Would Heath really appear leading the police through this little known access point to the medieval fortress? She figured he certainly would if asked. It was completely embarrassing for her to picture the moment though. Here he was, a suitor to a girl he just met, now being asked to put his life on the line to rescue her. Talk about your damsel in distress. But quite frankly he didn't have to *rescue* anyone, just lead the police in. How would she react when he arrived? It was all so awkward and high school.

Clive looked at his watch. "They should have been here by now."

"Perhaps it took them awhile to find Heath," she replied.

"Are you kidding? They can easily track him by his cell phone." He paced back and forth. She took a last bite of her cracker and fish eggs.

Clive reached into his pocket. "I've also got this." He pulled a wax-paper wrapping out and handed it to her.

She opened it up, revealing a squished sandwich.

"Marmite sandwich."

"Marmite? What is that?"

"It's yeast extract with spices on bread."

"Thanks but no thanks." She handed the wax paper back to him.

Clive took a bite. He savored it. Ashley grimaced as she watched him swallow it.

"Dad?" she said. "There's something I need to tell you."

He stopped and looked into her eyes, apparently concerned at the tone of her voice. "What is it?"

"I did something this morning..."

"Okay?"

"You have to promise that you will not hold anyone responsible but me."

"How can I do that if I don't know what it is?"

"Just say it."

"Okay fine. I will only hold you responsible. What is it? You're not pregnant are you?"

"No!"

"Then what?"

"You know how much I love jewelry."

"Yes. You got your mother's expensive taste. You used my credit card for something, didn't you?"

"No, dad. I did not use your credit card."

"You bought something on your own and you need help with the bill?"

"No, it's not that."

"Then what?"

"This morning I held the Kohinoor diamond in my hand."

"You what?"

"I got up early and Bernard was doing routine cleaning in the vault. I went down there and I got to hold it in my hands."

"I'll kill him."

"He is not responsible, dad! I am."

"I hardly believe that."

"You promised that you would not hold anyone accountable but me!"

"Do you know what kind of trouble I could get in if someone found out? I could lose my job! Bernard could lose his too and his pension!"

"I'm sorry. I wanted to tell you because I didn't want there to be any secrets between us."

"You could have asked me."

"I know what you would have said."

"Yes, because there are rules and regulations that I must adhere to!"

"It was a once in a lifetime opportunity. So I took a chance. To behold the mountain of light not through bullet proof glass but in my own hands! I got to hold history."

"It's a complete violation of policy! It doesn't belong to you! Nor Bernard!"

"No one will ever know the difference. But Bernard and I. And now you.".

She had felt comfortable enough to confess a big secret to him but rather than be happy he became angry and sulky. What difference did it make whether or not she had touched the Kohinoor without permission? No one would ever know. Given the circumstances of their current predicament did it even matter? They were not even sure they would get out of this ordeal alive!

Clive looked back again through the undulating subway tube, as if looking would make the white knights on their horses show up sooner.

"Can't you say anything?"

He did not reply. Suddenly she heard footsteps directly above. Clive pulled out the gun he had taken off the dead mercenary.

"I want you to go out." He pointed to the fiber optic lines. "Follow the cables it will lead you across the Thames."

"I know that, been there before. What about you?"

"I'm going back. I have to get above ground and see what's going on. The cops should have been here by now."

"You're angry with me. That's why you're sending me away."

The sound of the footsteps above grew closer. "I'm not angry with you. It's just not safe here."

"Can't we just talk about it? About the diamond..."

"There's no time for talk right now. You go through the tube and up the stairwell to the street level exit. I'm sure the Met has moved their command post to Potters Field by now. They will be right there when you exit. You tell them you're my kid, okay? They will want to debrief you. Tell them everything you know. Find Inspector Emma Winklough. She will make sure you're safe."

"I choose to stay with you."

"I've already placed you in enough danger. Your mother would slice my throat if she knew."

"I don't care!"

"I can't leave till the very end. You know that."

"You could have said that to me and mom all those years ago."

"That's not fair. There's much more to it than that."

She felt herself tear up. She couldn't help it. "If only you were as loyal to me as to this place."

The footsteps echoed behind them, gradually growing louder. Someone was approaching.

"I want you to survive. I can't worry about you now that we are entering this phase of the battle."

"But we were a good team! You told me that!"

"We were! But this is different."

Ashley backed out of the gate and into the tube. "Alright," she said.

Clive closed the gate firmly. "This is for the best."

She looked at him through the iron bars. It was as if the universe were manifesting their relationship. He turned back up the path towards the staircase. He did not notice that the gate had not completely shut. She had taken Heath's business card, still in her pocket, and placed it over the latch.

***

Clive watched Ashley's silhouette dwindle into the tube and felt a sense of comfort that she would be safe and no longer a witness to the killing spree that he could not avoid in this situation. He had never wanted to kill in front of his daughter. It was on one hand shameful that he had been trained to do such brutal acts but what choice had he had? In a situation where it is kill or be killed one does not "think" one simply must react and that's what he had done at the Bell Tower and the steps of the St. Thomas. Now he was prepared to do it again as he listened for the footsteps of what was likely another merc patrolling the Tower in search of him.

The footsteps sounded like they were traipsing through puddles of water which meant the interlocutor had made it off the stairs. Clive clung to the wall and waited. Was it safe to assume this individual was one of Bindar's men or could it be perhaps a cop? Maybe while he and Ashley were waiting they cops had entered a different way? He had to find out but he could not risk exposing himself to whomever was down here.

The footsteps drew even closer now. The individual had to be within fifty meters or less. Clive readied himself. A flashlight touched on the floor and a beam of light shone down the walkway.

A man's croaking voice emerged from behind the light. "Come on out, matey!"

Clive popped out from his concealment with gun drawn. He saw the stubble-faced man he had placed in the stocks. He carried an AK and had a look of vengeance in his eyes. "You should have killed me when you had the chance," stubble said. "Now you need to come with me."

"I don't think so," Clive replied. He fired preemptively, but not at stubble-face. He fired at the bare-bulbed light directly above them. It went out, plunging the tunnel into darkness. Then he dove to the floor.

Stubble lined the catacomb with bullets from his machine gun. Clive remained totally still. The merc pulled his flashlight out. As he lit up Clive fired directly at the source of the light. Stubble face went down hard and his flashlight dropped to the ground. Clive fired another round to make sure the deed was done. He crawled to the flashlight and shined it on his assailant's face. The bullet had ripped through his throat. He would not be coming back, not in this life anyway.

Clive grabbed the AK. He clambered up the stairs towards the cracks of daylight that bled beneath the doorway above. He pictured Victorian era passengers, women dressed in their corsets and petticoats and hats, men in frock coats and bowlers. He wished for a simpler time. He would go back to his perch on the Beauchamp Tower to get a lay of the land. The cops should have been here by now. Something was definitely wrong.

***

The gunfire reverberated through the underwater tunnel like an amplifier. Ashley covered her ears and dove for the floor. She immediately thought of Clive. She had been waiting for him to turn the corner before she backtracked to re-enter the Tower. But that didn't matter now.

The gunfire stopped and a light went out at the north end. There was pure silence. Should she call out to him or would that endanger him more? She chose to stay silent and clambered back through the tube, gripping the sides to guide her in the dark. She reached the gate which she had intentionally propped open and pushed it ever so slowly, to avoid any squeaks in the hinges.

She slipped through and let the gate close gently, then walked forward through the corridor. She stepped by Braille in the pitch dark. Was Clive okay? He had not called out to her. She approached the bottom of the subway staircase. A tiny shaft of daylight seeped in through a crack in the door above. In the dim light on the staircase landing she made out a body. Her heart pounded blood through her arteries. Could it be Clive? There was not enough light to be sure.

She pushed forward to get a glimpse. If it were an unfriendly did she have a way to defend herself? She reached in her pocket and gripped the mace lipstick tube that Clive had given her this morning. She scurried ahead on the balls of her feet. The sliver of light illuminated the person's torso. There was no rise and fall of breath. It could not be Clive. Or could it? She would never forgive herself if it were her fault that he had been killed, trying to shepherd her out of this castle. She drew closer still, her arm with the lipstick mace outstretched.

Ashley's position now afforded a glimpse of the face and profile . A man with a five o'clock shadow lay in a pool of blood. It was not Clive. Her shoulders slackened with relief. Her father had added another to his death toll. It was a gruesome sight. But she didn't care this time. She was becoming annulled to the sight of death. She rushed up the rest of the stairs towards the door with the light leak.

She carefully opened it a crack and looked side to side. The coast was clear. Clive was nowhere to be seen. The only thing she recognized was Herman the Raven circling above her.

***

Clive retraced his steps back through the tunnel that connected the White Tower and the King's House. For a moment he thought of Father John Gerard, for whom the tunnel was named. The Catholic was notorious as a Tower prisoner who found ways to give Mass and hear the confessions of other prisoners between his own torture sessions. Word was he had befriended and perhaps rewarded some of the yeoman warders of the time.

He approached the entry to the King's house cellar. It smelled of vinegary spilled wine. He stepped inside and sloshed across the floor. He ascended the steps to the cellar door. Where the hell were the police? Why had they not come through the subway tube underneath the Thames like he urged?

He pushed the cellar door open only half way and noticed a limping merc on patrol. The shuffle of the gimp struck him as a stark contrast to the normal grace of the Scots guards. Nonetheless he was a threat. Clive lowered the door quietly. Lame leg must have heard it because he shambled over with his AK drawn. Clive held his breath and waited.

The merc pulled at the door. Clive held it shut from the inside. He heard the sound of metal on metal and realized the cretin was going to plug holes into the handle in an effort to unlatch it. He had to act or get his hand blown off. He bashed the door upwards and it swung out towards the sky, smashing the merc in the face. Blood spurted from his nose but he did not lose grip of his gun. He leveled the barrel directly at Clive.

Clive placed his hands up in a submissive position.

"You're coming with me!" the gimper replied, blood oozing down his face.

"Sure, sure. Lead the way." Clive affected a shiver.

Now in close quarters with his assailant, he pivoted out of the line of fire and slapped the gimp's carbine to the right. The limper had not heeded a basic rule of close hand combat: never bring a long range weapon to a close range fight.

Clive flung his left hand up and over the barrel then elbowed the man in the face with his right arm. He wrenched the weapon free with his left and backed away. He rotated the rifle around from stock to barrel and pointed the gun at limpy now, keeping a safe distance between them.

Game leg pulled his sidearm. Clive pulled the trigger of the AK. Nothing happened. It was jammed and would not discharge.

Clive charged at the limper with the rifle. The only problem was it did not have a bayonet. He jammed the barrel into the merc's chest. The merc wobbled back and hit the ground, grimacing in pain. Clive flipped him over like a pancake and struck him in the back of the head with the gun stock. His body went completely limp. Clive was pretty sure that rigor mortis was the next phase but he didn't care or bother to wait and find out.

***

Ashley looked both ways as she crossed Tower Green. The coast was clear. She gazed at the Outer Wall. Where she had seen sharpshooters before there was no sign of them. Had they all been rounded up? Or called to another location? She took in the surrounding skyline of the Gherkin, Shard and Walkie-Talkie buildings. Some windows were now lit as office workers compensated for the setting sun. The sight calmed her nerves. She scampered towards the White Tower entrance. She would go back downstairs to the King's House tunnel and find her way back to the Beauchamp Tower. She was sure Clive had gone back to his perch.

As she passed the Tower gift shop she noticed its door was ajar. Someone was inside. She hid behind a kiosk. But it was not fast enough. A woman emerged from the shop and waved at her. She had an Eastern European look: slim, fit and dressed in fashionable, touristy clothes. Czechoslovakian perhaps?

The woman put her hands in the air. "Don't shoot!" she called out.

Ashley did not have a gun.

"I give up!" the woman said. She definitely had the Slovakian accent.

"It's okay." Ashley put her hands in front of her, palms out, to show she did not possess a weapon. "I'm not going to hurt you."

The woman walked toward her. "You're not one of them?"

"No."

The woman exhaled an apparent sigh of relief. "You were left behind too?"

"Yes, I was."

"I didn't hear the call to evacuate. I passed out in the torture exhibit, I don't know whether it was the horrifying pain devices, or the fact that I have low blood sugar...anyway I fainted. So the Beefeaters took me up here to First Aid. The medic checked my vitals but couldn't find anything wrong except the fact that I hadn't eaten. So he gave me some orange juice and cookies. I put my ear buds in and I was listening to relaxing music...Abba, it's my favorite. I guess I fell asleep and the medic forgot about me? Next thing I wake up all alone and I hear gunfire! Men in military uniforms charging around with guns so I decided to stay put. Until now. My name is Hedda."

"I'm Ashley." She shook Hedda's hand. She did not get weird vibes off this woman. Her story seemed legit.

Hedda rolled her shoulders back. "Do you know what's going on?"

"The Tower has been taken over by a gang posing as bomb squad operatives."

"Why?"

"Don't know."

"We've got to get out of here!"

Ashley gestured in the direction from which she came. "I will get you out. Come with me."

"You know a way out?" the woman asked incredulously. "Before you came I took a look around and I could not find any open exits!"

"When they shut this place up it's locked tight. That's why it was a prison."

Hedda paused and seemed to look at the place in a new light. "How did you get stuck here if you know a way out?"

"I didn't get stuck. I came back."

"Why would you do that?"

"I came back for someone."

"Are they still here? Can they help us?"

"Not right now. We're on our own. Come on. I'll show you the way."

Hedda pulled a pistol out of her jacket. "No."

Ashley felt a pit in her stomach. How could she have misjudged the situation? "What do you want?"

"I want you to come with me."

"Where are we going?" Ashley asked, even though she was pretty sure she knew the answer.

Hedda pointed toward the Waterloo Barracks. The location of the treasury vault.

"Is this a jewel heist?"

Hedda chuckled. "How can it be a heist if you're taking something that belongs to you?"

"I don't know what you mean." Or did she? Her mind raced. Was Hedda hinting that she was part of a movement to repatriate the Crown Jewels to some of their former owners? She had seen the protesters and heard the pleas of the Indian government to return the Kohinoor diamond, the very diamond she had held in her hands this morning.

"Just move." Hedda placed the gun at Ashley's back.

She walked across the parade ground towards the entrance to the jewel exhibit. Would Hedda really shoot her? She just didn't seem the type. Should she try to ditch her? There was a post in the arcade outside the Waterloo entrance and she could pretend to trip and fall, luring Hedda to help her up. Could she grab the gun? It might work. Might not. She looked up and saw that Herman the Raven was following them. Crazy bird. Swallowed an air tag.

No she had to go with the flow here. Dive into the belly of the beast and see what they were really up against. Maybe somehow she could get word back to Clive.

***

Clive entered the Beauchamp Tower and locked the door behind him. He ascended the circular staircase inside the tall turret. He had now killed four of the mercenaries. How many were there? He had seen five or six when he arrived. But there had to be more. Probably some had entered the Tower as tourists and remained after the evac.

Where were the police? That was the burning question. He told Winklough to locate Heath who could send officers through the old subway portal. It was only known by a few. But the British Telcom boy could easily guide the Met to the location. Had she contacted him?

He reached the top of the corkscrew stairs and opened the door just a hair. There was no sign that his nest had been breached. Everything appeared to be as it was. Bows and bolts all neatly stacked next to the embrasures. He gripped the AK he had taken and popped open the door.

He looked over the crenel. At the Byward Tower there was a hive of activity. Six or seven mercs were poised with weapons on the roof. Below them he saw activity on the moat bridge. A team of SAS troopers ambushed carrying a battering ram and possibly some charges? Behind them a team of commandos with rifles trained on the front buttresses.

What the hell were they doing? They were going through the front door? They had not heeded his advice? The mercs had the upper hand! He told Winklough this! They had RPGs they could rain down on the cops. This was going to be a bloodbath! He grabbed the radio in his pocket and keyed the mike.

"Inspector Winklough come in? Inspector Emma Winklough?"

The radio came back.

"This is Winklough, over."

"Inspector? It's Clive. What's going on? We waited for you at the rendezvous."

"There's been a change of plan, Clive."

"I can see that, over."

"I suggest that you use the aforementioned portal to evac yourself and anyone else you can."

"Negative, Inspector. I can't do that. I don't think you realize what you are walking into..."

"I'm not at liberty to go into further details. I suggest you stay out of harm's way and pray for the best. Over."

Clive clicked off. He knew Winklough and he could tell that she had been overruled. The SAS, or Strategic Air Services commandos and SO19 armed counter-terrorism police, had likely insisted on forging ahead with their own plans. There was nothing she could do. Her hands were tied.

The moment of silence was broken by gunfire. He looked down at the bridge and noticed three officers charge the Byward Tower entry. They carried riot shields. What were these guys thinking? Then he saw it. They had satchel charges on them. They were going to try to breach the entry door with explosives.

The mercs rained fire down on the commandos. They were sitting ducks. Clive took his AK and began to fire at the mercs on the Byward Tower roof. They fired back at him but had no good shot given he was above their position.

They turned their attention back to the Tower entry portal and showered more gunfire on the commandos. One went down, hit by a bullet to the neck. The demo guys worked furiously to set up their charges.

On the roof of Byward he saw a merc with an RPG take aim at the bridge. This would easily kill nine or ten cops who were now moving across.

He picked up his AK. He had to take this guy out. He took aim and squared his target in the gun sights. A deep breath and he pulled the trigger. But the clip exited the weapon. He was out of ammo! He grabbed a longbow leaning against the battlements. Next to it was a quiver of bolts dipped in grease. He placed the bow in an embrasure and lit the arrow.

The mercs turned their attention back to the entry below them. They blanketed fire on the bridge and took out two more commandos. The Met demolitions guys cowered in the entry alcove. They had not been able to blow the door because they had no way to retreat from the blast they were about to trigger. It was obvious Bindar's men knew that.

Clive had to take out RPG guy. He armed his longbow, aimed and plucked it like a harp. The arrow flew through the air and nailed him in the side of his leg. He dropped the rocket launcher and grabbed his knee, screeching in pain. Clive now lit several arrows in his quiver. He lit another flaming bolt and loaded it, plucked his bow again. His target: a box of ammunition the mercs had brought.

The flaming bolt landed and lit the box on fire. The mercs scattered like rats from the light. A loud sound echoed through the Tower as the ammo box went up in flames, popping like popcorn. He fired again at the Byward roof, dropping another flaming arrow. The mercs scampered to put it out.

The distraction allowed the Met demo guys to retreat. They took a safe position across the moat bridge and triggered their satchel charges. Boom! But the thick iron door did not fall. They had not rigged enough explosive to blow it.

RPG guy got back on his feet. He placed the launcher on his shoulder. The remaining commandos scrambled to get back across the bridge.

RPG guy leveled his warhead at the bridge.

Clive stood and aimed his longbow at the merc.

RPG guy fired. Whoosh. The grenade landed at the other end of the bridge and took out massive chunks of limestone.

Clive plucked his bow. The medieval projectile whooshed toward its own target.

RPG guy proudly surveyed the damage his grenade had created when the arrow reached its target. The bolt ripped into his side and he fell off the parapets to the cobblestone walkway below.

Clive hid below the crenellations and grabbed the walkie. "Winklough? Come in? How many casualties did you take?"

"Unclear," she replied. "But a lot less than what it could have been given what you just did."

Over the walkie speaker he heard a yelling in the background. Then static. "Winklough? Come in."

"I'm here, Clive." Then a crackle as if someone had grabbed the radio away from her. A gravelly male voice came over the mic.

"Who is this?" the gravel voice asked.

"This is Clive, Chief Yeoman Warder at the Tower."

"What the hell do you think you're doing? You're interfering with police activity."

"Who is this?" Clive asked.

"This is Ian Danforth of Met counter terrorism command. I am taking over on the scene."

It instantly became clear why Winklough had not been able to send men through the tunnel the way he had suggested. "Clive I am ordering you to stand down. You have no authority or jurisdiction here."

"Authority or jurisdiction? The Beefeaters have been guarding this Tower for nine hundred years!"

"I didn't ask for a history lesson. Your little bow and arrow show is not needed! You put our officers in danger!"

"I put them in danger? No that was you. And what made you think the iron door of his Majesty's oldest fortress would fall to a few satchel charges! That thing was hand forged by the best blacksmiths in the land to withstand Greek fire!"

"Get off this channel, Clive! If you continue to interfere in police business you will be subject to the steepest disciplinary actions including prosecution. Danforth out."

***

Ashley and Hedda snuck along the side of the Inner Wall towards the entrance to the Waterloo Barracks. Hedda kept her pistol trained at Ashley's back. She seemed shaken by the RPG blast and the gunfire. Perhaps this was not part of the plan when she signed up for this caper? She did not seem built for combat.

Ashley worried for Clive. Had he been involved in that gun battle? It was more than likely he was. She knew he could fend for himself but that didn't assuage her fears. The entrance loomed. A sign above read: *Crown Jewels Exhibit*.

"Go inside," Hedda ordered.

Ashley opened the door. The lead bomb tech, the man of Indian descent whom she had seen before, manned the security desk at the front. He gripped a rabbit's foot as if it were some type of comfort plushie. She had heard of superstitious OCD. This guy seemed like a candidate for the diagnosis. He held a radio and spoke into it.

"By now you must realize that the Tower of London is under siege," the lead bomb tech said.

Okay, Ashley thought. This guy is going to make some demands.

The radio responded with a male Scottish accent. "Is that what you call it?" He seemed to be doing his best to be bored. Was this a classic crisis negotiator tone?

"The Tower is in my control," the bomb captain replied as he stroked the rabbit's foot repeatedly.

The Scot on the other end of the radio crackled back. "But you are one of us, Officer Bindar. A tried and true expo who has defused numerous ordnance that placed the public in harm's way."

The rabbit's foot stroker's name was Bindar. She made a note of that.

Bindar put the rabbit's foot in his pocket, clicked the radio on and spoke. "I am afraid it has all been for naught."

"Tell that to the people who are still living and breathing because of you." The Scot had a soothing, lilting voice. He could have been a DJ, Ashley thought.

Bindar cleared his throat. "I was living a delusion, working for his Majesty and now I am done."

The Scot replied almost immediately. "I know you took some medical leave recently. Perhaps we can write all this off to a nervous breakdown induced by a bad combination of medications."

Medical leave? The bomb squad officer was removed from duty? This did not instill Ashley's confidence. This guy was an unstable head case. He continued to grip his rabbit's foot.

Bindar keyed the radio. "Do not attempt to invade the castle again. I have hostages."

The Scotsman volleyed back. "Who might those be?"

"You will get their names and passport numbers in due time. Just know that if you attempt any further advances on the fortress it will result in the immediate cessation of talks and certain death for the hostages."

"I see. May I ask what it is that you want?"

"I want justice."

"That's a very broad subject," the negotiator answered. "Can you narrow it down for me?"

"In the last four years, three Americans committed heinous crimes against UK citizens. Albert McKee stabbed and killed a British national. Ronald Holland robbed a convenience store at knifepoint and brutally slit the throat of the shopkeeper. Howard Callen smothered his British girlfriend while she was sleeping."

"Why are you so interested in the American criminals? There are plenty of Brits who commit the same kinds of crimes."

"These Americans have all been convicted in the British courts. What is to become of them? They are going to spend the rest of their lives in prison at the expense of the British taxpayer."

"I can't change our legal system," the negotiator demurred.

"That is precisely the problem, Inspector. That's why I want those men brought to me. Heads must fall in the Tower once more."

"So you are suggesting that I send you these Americans so you can execute them?"

"I'm standing right near the execution platform now. The very place that Anne Boleyn lost her head."

"I can't do that. They're American citizens!"

"They are British convicts! Why should they have any nationality really? They are human refuse of the highest order. Tell you what Inspector, since you seem to be overwhelmed with the enormity of my request, I will allow you to send one over to start: Albert McKee. He's in Belmarsh prison. Have him here within three hours or one of the hostages will die on this platform instead. Heads will roll in the Tower once more."

He clicked off and put down the walkie. Mic drop. The line went silent.

Bindar seemed proud of himself.

He turned to Hedda and noticed Ashley. "Who is this?"

"Another hostage," Hedda replied. "I came across her on my patrol."

"Where?"

"She was over by the gift shop. Offered to help me get out," Hedda answered.

Bindar took Ashley in. She was creeped out as he gave her the up and down. "Isn't that sweet. Put her with the other hostages."

"This one isn't your average tourist. She knew a way to an alternate exit."

"So what? I've got bigger problems to deal with right now! That Beefeater is on top of the turrets at Beauchamp Tower and he's just taken out two more of the men..."

Ashley's spirits lifted. Clive was alive! But they knew his location and would surely be sending more killers after him.

***

Clive kneeled behind the bullet-ridden battlement atop Beauchamp Tower. He contemplated the exchange he had just heard over the radio between Bindar and the new negotiator, Superintendent Danforth. When Danforth told him to stand down was that real or just a bluff to win over Bindar's confidence? Perhaps Danforth perceived he was interfering in the management of the crisis? Clive didn't really care. He would rather work with the Met than against them but he would do things his way, given his familiarity with the situation.

Clive was reasonably sure that Bindar was buying himself time. The demands for a hostage exchange were pure theater. He was here for the jewels, or a jewel. He had obviously not accounted for Clive's resistance and this had placed a hitch in his plan. Maybe he had not been able to access the vault as easily as he thought. Now he was using his hostage exchange card.

Clive looked at Herman, who circled above the turret. He descended towards him. Clive could see a paper attached to his leg. It was a note. Herman landed and Clive untied the note. He read it:

We take on the enemy of fate
A meal of beef we just ate
We shall repel the invaders
By sheer might defeat traitors
We Yeoman Warders true
Protect the heart of Britain
No matter the mission

The note could mean only one thing. John and the others had received his SOS. They were sending him a message of support. Or was it something else? A cryptic message for sure but he assumed that was because they could not be sure in whose hands the paper might fall.

Regardless of its intent, the missive invigorated him and he forged a new plan. He would use the Tower as it was intended, as a weapon. He could employ the two concentric circles of defense, the Outer Wall and Inner Wall as they were intended. He would seal off the two enemy factions from each other.

He heard two mercs rushing up the spiral staircase within the turret of the Beauchamp. There were obviously on their way to dispatch him now that he had revealed his position. But that was okay. He would go to the Devereux Tower.

Chapter Fifteen

The Devereux Tower, adjacent to the Beauchamp on the Inner Wall of the fortress, acquired its name from its most famous prisoner, Robert Devereux, also called the Earl of Essex. The handsome Devereux was a dashing and charming presence at court and he gained the favor of Queen Elizabeth I. She lavished him with land rights and privilege, not to mention a spot on her Privy Council. But their passionate relationship ran afoul when the Queen dispatched Devereux to quell a rebellion in Ireland. He negotiated a truce rather than battle to the death. His rivals declared him in dereliction of duty. The Queen deprived her former lover of his offices resulting in financial ruin. In an act of desperation he planned a revolt to depose her. Upon its failure he was convicted of treason and spent his latter days awaiting execution in an apartment of the keep which now bears his name.

Clive now occupied the rooftop space of the tower where Devereux had paced the halls those many years ago. He rattled the door that opened to the turret stairwell. It was locked. He heard the sound of heavy footsteps ascending the steps of the Beauchamp right next door. The mercenaries were on his tail. He grabbed a blunderbuss from the stash of weapons he and Ashley had borrowed from the Old Armoury.

He poured a handful of powder into the flared barrel. It looked like a trumpet rather than a gun. He wadded up a tissue and forced it down the bore. He took buckshot out of the ammo pack and poured it down the muzzle. He stuffed another tissue on top of that.

The footsteps were closer now.

Clive turned and loaded more ammo into the blunderbuss. Gunpowder. Wad of tissue. Buckshot. Wad of tissue. Layers like a cake.

The mercs banged at the door to the roof. The wedge he had placed there as a barricade held but he knew it would only delay them for a few moments.

He primed the blunderbuss with a rod.

The mercs splattered the door with bullets. Its hinges gave way and they emerged on to the roof. It was two stocky men in tactical gear with Glocks.

Clive pulled the trigger. The horn of the weapon sprayed buckshot. There was no aiming this thing.

The mercs went down. Their body armor only protected their chests. Their arms and legs were shredded by shrapnel. They dropped to the floor, helplessly grasping at their burning wounds.

Clive returned to the rooftop of the Devereux and fumbled for his master key. He inserted it into the lock of the rooftop door. It gave way and he darted into the stairwell and rushed down the circular steps to the lower floor. There he found the entry to a corridor. It was the passage to a series of apartments, converted to Beefeater lodgings. He beelined for Ridley's apartment. Ridley always left his door open. No reason to lock one's doors in a heavily guarded fortress...

Sure enough the lacquered door yielded to a turn of its handle. The apartment was very cozy with fashionable, modern furnishings: an Eames lounge chair and ottoman, a modular sectional couch in orange leather. Ridley was known as a furniture fashionista amongst the Beefeaters. Clive heard footsteps descending the staircase behind him. He grabbed the Eames chair and barricaded the front door.

He rushed to the cloak room. In the closet he saw a rack of coats hanging on a rod. Behind the rack he found a trap door. He thought of one of his favorite childhood books, *The Lion, The Witch and The Wardrobe*.

The tower had been rebuilt in the eighteenth century when these apartments were created. Ridley told him the builders must have found this ancient passage and decided to keep it. He ducked through the hatch and spread the coats back on the rod like a curtain behind him. Inside the passageway led to a narrow staircase.

Down the narrow staircase he plunged. Finally reaching bottom, he found a narrow door with a rusty handle. He turned it. The door opened into a stone vault lined with several tombs, a bust of Sir Thomas More and some religious vestments and artifacts.

He was underneath the Chapel of St Peter Ad Vincula. There was a baptismal font lit from above by an oculus at the apex of the domed ceiling. The passage was so that doomed prisoners could get the blessings of the sacrament before execution. The mythical Father John Gerard at work again, possibly?

He had no time to ponder the historical theory. He had to get to the Bloody Tower. The Bloody Tower had the portcullis gate that could cut off the main artery to the Inner Ward. He needed to shut off that artery as fast as possible to cut off Bindar from his men in the outer portion of the castle. Divide and conquer, the military and political strategy made famous by Philip II of Macedon, applied here.

***

Ashley and Hedda marched across the Inner Ward towards the Wakefield. Ashley knew where they were going: *The Torture at the Tower* exhibit. That's where the hostages were. If nothing else she could let them know Clive was within the Tower working to secure their release, one way or another.

She thought of the exchange between Bindar and Hedda. She could not help but notice there was tension (sexual tension perhaps?) between them. The way Hedda looked at Bindar was telling. She felt something for this man. She was not just another soldier in the platoon. They had some kind of relationship. Boyfriend and girlfriend perhaps? Maybe she could pry a wedge between them.

"What is it you see in him?"

Hedda sidled up next to her. "See in whom?"

"Boss man Bindar. If I'm honest he is good looking, but he doesn't exactly treat you with respect. Is it the power thing that attracts you? You go for the alphas right? I've been there. Done that."

"Spare me your psychotherapy."

"Fine. Stick with your bad boy. But think about this. You may not make it out of here to lay on the beach in Barbados with him."

"Ha. That's not our plan. You've seen too many movies."

"What is it then? You can tell me."

Hedda did not answer.

Ashley pushed around for trigger points. "Do you even know how you're going to get out of here? What's your exit plan?"

"You're a nosy bitch, aren't you? Let's go." She pointed to the door.

Ashley stopped in her tracks. She had definitely hit a nerve. "It seems like you're risking a lot for love. I hope he's not using you. I mean, I never went so far that I would risk being incarcerated—or worse for a guy, but I've put a lot on the line thinking my partner felt the same way about me. And then I was wrong."

Hedda simmered. "I didn't ask for your opinion!"

"He promised you a life together after this, didn't he?"

"It's none of your fokkin business!"

Hedda pushed her inside the door of the Wakefield Tower. Steps to the dungeon loomed. Bingo. Mission accomplished. She had broken Hedda's calm demeanor. She had wanted to place a little doubt in her mind, to hopefully break her allegiance to Bindar. The doubt was definitely there now. Hopefully she could build on it.

Chapter Sixteen

The nave of the Chapel of St. Peter Ad Vincula was empty. The five hundred year old church stood in all of her glory, decorative arches and windows letting in sunlight at perfect angles. A shaft shone down the center aisle. This version of the chapel was built around 1520 and the tomb of its builder, Sir Richard Cholmondeley, occupied the center of the nave. Clive took in the holy air within its walls.

He walked towards the chancel, paused and kneeled briefly. He was not normally one who called upon God but this seemed like the time and place. He thought first of Ashley and wished for her safety as well of that of the hostages confined here. After this moment of silence he rose to his feet and dashed behind a latticework screen to the left of the altar.

There was a postern, or rear door, in the the apse, for clergy to enter and exit quietly. He passed through the secret portal and it let him out on Mint Street, the cobblestone alleyway. He could picture mint workers of the day, making their way to worship on a Sunday morning. He hugged the Outer Wall to stay out of the firing range of Bindar's sharpshooters above.

Clive approached a blockade gate just below Legge's Mount, the northwest bastion of the the Tower's Outer Wall. He pulled the gate out until it blocked the street entirely. This would be a deterrent for any would-be pursuers.

On he went in an easterly direction, passing more castle keeps on the Inner Wall. He passed the Flint Tower, known for manufacture of arrowheads, the Bowyer Tower, so named because it was a residence of the royal maker of bows and then the Brick Tower, a keep that resembled a horse shoe. The street was completely deserted, littered with tricycles and bicycles of the Yeoman Warders' children, whose row homes were built into the Outer Wall, also called the Casemates.

He turned the northeast corner of Mint Street on to Water Lane and headed towards the south end of the fortress complex. The Tower Bridge loomed beyond. He looked up at the Broad Arrow Tower. Past that he reached the southeast corner of the fortress and turned to Water Street. The Bloody Tower and its portcullis beckoned.

***

The Wakefield Tower originally housed the King's apartments on its upper floors. Its basement was a prison. That basement now housed the *Torture at the Tower* exhibit. Ashley walked solemnly down the steps towards its entrance. Hedda opened the door with a key and shoved Ashley inside. She locked the door behind her.

Ashley faced Yeoman Warder Sheila Hansty. Behind her was another Yeoman Warder – Kincaid – she believed was his name. In the far corner of the exhibit was a gaggle of tourists.

Sheila bit her lip and bristled. "I wish you would have listened to me love, and stayed out of here like I asked."

"I'm sorry. But I wanted to make sure my dad was okay."

"Your father can take care of himself."

"He's killed four of them already," Ashley quipped. "Maybe more."

"How do you know that?"

"I was there."

Sheila paused. "I'm sorry you had to see that."

"I actually take some comfort in it."

"He'll get us out of here alive."

Ashley had wondered before if there were something between Clive and Sheila. Sheila was married to an insurance adjuster who spent a lot of time in Spain. He claimed England in the winter was not good for his health. So Sheila lived alone in her Tower lodgings. Of course Clive kept a respectable distance given Sheila's marital status but she had a feeling he held a torch for her. There was a latent chemistry between them.

Warder Kincaid piped in. "How did the rogues catch you?"

"There was a woman. She roped me in. Acted like she was trying to escape the castle when she was actually one of the perpetrators."

A man with gold bling and a cashmere hoodie approached Kincaid. "I'm sorry to break up your passionate family reunion but Mr. Doorman we need some leadership here. It's time for us to get out."

"We are working on it," Kincaid answered.

Ashley assumed this tool must be the billionaire her father had mentioned. He had a couple of assistants who flanked him. The other hostages were mostly tourists, a German woman in her thirties, a British teenager, her little sister, a cute girl of about nine and a couple of businessman types, one British and one American.

Suddenly the entry door burst open and Bindar barreled in. He beelined for Ashley with Hedda at his heels. "I understand you have a way out of here?"

"I don't know what you're talking about."

"Hedda says you told her you could get her out of here. How?"

Ashley wondered why now he so urgently needed to know about another exit. Hedda had told him this before and he lacked interest. Had his original exfiltration plan been foiled? She certainly was not going to help him. "She must have misunderstood. I never said any such thing."

Hedda broke in. "You said you know someone that works here."

"No. I think she's got me confused with someone else."

Bindar glared at Hedda. He was not pleased. Apparently he felt she had led him down here on a wild goose chase.

Hedda folded her arms. "She's lying."

Bindar looked at the metal door that said: Little Ease. He smiled. "So this is the torture cell so small that a prisoner could neither sit nor stand?"

No one answered his question. He opened the squeaky iron door to the small torture box. The answer was obvious.

Bindar stared at Ashley. "You sure you don't remember anything about this escape route?"

Ashley adopted an apathetic air. "No idea."

Bindar opened the door to Little Ease. "Then you go inside."

Was he really going to do this? Go medieval on her? Ashley's heart sunk. Her palms started to sweat. But somewhere from deep within a calmness took hold. It rose up from her knees to her chest. She breathed deeply. She turned to Hedda. "Is this what you signed on for?"

Hedda gave her a sheepish look. "Just tell him where you were going to take me."

Ashley put on her best poker face. "I don't know what you mean. I was locked in here just like you."

"Liar! You came back here to rescue someone!"

Bindar took Ashley by the arm and pushed her toward Little Ease.

Warder Kincaid stepped between Ashley and the entry to the chamber. "You can't put her in there. Put me in instead."

Bindar laughed. "You're too fat!" He shoved Kincaid to the ground. Kincaid rose to his feet and once again blocked the entry to the small chamber. Bindar smashed him in the face. He stumbled to the ground. "Do not do that again, Beefeater."

He shoved Ashley into Little Ease and closed the metal door.

She was plunged into darkness. Her first instinct was to bang on the metal door. "Let me out!"

She heard Bindar's cold voice. "I'm going up top. Hopefully when I return your tongue will be a bit looser."

Then she heard Hedda.

"I can make her talk. Just let her out."

"Are you going soft on me?" Bindar snapped.

Hedda was silent.

"You can't leave here in there!" Kincaid chimed in.

"I can't?" Bindar replied.

Ashley heard a gunshot. Gasps and moans from the hostages.

"What happened?!" Ashley asked.

No one answered. She only heard receding footsteps and what sounded like a body being dragged across the floor, then the sound of a door slamming.

***

Clive approached the three-story Bloody Tower and stopped at the archway. Above him, the famed portcullis gate hung from thick ropes on a pulley system. It was probably the heaviest gate in all of the United Kingdom, designed to impede the penetration of armies and raging populaces into the inner sanctum of the monarchy itself. The mechanism to lift this impossibly heavy barricade was simple physics: a system of ropes, chains and counterweights. It was set within grooves in the archway walls. Using this system, two men could lift two tons by hand. It was also designed to drop smoothly to the ground, thus sealing off the Inner Ward.

Clive stepped into an alcove and gripped a lever which attached to the pulleys. He unlatched it and rotated the crankshaft . The giant gate shuddered and lowered steadily to the ground. It was done. Clive had sealed off the Inner Ward. Bindar was cut off from his men on the Outer Wall. They had no way to rejoin him.

Clive rushed to the Develin Tower, which faced the river.

Next to the Develin was the rectangular tower called: The Well. It was originally connected to the Tower's water well. It featured a square keep with crenellated battlements and arrow loops. Clive spotted one of Bindar's snipers on the walkway between the Develin and the Well.

He opened the door to the Develin and lightly tread up the corkscrew stairs. He emerged on the roof and hid behind battlements. He popped his head above a merlon and got another glimpse. The enemy sniper was looking out towards the Thames and had no idea an ambush was imminent. Until he turned and saw Clive's Beefeater bonnet.

He unleashed a barrage of fire at Clive's position. Clive dove behind the masonry. He removed the quiver from his back and loaded a bolt. He mounted the bow in between merlons and pulled the string.

The bolt pierced the sniper's right shoulder as he took aim at Clive. He pulled the arrow out and winced in pain. In a burst of adrenalin he ran from his position toward the merlons of the Well Tower, keeping to the inner side of the Outer Wall. Clive fired again. Another arrow grazed the sniper's left leg. He sprinted the rest of the way toward shelter.

Clive armed and fired again. This time his arrow lodged in the back of the sniper's neck. He dropped to the ground. Man down.

Clive's mind was on Ashley. Surely she was upset with him for chastising her about the Crown Jewel vault. It really was the royal jeweler's fault. The fact she took full responsibility was quite mature. He should not have reacted the way he did. He wished he could join her behind police lines and apologize over a cup of hot coffee with blankets draped over their shoulders.

He noticed Herman the Raven caw-cawing as he ascended over the Inner Wall and above Tower Green. Caw-caw, caw-caw. The ravens were frequently seen as harbingers of death. Was someone dead? Clive wondered. Clive looked into the sky where the jet black bird circled. It was right over the Waterloo Barracks.

He noticed something on the ground.

It was a cell phone. He bent over to pick it up and pressed its button. The screen was black. It was out of power. He turned it over to see a sticker photo of Harry Styles. It was Ashley's phone. What's her

phone doing over here? Clive put the phone in his pocket and headed to the last entrance he had to seal off: the King's Gate.

***

Little Ease was an abomination of a torture chamber many times
over. The windowless cell was a small four square feet, designed so
that a prisoner could not stand nor lie down. The victim was destined
to crouch over in stages of increasing agony, stuck in complete, suf-
focating darkness. Guy Fawkes, errant Tower guard John Bawd and
some of the Knights Templar, had been subjected to its rigors. Now
Ashley was inside it.

"Hello?" she yelled.

No answer came. What had happened to everyone? What happened to Kincaid? She sat there in the dark of Little Ease, thankful
her yoga classes made her as limber as possible. She was also thankful
she was not claustrophobic. She breathed deeply to calm herself.
Nonetheless her heart raced. Then she remembered something. Her
father had said the last person locked in Little Ease had escaped.

"How could that be?" she had asked.

"He's a magician named Peter Rutherford. An escape artist. He
had the yeoman warders lock him in overnight. The next morning he
was gone."

"How did he get out?"

"The rumor was there is a trap door. Rutherford showed up for
lunch at his favorite pub in Soho the next day."

Ashley poked around the walls of the cell. Could there actually
be a trap door? It was likely an apocryphal story or a hoax. Probably
not.

Then she felt an indent in the wall. She pushed against it. Nothing. There was no door. But the idea of one gave her comfort at least
momentarily.

"Hello!" she yelled again. No one answered.

***

Clive huddled beneath the archway of St. Thomas Tower. The building was rectangular, long and wide with two corner turrets facing the
inside. It afforded a perfect shelter to stay out of harm's way when
awaiting the outcome of battles being waged above. Clive paced back
and forth next to the stone walls, thinking of Ashley. He kept envi-
sioning her, perhaps in a hotel now or maybe at the hospital? Maybe
the medics wanted to check her out as a matter of protocol. The
thought comforted him.

He emerged again and walked down Water Lane towards the
Henry III watergate. King Henry III, known as the most obsessive
patron of art and architecture who ever occupied the throne of England had a passion for rebuilding his royal castles and properties.
He rebuilt the royal palace at Westminster and Westminster Abbey,
Winchester and Windsor Castles and last but not least part of the
Tower of London. Henry greatly expanded the fortress, fortifying its
concentric circle within a concentric circle design with the addition
of huge new curtain walls with their smaller towers. He also enlarged
the Tower moat. Consequently, the third entrance to the Tower of
London, after the main gate at Byward Tower and the Traitor's Gate,
was named after him.

Clive turned a corner and walked beneath the archway that led
through the Outer Wall and on to a pontoon that crossed the moat
and led over to the Wharf. This was how Bindar and his men had entered earlier in the day.

On either side of the bridge over the dry moat there were two
pulleys and counterweights. Clive pulled on the windlasses connected to the pulleys and slowly the counterweights moved down into
two slots on either side of the opening. In synch with that motion
the portion of the bridge connected to the castle rose into the air.
Clive continued to rotate the windlass and the huge oak planks that

were the drawbridge sealed the opening to the castle. The drawbridge was now vertical. Clive pressed a lever, locking it into the closed position. The second gate to the Tower was now sealed tight.

He walked back toward Water Lane. He looked down the street and noticed a bridge over the cobblestone street. It was the bridge from St. Thomas' Tower to its sister keep, the Wakefield Tower. He had one more access to seal off.

***

Ashley felt a crick in her neck and lower back. She was starting to get stiff. Her feet were pins and needles. She squeezed and unsqueezed her toes to keep the blood circulating. It was cold down here in the reprehensible box called Little Ease and she was confined to one position. She didn't know how long she could last.

"Help!!" she called. But no one answered. She knew that Sheila or Kincaid would answer if they could. Something was terribly wrong.

Would she die down here? She pushed the thought out of her mind. No. Bindar or one of his minions would be back. Maybe Hedda would take pity on her. They would let her out. She would have to promise to show them the secret exit of course.

As she leaned against the wall she felt a vibration in the masonry. Was that a drill? A jackhammer? She thought of her dad. He was right. This was a jewel heist. She was sorry they quarreled. It was understandable he was upset about her unauthorized trip to the jewel vault. In the ensuing investigation all security tapes and cameras would be looked over with a fine tooth comb. Her unauthorized presence in the vault would surely be noted. Would she be accused of involvement with the mercenaries? That would be a good problem to have at this point. It would mean that she had gotten out of this oubliette.

She got a sore feeling in the pit of her stomach. Keep calm, keep calm. Yes she was stuck in a box meant to break her. This guy Bindar obviously meant business. She thought of that 80s song her mother listened to, *Only The Good Die Young*. No, she would not die young, she made up her mind. She was not *that* good anyway. The thought made her chuckle and she relaxed a bit.

She thought of a TV talk show she had seen about airplane phobias. A therapist had suggested an exercise to ease the anxiety: *visualize a place that makes you feel calm*. Instantly a mental image popped into her head: the tent that she and Clive had pitched in the backyard of their family quarters at the Imphal Barracks in Fulford, York. The flash memory surprised her – she had not thought of that place in years. Picturing it gave her great comfort. She thoroughly visualized their tent, the beautiful birch trees that lined the green lawn and the lantern that hung from a branch. Her mother brought them marshmallow biscuits with chocolate coating. Tunnocks Teacakes she remembered they were called.

She heard the creaking of an iron handle and the door opened. She squinted into the light and saw Hedda's face. "Get up."

That was easier said than done. Ashley pushed herself up little by little, as the blood began to flow into her veins. Hedda offered a hand. Ashley could see that she was alone.

"Where are the others?" Ashley asked.

"They have been moved."

"Why?"

"Never mind that. Are you going to show me where this exit of yours is?"

"Yeah, let's go," Ashley staggered to her feet. The blood rushed to her head. She felt like she was going to pass out.

Hedda caught her. "That can't have been easy being locked up in there."

"No," Ashley gasped. "Thank you for getting me out." She was relieved at the empathy. Perhaps she had created a rapport with Hedda after all. She had established a beachhead in her mind. It was something she could build on.

She limped toward the door. The blood was starting to flow again as she walked. Her limbs were still there.

"Show me," Hedda warned. "If you don't he will put you back there."

Ashley emerged into the twilight from the exit to the Wakefield Tower. They were in the Inner Ward. Above the high walls that confined them she could see some stars in the sky. She walked towards the Bloody Tower and its portal to the Outer Ward. She stopped in her tracks.

"What is it?"

"We can't get out," Ashley said. She pointed out the portcullis gate.

Hedda flashed on the heavy iron cross bars that now barred the entrance. "Someone closed it!"

"We're locked in. The secret exit is in the Outer Ward, on the other side of this portcullis."

Hedda approached the giant portcullis gate and rattled it. Its two tons didn't even budge a micromillimeter.

***

Clive rushed back to St. Thomas Tower. It sat over the Water Gate. King Edward built this gate in the late 1200s as an alternate entrance, given the main entrance was subject to the protests of unruly citizens or other security concerns. The Water Gate enabled the King to arrive off the Thames, moor his boat and head directly to his lodgings above. It was equipped with all the features of a proper castle entrance: arrow loops, murder holes and a portcullis. The only difference: you had to swim or sail through it.

The Water Gate was later renamed Traitor's Gate due to its frequent use as an entry point for Tower prisoners rather than the monarch himself. These prisoners were brought up a flight of stairs where the St. Thomas was connected to the Wakefield Tower by a bridge. They crossed the bridge which led them to the Inner Ward and its facilities. Clive wanted to make sure that portal was sealed off to Bindar and his men.

He climbed the very same stairs many illustrious prisoners had climbed before. This corridor was normally closed to the public. He opened the heavy iron door to the bridge on the St. Thomas side and looked through the chamber. There were portcullises suspended from either side. He approached the thick hemp rope that held up the portcullis on the inner side. He took out his partizan axe and hacked at the rope.

He heard footsteps behind him. Someone was coming up the stairs. Certainly one of Bindar's unfriendlies.

He hacked away at the hemp rope.

The footsteps grew louder. His assailant was near. He heard the click sound of a trigger resetting. It was an unmistakable sound. Likely a Glock.

He hacked away some more.

A merc emerged from around the corner and pointed his gun at Clive.

He hacked once more at the hemp.

The merc fired and Clive hugged the wall.

The man rushed Clive.

One more hack and the hemp gave way. The latticework iron gate fell directly on the merc, impaling him from above. Its spiked iron grates pierced his shoulders on either side.

The bridge was effectively blocked with a human gargoyle.

***

Ashley looked at the pistol in Hedda's hand as they embarked on the long walk back across Tower Green. It did not faze her much. The weapon almost appeared to be a formality at this point. After all Hedda had to keep up appearances. The leaves on the Green crackled as they broke under Ashley's feet. Her body was coming back to life. So someone had closed the Bloody Tower portcullis? It had to have been Clive. Bindar and his men were now locked within the confines of the Inner Wall. This was a good development and gave her hope. There was a strategy at play. She was not sure what it was yet but there was something happening.

Hedda pushed her through the door of the Waterloo Barracks. Bindar paced in front of historical photographs of the Cullinan diamonds. Ashley's eye was caught by the photo of the Cullinan I. It was much larger than the Kohinoor but it just did not have the same mystique or allure.

He approached Hedda and got in her face. "That was quick."

Hedda looked into his eyes. "She tried to show me the exit but there's a problem."

"What's that?"

It was obvious Hedda did not want to be the bearer of bad news but she had no choice. "The gates are closed."

"What gates?"

Ashley intruded. "The gates to the Inner Ward. They've been closed off."

Bindar gripped his rabbit's foot. He stroked it as if it were a worry stone. "It's probably that Beefeater."

Ashley shrugged. Bindar stared at her for a moment. Was he studying her features? He had met her father. People did from time to time comment on the obvious resemblance between them.

Bindar picked up the radio. "Noxon? Bates? Come in."

"This is Bates."

"The Beefeater has closed off the gate to the inner ward of the castle."

"I see that, yeah. Isn't there another?"

"No there is not another! That's why it's a fortress you fool! Get down there and open it!"

The radio went silent. Bindar proceeded to pace once again. There were clouds of smoke and dust coming from the end of the corridor where the treasury and jewel display were located. They were definitely drilling. It seemed like it was taking much longer than they had originally planned.

Bindar picked up the radio again. "Bates are you there? Over."

Bates replied immediately. "Yes I'm here."

"Did you get the gate open?"

"No. It weighs two tons."

"There must be some hydraulic lift, some button that will take it up."

"No. It's a system of weights and ropes and pulleys."

"Well, use it!"

The radio went silent again.

"It's not working. We have no idea how it works. We'll have to blow it."

"Fine! Get on it!"

"Copy."

"After you have the gate open you track down the Beefeater and bring him to me."

Do not execute him. Is that clear?"

"Yes. Over."

Bindar turned to Ashley. You will have your chance to show us this special information you possess. That is if you are telling the truth. If you are lying, then your fate will be much worse than the Little Ease cell.

Hedda gripped Ashley by the arm. "Shall I put her back there?"

Ashley knew this had to be a bluff. Hedda was putting on a cut-throat façade for Bindar. She could not show that she was the weak pirate.

"No," Bindar replied.

"With the other hostages?"

"No! I want her right here with us." He handed Ashley one of the blueprints that Clive had given him. "Draw me the location of this portal on the map."

Ashley looked the blueprint over. The old subway tube was not on the schematic.

***

Clive looked back at the Inner Ward from his roost on the roof of the St. Thomas. He thought of this tower's namesake, St. Thomas Becket, the Archbishop of Canterbury who was murdered by knights after a dispute with Henry II. He became the patron saint of London after his death and some had visions of him appearing alongside the very walls upon which Clive stood. Clive could certainly use his help now. He took some small solace in the fact that the interior of the castle was completely sealed off now. There was no ingress or egress. The two entries to the Inner Ward were effectively blocked.

Clive surveyed Water Street below. He could see two mercs lurking outside the archway to the Bloody Tower. One of them planted C4 putty explosive on the iron bars of the Bloody Tower portcullis. The other rigged a remote detonator. This bomb squad was truly a group of bombers not bomb defusers. They were not explosives and ordnance disposal, they were installers. That much was clear. Why had he missed this? He was monitoring Bindar's transmissions over the radio. It must have been on a different channel.

No matter. He looked around and noticed the trebuchet down the wall walk. It was staged for the exhibition which had been planned with the stuntmen. A pile of rocks were stacked neatly next to its counterweight bucket. Clive began to place the stones into the counterweight. He piled stone after stone in and tried to arm the spring mechanism but the counterweight was not full enough.

Clive piled more stones into the bucket. He was able to turn the winch this time, winding it up to trigger the giant slingshot. He placed a large round stone about the size of a bowling ball inside a pouch at the flinging end and turned the winch again. The arm of the trebuchet inched back, the torsion on it became tighter. He pulled back on the floating arm as far as it would go. Then he pulled the pin on the counter-weight and the heavy basket dropped to the roof of St. Thomas' Tower with a thud. The energy of the weight pulled on the floating arm and it swung through the air with its payload. The rock soared through the air and descended on its trajectory towards the portcullis. As it landed it took out the merc with the detonator, slamming him with the force of a bulldozer. His body flew into the other merc and the two hit the ground hard. They lay still, bloodied and crushed, two barely human limp sacks of flesh. The portcullis was undamaged.

***

Ashley looked up from the blueprint of the Tower to see that Bindar had a visitor. It was one of the hostages, the brash American billionaire she had seen in the dungeon. He was accompanied by Bindar's right hand, the one they called Sedgewick.

The billionaire faced Bindar. "I see that you have reached some kind of an impasse with the police and I want to be your intermediary. The Home Office loves me. They do not want me to be stuck in here. I am your most valuable asset right now. I am your trump card."

Bindar laughed and turned to Sedgewick. "Why did you bring this clown up here?"

Sedgewick went to open his mouth but the billionaire spoke for him. "Because he understands my value. My name is Robert Slater. I am a visitor here, a VIP guest of the Ministry of Tourism. I am developing a replica of this place as a hotel in Las Vegas."

Bindar looked at his watch. "I don't care."

"But you should, Mr. Bindar. Because I can get you exactly what you want. You let me be your negotiator. I will have you out of here in no time with complete compliance to your demands. They do not want me to be unhappy, don't you see? Because I represent money. My hotel will represent this place and create a heavy revenue stream into the future. It's all about licensing trademarks now. I am the brand builder for this place and the higher ups realize that."

Bindar grabbed Slater by the throat. He pressed his finger into his

Adam's apple. He started to choke and cough. Ashley pondered how she could defuse the situation. She had no interest in seeing this man killed before her very eyes no matter how repulsive he might be. Maybe if she ran away it would provide a distraction? But they would surely shoot her in the back...or would they? She got up from her chair and prepared to sprint.

Hedda was immediately on her. "Where do you think you're going?" She took handcuffs and slapped one on Ashley's wrist, clipping the other side to the desk.

Bindar barely gave her a moment's notice. He continued to throttle the sleazy billionaire. Until the radio crackled to life.

"Richard Bindar. Come in?" It was Clive!

That caught Bindar's attention and he released Slater's throat to pick up the radio. "This is Bindar."

"This is Clive Bellamy. Chief Yeoman Warner at the Tower."

"I know who you are."

"You need to give up now. There is no way out. I have sealed off all the exits. The men you sent to open the portcullis are dead. You are cut off from the Outer Ward. Any stragglers have no way to get to you and you have no way to get to them."

Bindar quietly seethed as he let this news sink in. Slater rose to his feet. "Mr. Bindar. I know that guy. I recognize his voice. He's a useless flea buzzing around nipping at your heels, that's it. He was my tour guide this morning. He's a nothing, a nobody. Don't worry about him." Ashley had to swallow her tongue. Her instant reaction was to defend Clive, to say he was better than any of these men would ever be. But it would not help matters to lash out at her captor. Nor did she want to give away her identity.

Bindar looked daggers at Slater. "Why shouldn't I worry?"

"I will tell you but first you have to promise not to hurt me, Mr. Bindar. Please don't do what you just did to me again. I'm asking for your word."

"Fine. You have it. What is it? Why shouldn't I worry?"

Slater pointed at Ashley. "Her." Her spirits plummeted. This son of a bitch knew who she was!

"What about her?"

"She's his daughter."

Bindar gazed upon her face again. "I knew she resembled someone I knew!" He grunted and picked up the radio.

"You are actually quite clever, Clive. You obviously know this castle backwards and forwards."

"I do. And I'm here to tell you there is no way into that vault. Better people than you have tried. And even if you were able to get in there, which you are not, you would have no exit."

Her father was walking into an ambush. She wished she could tell him.

"That's all well and good Clive except there is just one problem. I will get into that vault and I will get out because I have you."

"You are crazy if you think I would help you."

"Oh, you will."

"Why on God's green Earth would I do that?"

"Because I have someone here that I think you would do any-thing for and she needs your help."

"Who is that?"

There was a jumbling as if the radio was being passed over or per-haps dropped. "Dad..."

There was a long pause. She could only assume Clive was digest-ing this news. "Honey? It's going to be okay."

She could hear it in his voice: his heart tumbling into the deepest depths of his body. He had obviously thought that she was safely out of harm's way and in police custody. After all, he had locked her out at the gate at the subway portal!

"You're mad at me."

"No I'm not mad at you. Okay? Just sit tight and do whatever they say, alright?"

"I'm sorry."

"You have nothing to be sorry about."

Bindar grabbed the radio out of her hand. "Listen closely Clive. I know exactly what's going on right now. The cops are planning a full scale invasion. They know I have hostages but they are willing to risk collateral damage. They are going to come in here with guns full bore and it's your job to hold them off. It's your job to make sure they do not penetrate the barriers of this castle because if they do, Ashley will pay. Do you understand me?"

"Yes, I do."

"From now on I only deal with you. I don't want to speak to the Met negotiators any more. I only deal with the Chief Beefeater. Is that clear?"

You could hear Clive swallow. "Crystal."

Slater approached Bindar. "You see? I'm on your side, aren't I? I helped you. You owe me! I'm on team Bindar, don't you get it? You and I, we can do great things together."

Ashley could not believe she had considered risking her life for this guy.

Bindar pushed Slater away. "Sedgewick! Get this worm out of my face before I throttle him again!"

Slater protested. "You need me, Bindar! Admit it! I can fix all of this for you!"

Bindar waved him off. "You're lucky I let you live."

Sedgewick yanked the billionaire by the arm and dragged him down the corridor.

Chapter Seventeen

The Waterloo Barracks building was erected in 1845 to house 826 soldiers. In 1967 it was converted to house the Crown Jewels. In the course of 120 years it went from sheltering infantry to sheltering the most precious gemstones of the royals. Ashley sat handcuffed to the security desk and pored over the blueprints given to her. With her free hand she penciled in an escape route under Hedda's watchful eye. Down the hallway, smoke and dust billowed out of the ante-room to the jewel treasury.

She heard the sound of a high-pitched drill. She thought of her dad. He was right. This was a jewel heist. She was sorry she had come back and caused this problem. She might have walked away if he had forgiven her for this morning. It was understandable he was upset about her unauthorized trip to the jewel vault. In the ensuing investigation all security tapes and cameras would be looked over with a fine tooth comb. Her unauthorized presence in the vault would surely be noted. Would she be accused of involvement with the mercenaries? That's what Clive was concerned about. Despite her innocence she might require a lawyer – a barrister – as they said over here. Clive could hardly afford that on his civil servants' salary.

Bindar emerged from the vault area wearing a mask to filter out the dust in the air. Once again he gripped that rabbit's foot. Was it some kind of trigger perhaps? Some kind of weapon like in the *Mission Impossible* movies? She stole several glances at it while pretending to pore over the blueprints. No, it was just a regular rabbit's foot. She had heard stories of famous people who swore by the power of the rabbit's foot charm: Franklin Delano Roosevelt, Ernest Hemingway, Michelle Obama, the actress Sarah Jessica Parker. Obviously Bindar was a member of this club. He was superstitious.

A short man in a welder's mask emerged from the vault. He was clad in leather gloves and a welder's mask. He held what looked like

172

a welder's torch. He put down the torch and lifted his mask. "They said you wanted to speak with me?"

"Yes, Nick. That's right."

"Stop calling me Nick. It's Niko."

Bindar spun around and laid into him. "Excuse me. Why don't you put it on a name tag so we can all make sure we spell and pronounce it correctly?"

"What do you want? We're wasting time."

"You have only opened three doors!"

"What did you expect? They aren't exactly fastened with chewing gum." Niko shrugged. He did not appear to have much fear of the ringleader.

"You were supposed to be in by now!"

"Yeah, that was based on the plans that we saw before the coronation. They have changed a lot about this place since then."

"What about the treasury room?"

"I won't know until I get there."

Bindar shook his head. "Get back to work."

Niko took his mask and torch and disappeared back inside the vault.

Bindar walked toward Hedda. Hedda tensed up as he approached. There was an obvious rift in their relationship. Ashley quickly put her nose back in the blueprint and hastily drew a line for the escape plan she was proposing.

Ashley raised her hand. "I have to go to the bathroom."

Hedda grimaced and walked across the room to confer with Bindar. There was a quiet conversation between them and then she returned. She pulled a key out of her pocket and unlocked the handcuff. Ashley massaged her wrist as she got up.

***

Clive looked out across the Thames from the St. Thomas parapets. Across the river Potters Field Park now had a police presence not seen in this part of London in decades. Whereas before the park had been empty, now The Met had it cordoned off. Clive noted a fleet of Marine Policing Unit (MPU) speedboats on the waterfront near the river walk. In and around the cherry trees SAS commandos prepped amphibious gear. A squad of army techs readied more drones. This gear was next-level. Unlike the earlier drone sent, there were black combat octocopters: eight rotors apiece.

The fog was coming in. He could taste the saltiness of the mist on his tongue. Clive knew he had to hold off these battle ready squadrons to keep his daughter alive. It was going to be a heavy lift.

He wished this all could have been avoided.

He recalled the last time he brought Eva to the Tower. He was about to finally retire from the Royal Marines. She was so happy. She had been a faithful Army wife for the first eight years of their marriage, moving with him from base to base each time he was transferred. Finally after twenty three years he was done.

Eva was looking forward to settling down to a life of normalcy. He had an offer to work for BAE Systems, a defense contractor in Sheffield. They started to look at quaint cottages to purchase. It was a hopeful time.

Then he got the phone call. He had applied for the job of yeoman warder two years earlier on a lark. He never in a million years thought they would choose him, so he had not even told her. But then they called. He went to London for the interview, again as a lark. He was sure they would not want him. Again he didn't tell Eva. Then they called him for a second interview. Again, he did it for fun, nothing else. He did not take it seriously. Then they offered him the job.

So he brought Eva and eleven year old Ashley to the Tower under the guise of tourism. That's when he broke it to her. Would you like to live here? She hit the roof. If there had been a roof she would have, anyway. They were outside at the time. He said he didn't tell her because never in a million years did he think he would get the job. But he had decided that he really wanted to do it. He didn't want to work for the bomb-builders. Could they make their home here at the Tower of London?

I will never allow my child to grow up in this prison!

It's much more than a prison, he tried to explain. It's more than a place of execution. It is a living museum of the history of this country! But there was no convincing her. And he didn't realize how selfish he had been at the time, how ignorant he was of what she had gone through, raising their daughter in a country not her own, going from military base to military base, no plot of land to call her own.

This is too much of an honor, he had said. It's too much of a duty to pass it up. If you don't want to live here then we will find a flat for you and Ashley nearby and we can be together when I'm off.

That arrangement just hadn't worked out. They grew apart quickly as Eva was left to contend with Ashley and the trials and tribulations of a new school and big city life after growing up on military bases where everything was provided for you.

Six months later she told him she wanted a divorce. She wanted to take Ashley with her back to California. In a custody hearing Ashley said she did not want to stay in London, she wanted to go with her mom.

It broke Clive's heart but he agreed to their relocation as long as she would visit in the summers. That first summer Ashley came to stay it had been fun. He taught her to ride a bicycle right there on Mint Street, in front of his cottage on the Casemates. She became bold and sped around the castle after the crowds exited each day. But one hard turn on wet cobblestone and she broke her arm. Eva's attorneys claimed parental negligence. Clive did not fight it. Ashley did not come to visit after that with the exception of twice for Christmas tea at Harrods while Eva shopped.

If he could have gone back to change the past he would have. He would have changed his mind, never become a yeoman warder. He would have taken that job with BAE Systems. Maybe they might have been a happy family, living in Sheffield. But none of that mattered now.

He reached the yeoman warder offices and beelined straight to a locked blueprint cabinet. Its drawers were shallow and wide. He inserted his key and opened one of the lower drawers. He rummaged through stacks of paper renderings for sections of the Tower until he found one for the Waterloo Barracks. It featured some design plans for the treasury room, aka the jewel vault.

***

Ashley walked towards the ladies room. Hedda fell in behind her. They entered the restroom door. It was the cleanest public restroom Ashley had seen: spotless mirrors, tile with grout scrubbed toothpaste white, stalls made of a warm stained oak. It even smelled good. Ashley whirled around and parked herself against a sink. She washed her hands. Hedda did not betray any reaction.

Ashley splashed cold water on her face and daubed it with a paper towel. "Where are they?"

"Where is who?"

"The hostages? That slimeball Slater? Kincaid? The Beefeater who tried to prevent my entry into the torture chamber? I thought they would be here in the Barracks but they're not. Where are they and what have you done with them?"

"*I* haven't done anything with them."

"You have allied yourself with that monster out there. You are a co-conspirator, an accomplice, an accessory. Where are the hostages? Is Henry Kincaid dead?"

Hedda held up her Glock. "You are not in any position to be interrogating me."

Ashley threw her paper towel away. She realized she needed to soften her tone. "If you help us get out of here I'm sure you will get leniency."

"Leniency? Ha. I'm past the point of no return. You just said so yourself."

Ashley suddenly remembered a *London Times* article decrying excessive leniency by the Crown Prosecution Service in the face of heinous crimes. "Cooperation with law enforcement is the most valuable way for criminal conspirators to gain leniency in sentencing," she repeated.

"What are you? A barrister now? We broke into the Crown Jewel vault, okay? No one's going to let that go. They will make an example of us."

"Just tell me where they are."

"What would you do even if you knew? It makes no difference."

"Together, the two of us might be able to help them."

Hedda hesitated, as if she were considering the scenario. Then reality apparently set in. "You have no idea what he is capable of if I step out of line."

"Is Henry Kincaid dead?"

"Yes, I think so. He was clubbed over the head and dragged away."

"And the others?"

"I don't know exactly where they are. I only know he is negotiating a deal to trade them."

"Why not keep them close until the exchange is made?"

"I don't know."

"He doesn't share much with you, does he? So much for pillow talk. I guess you're just a pleasure toy."

Hedda reached out and slapped Ashley. Her cheek immediately burned with fire. But she was happy that it had happened. She wanted Hedda on edge.

***

The air was heavy with moisture now. It was not a rain per se, nor a drizzle, it was not a fog either. Tiny globules of moisture soaked Clive's face. He peered over the parapets of the St. Thomas to see more Met police congregate on Potters Field. Met Police logistics erected a canopy over what looked like a command post.

The canopy transported him to a happier time. He had attended a flea market at Potters Field with Eva. Vendor canopies had dotted the lawn. One such canopy sheltered a rack of beautiful tapestries. They had bought one for their flat. But that was a long time ago.

The police logistics crew appeared to be finished with the canopy.

Clive keyed his radio. "Met Police command post? Come in. This is Inspector Clive Bellamy, Chief Yeoman Warder calling. I have good news. We have recaptured the outer ward of the Tower. We have the enemy contained."

The voice of the man who had identified himself as Superintendent Danforth rang back across the airwaves. "You had no authority to do that!"

"Since the Duke of Wellington. The Tower is Yeoman Warder jurisdiction."

"I want you to stand down, do you hear me? We have a strategic plan and you are interfering!"

"May I ask what your plan is?"

"No you may not! You do not have operational security clearance. You must stand down and evac the premises immediately! Is that clear?"

"The survival of the hostages is on your head," Clive warned. He spoke in general terms because he did not want to reveal that Ashley was among them. "I know what your plan is. You come in with helicopters, SAS commandos and gas," he noted blandly.

"I can neither confirm nor deny anything you are saying."

"What is the casualty rate with your plan? I am sure you have war gamed it out?"

"This is an open radio channel Clive!"

"It's nothing Bindar doesn't already know. I'll answer for you. Maybe twenty percent hostage casualties. If we're lucky. I'm sure you ran your computer model for the projection. The AI takes into account all past situations with similar circumstances."

"AI does not make life and death decisions for us!"

Clive chuckled. "No. But it can assist in mapping out certain scenarios. I suppose your other option is a guided smart missile attack."

"This castle is England for God's sakes. You think we would drop a bomb on the Tower of London? A UNESCO world heritage site?"

"Option number three: launch a stealth attack rather than a full frontal assault with helicopters, but it will take time. It will also kill the hostages. I suggest that you comply with Bindar's demands. He has the means and the will to do what he has promised. In the meantime I have him contained in the Inner Ward. All entrances to the Inner Wall have been sealed. The besiegers have become the besieged. I suggest you play castle warfare and wait him out."

Clive knew that at the very least Danforth would have to delay whatever he had planned while he relayed the latest circumstances to his superiors. He had bought a little time but he wasn't sure how much.

***

Ashley walked out of the ladies room and set foot on Tower Green. Hedda was at her heels. Ashley was absolutely wrought with sadness for Henry Kincaid, who had died defending her. He was a kind man whom she knew only as an acquaintance. She had seen her father interact with him several times and had been introduced briefly, but that was about it. Once again she was haunted by the fact that she should not have been there. She should have obeyed orders and if she had Kincaid would likely be alive. But then again, would he? There was no guarantee that his life would be spared in another version of the multiverse. She tamped down her guilt as much as she could.

She thought of the hostages. She and could not understand why Bindar had moved them out of the Wakefield Tower, before a proper hostage exchange had even been negotiated. It did not make sense. Unless he had some other intention. What could that be?

Hedda's voice bellowed behind her. "Stop!"

She checked herself dead in her tracks. Hedda marched over and frisked her. Evidently she had noticed something shiny underneath her shirt.

What are you wearing?" Hedda asked.

"Harquebusiers Armor," Ashley replied. "They were the first armed cavalry back in the day."

"Take it off!"

Ashley pulled the chest plate out from under her shirt and handed it to Hedda. "This one was designed for a child. A prince most likely."

"Why would you wear this?"

"It's better than nothing considering all of the bullets flying around here."

Hedda dropped it on the ground. "Let's go."

She pointed toward the entrance to the Waterloo Barracks and they trooped across the parade ground.

Ashley took note of Anne Boleyn's execution platform. Where the remembrance memorial had stood there was now a headsman's block and an axe. She turned to Hedda. "So this is all a distraction, is it? He could care less about a prisoner exchange or executing those three American prisoners. He wants the Kohinoor. You want the Kohinoor."

Hedda paused, as if pondering whether to share more with Ashley. "I don't want it for me. I want it for my country."

It was all starting to come together now. The Kohinoor was an object of contention between Britain and India for years. "So that's it. You are here for the romantic notion that you will take the diamond back to your country as a hero."

"It does not belong here."

"So yours is a noble cause, then? Only problem is you have allied yourself with a madman."

Hedda turned and looked straight into Ashley's eyes. "Sometimes it takes a madman to get the job done."

"Never love a psycho. I can tell you now he's not in it for the cause. He's in it for the money. How much is the reward?"

"Enough."

"That's the only thing he cares about."

"No. You don't know him like I do."

Ashley shook her head. "Dream on, sister." They walked into the vestibule of the Waterloo Barracks. Bindar appeared to be awaiting their return.

He targeted Ashley.

***

Clive looked out from the St. Thomas Tower across the Inner Wall. He could see Tower Green. He noted the execution platform with the pilfered executioner's block and headsman's axe. Would Bindar go through with the act of executing a convict offered to him by the police in exchange for hostages? He did not know. Bindar seemed capable of anything. But he was convinced that it would be not for retribution or justice but purely as a distraction from his true goal: a heist for the Crown Jewels.

The other question was would the police legitimately go through with a prisoner exchange for the hostages? He was pretty certain they would not although they were playing coy about it. He tried to imagine them going to Belmarsh prison in Woolwich and meeting with the American prisoner.

What would they say to him? We need you to save hostages' lives? They could say they would use him as a Trojan horse to buy them time and once inside they would rescue him before the terrorists lopped off his head.

They could say that they would grant him a full pardon and extradition to the US if he cooperated. It was a long shot. The prisoner would have to trust them at their word. But then again what other option would any of these requested American convicts have? What would be the better alternative? Rot in prison for the rest of your life or take a shot at a ticket out?

Clive had heard the term Hobson's choice before. Named after Thomas Hobson, a stable owner in Cambridge, England who despite having a whole stable of horses always insisted that his customers take a weak horse tied up closest to the door or take none at all. It was a choice that really was not a choice.

It was entirely possible that the cops might give the prisoners over to Bindar. But it would only be a temporary means to appease him while they got their ducks in a row to go in guns blazing.

He heard the scuffling of feet below him. Underneath the St. Thomas there was an archway over the Water Gate. After disembarking the barges which delivered them, venerated prisoners such as Queen Elizabeth I and Anne Boleyn walked beneath the arch and up steps to become prisoners of the royal fortress and prison.

Clive descended these very steps towards the source of the footsteps he had heard. Or had he? The stairwell was silent now. But that was no comfort. He knew that Bindar had likely alerted men on the Outer Wall to come for him.

He pulled his crossbow as it was better at close range. He locked and loaded a bolt in case of a fight. Another footstep echoed through the archway and he darted behind a pillar.

He triggered the crossbow and bolted out into the open.

He was faced by an unarmed man. A friendly face. A Beefeater. It was John the Ravenmaster.

John smiled. "Thank God you're okay!"

"How did you get across?" Clive asked. "Swim the Thames?"

"We came through the subway tunnel," he answered. Several more Beefeaters surrounded them. Clive felt a sudden sense of relief.

Emma Winklough trodded up the steps.

Clive smiled. "Inspector? I was trying to reach you on the radio!?"

She shook her head. "I was relieved of duty."

Clive put his hand through his gray locks. "So you decided to come here?"

"Yes. I have a serious disagreement with how the police are handling things. The intelligence services are involved."

"How did you get in?"

She pointed out Heath, who trotted up the steps behind her. "I found Heath, like you suggested. He brought me here."

Heath put his hand in Clive's. "Heath Glennon at your service. I am a friend of your daughter's."

Clive smiled. "I heard something about that. You met last night at the karaoke?"

"Yes, that's me. Did she mention it?" He brightened.

"Never mind that."

"I work for BT. When Ashley mentioned that she had come back to the Tower to fetch you I got worried. I went to the Met command post to tell the coppers she might be a hostage and that's when I met Inspector Winklough."

"They had already replaced me."

John the Ravenmaster huffed and puffed up the stairs. "I was with her at the command post at Potters Fields, commiserating."

Emma smiled. "He had just received your pigeon post message."

John corrected her. "It was a raven's post."

Clive faced Heath. "Thank you."

Heath beamed.

Clive addressed the assembled Beefeaters. "I must tell you that we don't have much time. We must get the hostages out before the Met and Counter-Terrorism come in here with guns blazing. Then it's lights out."

John raised his hand. "The CTC is going to use the prisoner exchange for the attack?"

Clive nodded. "Yes, I believe that's correct."

Clive addressed the rest of the group. "I have sealed off the Inner Ward to restrict the movements of the mercenaries. But there is a contingent still on the Outer Battlements. They are heavily armed so move with caution. Our first step is to eliminate their presence on the Outer Wall."

John pointed toward the end of the corridor. "You should all proceed to the New Armoury for your weapons!"

Clive shook his head. "New Armoury has been purged. Go to the Old Armoury to equip yourselves."

John's eyes lit up. "You heard the man! Old instead of new." There was murmuring amongst the men. They were obviously not quite sure how centuries old weapons of yore would help.

"Follow me. Stay close to the wall!" Clive ordered. He and John led them beneath St. Thomas Tower to Water Lane.

***

Back in the lobby of the Waterloo Barracks Ashley sat at the guard's desk. She wondered what it had been like when this building was the home to over eight hundred soldiers. She thought of the Duke of Wellington, who defeated Napoleon at Waterloo and named this structure in honor of that victory. What would he have thought of her current predicament, held captive by jewel thieves – not the elegant type dressed in black sneakers and tights—but cold hearted terrorists hiding behind a political cause to justify their crimes. Bindar glanced over at her and she pored over the Tower blueprints again. She picked up her pencil and sketched the route out across the river.

Bindar turned on the television behind the guard's desk. Sky News came on. They broadcast an aerial shot of the Tower then cut to a news reporter in the Tower Hamlets. The White Tower loomed from a distance. .

"Unconfirmed reports are coming in that the Tower of London is not under bomb threat as originally thought. Instead the bomb threat was perpetrated by an ex-EOD employee as a means of entry to the fortress. He is now holding hostages and has made demands to provide him with three American convicts for execution. If true this is a huge story as the Tower has not been used for any executions since 1941."

Bindar beamed with pride. "Brilliant! Public pressure will build for us. There is no reason why the public would stand for UK lives to be sacrificed in the interest of saving some American criminals from execution."

Ashley wondered if Bindar himself had leaked these details to the press.

"Where is my map?" Bindar asked her.

"Almost ready," she replied.

***

Clive reopened the bridge over Water Lane so the men could pass inside the Inner Ward to the White Tower on their journey to the Old Armoury. They crossed it in stealth, staying out of view of Bindar's outer guards. They descended down the Wakefield Tower stairs and emerged within the Inner Wall, back on the Green.

Clive's mind was on Ashley. She was in the custody of a certifiable madman. His baby girl, the one he had held in his arms as an infant, was here because of him. He wondered if her mother had seen the news. Hopefully not. She was not a fan of BBC. Come to think of it she was not a fan of anything British in nature. That was because of him.

He led John and the men towards the White Tower in the shadow of the Inner Wall. He took note of the Tower's iconic K2 red phone booth with a Tudor crown at the top. *There was someone inside the booth.* The person's back was to him.

He drew closer and discerned it was the red tunic of a Beefeater. Who could it be? All of the Beefeaters were queued behind him. Unless it was Sheila, or Kincaid? Or perhaps someone posing as a Beefeater? Was the phone line working again?

He looked around for lingering unfriendlies. The coast was clear. He approached the booth and tapped softly on the glass. The nameless Beefeater did not respond. He did not have his hand on the phone receiver. He was simply leaning against the glass. Clive tapped again.

The Beefeater did not budge. Clive circled to the booth's entry door. There he saw Yeoman Warder Henry Kincaid, dried blood on his head and chest. He was not standing on two feet, he was collapsed against the side of the booth. Clive opened the door and placed his hand on his neck. His body was cold to the touch. Kincaid was dead.

Clive looked up and noticed Herman the Raven, circling overhead. He thought of Poe. *Quoth the Raven, 'Nevermore.'*

John the Ravenmaster drew near.

Clive made the sign of a cross across his chest. "He's dead." He pointed at Kincaid.

John bowed his head in shock. "The eternal God is thy refuge, and underneath are the everlasting arms."

"Amen."

John shivered. "They're not your ordinary thieves, dealing out death like this."

"No, they're not."

John covered Kincaid's eyes with a handkerchief. "What shall we do with him?"

Clive pointed out a first aid sign next to the souvenir shop. "Let's take him in there and lay him out."

The two men extricated Kincaid from the phone booth. They carried him past the shop into the medical station. They laid the body on a cot. John placed a pillow underneath his head and a sheet over his face.

They re-emerged to find Herman the Raven caw-cawing a eulogy. He finished the impromptu paean and ascended over the Inner Wall and above Tower Green. Caw-caw, caw-caw.

"What's he trying to say?" Clive asked.

John shrugged. "I don't know. He usually stalks Ashley when she's around."

Clive looked into the sky where the jet black bird circled. It was right over the Waterloo Barracks.

***

Ashley heard the sound of a high-pitched drill. It reminded her of a dentist's office and set her teeth on edge. Smoke and dust billowed out of the anteroom to the jewel treasury. Bindar appeared out of a dust cloud with a respirator on. It gave him a particularly menacing Darth Vader look. He marched toward the counter. She put her nose down to the blueprint. She was pretty sure her penciled markings of the path to the old subway tube were accurate. She had thought of falsifying the location but changed her mind. She did not dare try to double cross Bindar. If he were to actually use the map and found out she misdirected him there would likely be hell to pay. No, he was too volatile. She had no choice but to do exactly as she was told.

Ashley handed the blueprint to Hedda. "I'm done."

Hedda looked at the path she had drawn. "This is it?"

Ashley nodded. "That is the site of the old subway tunnel."

"I never heard of such a thing."

"It was built in the mid-1800s. First one of its kind. Stayed open only a short while until Tower Bridge was built. Then it was no longer necessary."

Hedda waved the blueprint at Bindar. "She says there is a subway tunnel that goes under the river."

He grabbed the scroll and pored over Ashley's mapped route. "Why have I never heard of this?"

"It's been closed since the late 1800s. But it's still used as a tunnel for telecommunications."

Bindar pondered. "This might work."

One of the men called him back to the vault patrol passage. He donned his respirator again and walked off.

Ashley made a heart symbol with her fingers. "I'm assuming you two met at one of the diamond repatriation protests?"

Hedda shook her head. "No. We met at a pub where I bartended. He regaled me with stories of bombs defused in the nick of time, women, babies and puppies saved from imminent destruction. He had a fervent energy about him. There was an animal attraction and it led to a tempestuous affair, which ended when I found him in my kitchen texting his wife that he was called in last minute to defuse an IED."

Ashley was surprised at Hedda's sudden candor. "Yet you went back to him anyway."

"He came back to me, six months later. Showed me his divorce papers. He said he could not stop thinking about me. So we moved in together. We adopted a cat. It was all very cozy until I found out he seduced a young constable after a long night at a nightclub bombing. He told me it was just built-up tension and that it meant nothing. I threw him out."

Ashley sassed back. "Yet here we are."

"A year later I got a phone call. A social worker rang from the local hospital. She said he was in intensive care and had asked for me. I visited him in hospital and saw his injuries. He had been in a bomb-maker suspect's flat gathering explosive materials when a spark ignited one of the chemicals. He had second degree burns and a dislocated shoulder. It was obvious he had come within a hair of losing his life. He told me I was the only one, he had no one else to call, nowhere to go."

"It's always a sob story, isn't it?"

"I could not leave him in that condition. I took him back and nursed him to health by day while tending bar at night. But he was not the same. He became increasingly agitated by politics. He tried to go back to work but they put him on leave for mental health reasons. His leave meant plenty of spare time to watch football at the pub. He fell in with some rowdies. I had an inkling he was participating in petty crimes but refused to entertain the possibility. He took several trips to India on his own. He had family there, he said. He promised we could go and live out our lives in peace and relative wealth to the rest of the country."

"So that's the plan?"

She paused as if carefully composing her answer. "Tarkarli. It's just as beautiful as Goa, but not as crowded. South coast of Maharashtra. It's got it all, fine white sand, fun villages with outdoor markets where we will pick up the most delicious fruits and vegetables, there's temples for meditation, it's all there."

"Sounds beautiful."

"We will live off the grid."

"What if you want to travel?"

"We can go wherever we want within India."

Ashley looked at her. It was blue skies and fair weather forever. Alluring but too much of a fairy tale.

Bindar wasn't interested in Hedda. He would get to India with the gem, hand it over and revel in his hero status. He would likely have beautiful young women throw themselves at him. He would not need her. He would leave.

***

The glass display cases of the Old Armoury exhibit shook and rattled as the Yeoman Warders crossed its aisles. It might as well have been a shopping mall on Black Friday. Some grabbed longbows, crossbows, spears, axes and even slingshots from various cabinet. Others undressed medieval mannequins and adorned themselves in chain mail, helmets and gambesons, the medieval precursor to Kevlar.

Clive followed John into the room. He was deeply distraught over Kincaid. He could not stop thinking about the fact that if he had not assigned him to escort the billionaire on his tour he might still be alive. Yes, Kincaid was a military veteran. Yes, he was aware that he might have to sacrifice his life for his country. But that was on the battlefield, not here as a tour guide at the Tower.

Clive tried to suppress his feelings of guilt but it seemed to make them stronger. He thought of the American General Ulysses S. Grant, whom he had studied in military training. Grant had expressed crippling distress over the loss of his men in the Wilderness in 1864. He overcame it and ultimately won the war.

Clive would have to do the same.

The Beefeaters were now outfitted with medieval weapons and old regalia. They were quite a sight, these 21st century custodians of the Tower. He looked around for Yeoman Warder Hansty but did not see her.

He turned to John. "Where is Sheila?"

"She never came out."

"What? Are you sure?

"Yes. She and Kincaid never arrived for roll call across the river."

"When is the last time she was seen?"

"Down at the Wharf assisting tourists in the evac."

"You think she came back? I expressly ordered all warders to leave the premises."

"You can court martial her for insubordination later. Hopefully."

Clive shouted in a whisper. "Yeoman Warders gather!"

The warders quickly assembled around him. They were now a motley crew, reminiscent of Robin Hood and his band of merry men, the Knights of the Round Table or even the Knights Templar.

Clive briefed the troops. "I want four teams to take out the snipers at the four corners of the Outer Wall. They have automatic weapons but you have a knowledge of this castle. The Tower will afford you many defenses, so long as you use them. Embrasures, arrow loops, murder holes and machicolations are all at your disposal. This is our time because we know them. The enemy does not. Ravenmaster John will assign you to the proper quadrants. Are there any questions?"

A man in chain mail tunic rose. "When will we have the opportunity to secure the hostages?"

"In due time. Our first step is to control the Outer Ward. That way we can confine the kidnappers in their movements. Stay off walkie communications as the enemy may be monitoring them. If you need to communicate send a messenger to my location under St. Thomas Tower, is that clear?"

The men nodded and saluted.

"Be careful. The snipers on top of Byward, Develin and Brass Mount have the high ground. You will need to enter the keeps stealthily and engage them by surprise."

Several men whisper-shouted their assent. "Yes sir!"

"Once you have re-secured those four outer towers hoist your partizans. Remember, these men are trained killers. Do not hold back. That's all. Dismissed."

The men dispersed out of the White Tower and headed down the stairs toward Tower Green.

***

The lobby of the Waterloo Barracks reminded Ashley of a documentary she had watched about the Dust Bowl in the 1930s. Drywall powder, metal shavings and lord knows what else floated in the air. A layer of this dust coated everything in sight. Her lungs burned. Was Bindar's crew making progress in getting through to the vault? She had no idea and she certainly wasn't going to bring up the subject. She and Hedda sat across from each other at the counter normally manned by a Scots Guard.

Bindar emerged from the vault patrol passage. His phone was ringing. He removed his mask and swiped right. "I hope you have good news."

Ashley could hear the voice of the negotiator who called himself Superintendent Danforth. "We are prepared to do the hostage exchange."

Ashley figured that news coverage of the hostage negotiation must have done its trick. Public sentiment would surely pressure the Home Office to act to preserve the lives of British citizens. They would not care if it required the sacrifice of American convicts in return. The government had to at least give the appearance of offering the American criminals in exchange. Nonetheless Ashley was sure this entire subject was a misdirect.

"We will plan the rendezvous for 1900 hours in the moat," Bindar replied.

Danforth radioed back. "We will have a helicopter land at the appointed place with the prisoners."

This was all going too easily, Ashley thought. There had to be some hitch in the plan.

Bindar clicked on the radio again. "By the way, you have a rogue Beefeater here that claims to speak or negotiate on my behalf. Know that is not true. It's a ruse."

"Copy that," replied Danforth.

Ashley could not believe her ears. Bindar had told Clive that he was the only one he wanted to negotiate with! And now he was telling the cops the opposite. He was setting her dad up. Would the police fire on him? Why was Bindar so adamant that the hostage exchange take place in the dry moat? She had so many questions.

"Why are the prisoners in the moat?"

Hedda shook her head. "I told you, I don't know. That's where he wants the prisoner exchange."

"You don't honestly believe that he is going to let the hostages live?"

"I have no reason to believe otherwise."

"He's going to kill them."

"If he wanted to kill them don't you think he would have done that already?"

"He killed Kincaid."

"That's because he crossed him. You never cross him."

"If he kills those hostages will it have been worth it?"

"Worth what?"

"Getting the diamond back to your country. Is it worth their lives? There's a little girl among them."

"He's not going to kill the hostages."

Bindar re-entered the Barracks with a spring in his step.

"Why don't you ask him?"

"I don't need to do that!"

"You're scared of him, aren't you? Great relationship. Built on mutual trust."

Hedda turned on a dime and marched toward Bindar. It was as if she had been dared and she did not back down from a dare.

She pulled him aside. He still gripped his rabbit's foot. "What is it?"

"Promise me," Hedda said. "Killing hostages was never part of this plan. I want your commitment..."

He seethed and looked at Ashley. "Did she put you up to this? You're so easily manipulated." He walked over and lifted Ashley out of her chair.

Hedda slammed her fist on the desk. "It was my question, not hers. We are so far deviated from the original plan."

Bindar released Ashley. "You let me worry about the plan. You know I do not want to end innocent lives. You know how hard I have worked, how much I have put on the line to save lives. It's an insult, frankly, that you would ask me that."

Hedda lowered her gaze. "I'm sorry."

He walked back towards the patrol passage with his respirator in hand. "Be ready. Do not let this one distract you! Once we extract the Kohinoor you have an enormous responsibility."

Ashley massaged her neck. Her breathing settled. So it was the Kohinoor they were after. What was this responsibility? Did Bindar know about the diamond's curse? He likely did, given his tendency toward superstition. Maybe it was Hedda's job to carry the diamond. It was quite possible he believed it was only safe in the hands of a woman.

***

Clive manned a post atop St. Thomas Tower and trained his binoculars on the Develin. One of Bindar's men, a sniper in bomb squad uniform, stood watch behind the turrets with an HK G36. He faced the river. Three Beefeaters with longbows silently popped up from the battlements of the Well Tower, which was a higher elevation. They showered bolts on the sniper, catching him off guard.

He fired back but it was to no avail. The bullets pinged against the merlons of the turret, the Beefeaters safely ensconced behind them. It was a battle of automatic weapons vs. longbows. The Beefeaters reloaded and rose again, firing down at the sniper. One of the arrows struck him in the shoulder.

He tugged at the shaft with his uninjured arm, seeking to remove it from his skin. Blood flowed down his shoulder. In a burst of adrenalin he ran across the wall walk toward the turret of the Well Tower. He stopped directly underneath one of the arrow loops and fired blindly inside.

One Beefeater materialized on the turret above and fired directly down. His arrow pierced the sniper's neck . Blood gushed from the second wound. He collapsed, dropping his weapon.

Clive sighed in relief. He turned his attention to the southwest corner. There was activity atop Byward Tower. A gunman manned a post on the riverside keep. Three Beefeaters bearing crossbows ambushed from the inside. Caught by surprise he whirled around and sprayed bullets. The Beefeaters dove for cover but not before one of them got off a crossbow bolt. It struck the gunman squarely in the chest.

John the Ravenmaster appeared next to Clive, startling him. "What is it?"

John shook his head. "Bindar has moved hostages to the moat. Looks like they are in preparation for some kind of prisoner exchange."

Clive followed John along the wall walk to a vantage point on the westward moat. It was a grassy park area, most days calm and sedate. Today the hostages were arrayed across it, anxiously awaiting their release. This did not make sense. Why would Bindar want do a hostage exchange there?

Yes it was a fairly wide open space and certainly a helicopter could land within its wide confines but why not the main bridge by Byward Tower? Prisoner were usually conducted on bridges. Or why not the Tower Green? There was plenty of room for a helo.

He thought of the vault, obviously Bindar's main objective. This vault was foolproof. It was designed to withstand a nuclear attack. It was sealed against flooding, *except* earlier this year in doing some cabling for closed circuit TV one of the techs had noted the electrical, lighting, security and telephone line conduits were not. In other words, in the event of a normal rain this was no problem. But in the event of a flood, water could seep into the vault via holes in the wall drilled for the cabling. But even in that instance, there was a failsafe. In the event of water detection, the vault floor was designed to elevate as high as eight feet to keep its contents dry.

Was it possible that Bindar knew this? Was he going to flood the moat? Was this why he was locating hostages there? It was a very big if but it made sense. A flooded moat would give Bindar cover. As the Met attempted to rescue the drowning hostages, he would have more time. He would also have a vault that was lifted high above its reinforced sheathing.

Clive wondered if he should get on the radio and share his theory with the cops? He doubted they would believe him.

Chapter Eighteen

Clive looked down from the parapets of the west outer wall. Below was the dry moat. It was arrayed like the demilitarized zone between North and South Korea. On one side was the landing pad for the incoming Met helicopter. Its rotors could be seen on the horizon as it approached the Tower airspace. On the other side, the hostages were assembled in a group, guarded by three mercenaries. Clive quickly scanned each of the hostages' faces. Sheila Hansty was there along with Slater and a small group of tourists including a young girl. Ashley was not among them. Clive was not surprised by this. He had an inkling Bindar would not release her with the rest, knowing that was a trump card. And Bindar was correct. He would do anything possible to ensure Ashley's safety.

Clive looked above to see a small group on the Inner Wall. They were on the roof of the Beauchamp Tower. He made out Bindar, with binoculars. He was on the phone. Next to him was the female expo officer that arrived in the van. There was another female behind them, although hidden from view. Could this be Ashley?

The helo approached. Bindar's mercs kept the hostages at gunpoint to ensure the Met did not make any false moves. Clive knew they would be if any signs of foul play on the part of the police.

The helo landed, its rotor wash kicked up dirt and debris. The hostages, kept at a safe distance, turned their backs as the air kicked up. The passenger hatch to the helo opened and three prisoners emerged in prison scrubs. They marched toward the halfway point between the helicopter and the hostages. Two of Bindar's mercs walked forward to meet them. The lead merc spoke on the phone. He motioned for the three prisoners to stop. They did so and began to strip down to their underwear. Apparently Bindar was concerned they might have weapons planted on them.

The three shivering prisoners moved away from the police toward their new minders. Bindar's merc took a photo of each prisoner. Clive assumed Bindar was verifying their identities? He wanted to make sure he executed the right people?

Another moment. The unclothed prisoners were marched towards a ladder that extended up the lowest portion of the Outer Wall. At the same time the hostages were marched towards the helicopter.

Clive scanned the dyke that kept the Thames out of the dry moat. He could not see any explosives. Just mortar and rocks and…a small sand colored box attached to the vertical bricks? He looked over to the left of the moat and spied another box. These had not been there previously.

***

High atop Beauchamp Tower, Ashley watched the first of the three unclothed prisoners climb up the ladder and ascend into the fortress under guard. She assumed they would be escorted to the execution scaffold on Tower Green and be summarily executed. That didn't really concern her. It was the hostages. They were slowly walking towards the police helicopter but something felt off. Why would Bindar give up all of the hostages? It didn't make sense. They were his leverage. Unless this was all part of a plan.

Hedda looked down at the hostages too, she seemed focused on the nine year old girl who walked hand in hand with her sister. She turned to Bindar. "You said you wouldn't do this!" He laughed. "I'm not *doing* anything," he said. "Whatever happens now is on the police's head."

Hedda wasn't buying it. "This was never part of the plan!"

"Plans change, my darling."

Ashley saw Bindar had his hands on a rabbit's foot that he perpetually stroked. Up close she could see it was no ordinary rabbit's foot. It had a small antenna protruding from the furry foot. It was a radio controlled detonator. Bindar's thumb was on the switch.

Ashley could see Herman the Raven in the gray sky, circling.

Hedda grabbed for the rabbit's foot or remote control device (?). "Whatever you are going to do, let the hostages go!"

Hedda looked down at the hostages and yelled. "Run! It's not safe there! Get out of the moat!"

A couple of hostages looked up but it was unclear if they heard her.

Bindar grabbed her by the throat.

Hedda choked. "You and I are over."

"I can't let you go."

"Then you are going to have to kill me."

Bindar softened his expression. "There is no problem! Once we get to India you and I will live like king and queen in Takarli."

"It was a stupid romantic idea. The two of us in that village, me in a sari, making house and cooking curries. It's not in the cards. You never cared about me. And this is obviously not some noble cause for you."

Bindar pointed his gun at Ashley. "She has poisoned you against me. I should kill her right now!"

Ashley peered at the gun. No one had ever pointed a gun at her before today. Maybe there was a water pistol or two. But this was not water and this was not a sassy pre-teen boy holding her hostage at the peril of a drenching. This was real life.

Hedda darted in front of her. "No!"

Ashley blinked and dove to the ground. A shot rang out. She was frozen in time, fear, shock. There was an echo – a clap against the stone walls of the moat. The moment seemed like an eternity. She was frozen in time, not knowing if she was injured or not. She felt her hands against the cold damp stones of the wall-walk. She opened her eyes. Her first glimpse was of Hedda. She was on the ground in a pool of her own blood, a bullet through her heart.

"They killed her," Bindar muttered, as he crawled to her side.

She saw the glint of a sharpshooter's reticle, like what Clive described previously. Had Hedda been killed by a Met sniper lodged in one of the modern buildings that surrounded the Tower? No. They would have no incentive to fire shots while the lives of the hostages were in jeopardy. Bindar had obviously done it. He had killed her in cold blood for defying him.

Yet he cradled her bloody body in his arms. "For the curse has come on me, not with my own death but with yours. Now they kill me with a living death."

He kissed her on the lips. Then he gripped his rabbit's foot/remote trigger.

***

Clive heard the gunshot ring out. He triangulated it in his head and figured it came from an SAS sniper nested on the roof of the Tower Place shopping mall, across the street. It was directed at Beauchamp Tower, where Bindar had been watching the hostage exchange. Had they been able to take him out? It was unclear. Bindar was now out of view. There was no one visible on the Beauchamp roof.

Below in the moat the hostages moved toward the Met helicopter. Clive keyed his radio. "This is Clive Bellamy, Yeoman Warder. Get the hostages out of the moat as fast as possible! They are in danger..."

Danforth's voice came through. "Clive!!! I told you already to stand down! Get off this channel!"

Clive could not take it any longer. He backed out of his embrasure and rushed down the stone corridor. John followed. "Where are you going?"

"To the wall walk."

"But the sharpshooters will shoot you!"

"We have to get the hostages out of there. There is no time to waste."

Clive darted over the cobbled wall walk and turned right at a landing. There were several ladders and bags of mortar patch mix along with a roof sealer. He took an extension ladder and carried it over to the side of the outer wall and hung it over the side, dropping its extension so it spanned the entire distance from the ground up to the outer wall.

He watched as the hostages below moved quickly towards the helicopter.

Clive yelled at Warder Hansty. "Sheila!! Do not get on the helicopter! You need to get everyone out of the moat right now!"

John and another Beefeater emerged with another extension ladder. They proceeded to lower their ladder down into the moat.

Clive screamed at the top of his lungs above the pounding pulse of the helicopter rotors. "Come up here! We have these ladders for you. You must climb up here right now!"

Several of the hostages recognized him and ran over. Slater tried to dissuade them.

"Don't listen to him! We are here because of his incompetence!"

"Mr. Slater, please. It is not safe here in the moat. There are explosives rigged at the end. They are going to blow it up."

Sheila hastened the other hostages towards Clive's ladder and they climbed up one at a time. John took their hands and helped them on to the top of the wall. Clive lifted the young girl over the battlements. She smiled at him. Sheila then climbed up herself.

But Slater stood did not budge. He stood in the center of the moat. He glared at Beckford, who climbed up John's ladder. "You're going up there too?"

Beckford offered a sheepish grin. "I don't like helicopters."

"You can look for another job when we get back!"

Beckford shrugged and continued up the ladder.

Slater shook his head. "I'm going to the police." He walked toward the helicopter.

Clive raised his hands in protest. "The police don't understand that there is a bomb! It's at the end of the moat. You need to get up here right now Mr. Slater!"

Slater looked toward the stone wall that held back the Thames. "You don't know what you're talking about!" He kept walking.

The other hostages were pulled to safety. Clive followed Slater from atop the wall.

"None of this will ever happen at my hotel!" Slater yelled. "Except in the escape room which I will personally design, inspired by this shitshow!"

Clive lifted his leg over the parapet and on to the ladder. "What are you doing?" John asked.

"I'm going down there. I have to get him out."

John bridled. "You can't do that!"

Suddenly there was a loud explosion. The rocks, mortar and brick of the moat's outer wall came tumbling down. The Met helicopter immediately ascended. A cascade of broken masonry was followed by a wall of water.

Robert Slater was crushed by rocks and then swept up by a flash flood, his body caught in the heavy current. Clive's ladder crashed down into the surging water.

John the Ravenmaster turned to the hostages. "We have a way out of the Tower. Please follow me. I will escort you to safety."

***

Ashley leaned against the parapets of the Beauchamp Tower listening to the sound of water rushing through the moat. She knew she was in deep trouble. Hedda lay lifeless just steps from her. She glanced over at Bindar who kneeled beside her body as if he had nothing to do with her death.

He did not cradle her in his arms, he methodically checked her pockets to remove any valuables or clues to her identity. He was not overly distraught. This was business. Hedda truly didn't really mean much of anything to him. She was a means to an end. But he had not killed her. She could see that the shot had come from outside the Tower. It was probably meant for him.

Now what to do? Should she make a run for it? Take off down the wall walk and head towards the bridge at the Wakefield Tower? But it was not open. Clive had closed it to seal off the Inner Ward.

She started to hear a song in her head. A song that was on a continuous loop and would not go away.

A kiss on the hand may be quite continental
But diamonds are a girl's best friend.
A kiss may be grand but it won't pay the rental
On your humble flat
Or help you at the automat
Men grow cold as girls grow old
And we all lose our charm in the end
But square cut or pear shape
These rocks don't lose their shape!
Diamonds are a girl's best friend

Why the hell am I hearing this song? She rolled over and looked down the wall walk that led to the Wakefield Tower and its bridge. Even if it were closed maybe she could climb up over its roof.

Diamonds are a girl's best friend

Ashley decided to make a break for the bridge. She inched away from Bindar, still on his knees emptying Hedda's pockets.

Bindar broke his silence with a click of his pistol. "Don't even think about making a run for it."

Diamonds are a girl's best friend

"You can't kill me. You need me now more than ever. If you or any man touches the diamond the Kohinoor curse will kill you faster than a lightning bolt."

"How do you know about the curse?"

"Anyone who knows a little history knows about the curse. The diamond in male hands is death. They are driven insane with greed and power by its allure. Ring a bell? It's well documented. Men have raped, plundered and savaged kingdoms in their pursuit of the Kohinoor. Why do you think the Khiliji empire fell? Or the Tuglaq Empre? The Mughals? Even the East India Company – in charge of shipping the Kohinoor here was nearly destroyed by contact with it. The British royal family knows this. Have you ever seen a male British royal wear it on any occasion? No! It was and has been only for the women to wear. Some say even the present King has been doomed by its inheritance, though he never touched it."

"You call that a *little* history? You are very well versed," Bindar replied.

Ashley realized she was ingratiating herself with him. "I am a diamond fanatic. The ultimate fan. There's nothing about famous diamonds that I don't know. Why do you think I came here?"

"To see the Crown Jewels..."

"Specifically the Kohinoor. It's been my life's dream to see it."

"Did you?"

"Not yet," she lied. "I always thought I would be seeing it through thick bulletproof glass, not up close and personal."

"Oh you're going to see it much closer than that," Bindar replied.

He grabbed her by the arm and pulled her into the turret stairwell. They descended the steps coiling down towards ground level.

Part III
After The Flood

-

Chapter Nineteen

As the Tower evolved from its identity as a royal residence to a military fortress, it received more soldiers. Soldiers required berthing. A devastating fire in 1841 destroyed several structures on Tower Green creating an urgent need for more bunks. So the Duke of Wellington decided to address this by erecting the largest structure ever built within the Tower's walls. He named this the Waterloo Barracks, after his decisive victory over Napoleon.

Bindar led Ashley into this imposing structure at gunpoint. He led her down the corridor to the treasury room. The clouds of dust were gone for the moment. There was a gaping hole in the outer wall where his team had breached the outer wall of the depository. The inner wall stood firm despite various drill bit marks where they had tried to penetrate its shell. It was solid stainless steel.

She heard water trickling, like the sound of a stream or a brook. Was the water a threat? Ashley doubted it. She was sure that the engineers who had rebuilt this high tech security vault had allowed for any eventuality including the refilling of the moat. But if that were the case then why was she hearing a gradual increase in flow? This thing was supposed to be water tight. Had the engineers missed something? It was entirely possible, she thought. History was littered with engineering mishaps, mistakes and disasters. There was even a television program about them. Her former boyfriend had her watch it with him, although she found it dreadfully boring.

Bindar put his ear to the inner wall. She heard the sound of a hydraulic lift beneath them. Was it a lift or a pump? Or maybe both? She was not sure. But all she knew was that she could hear the sound of something rising from deep in the ground beneath them. Bindar perked up to the sound of the water. Why was he so excited? He was certainly aware he was surrounded by a police presence.

Bindar smiled as he put his ear to the sheathing that surrounded the depository. The floor to the vault was rising. It must have been designed to rise when any significant moisture level was detected.

Niko entered the patrol passage carrying goggles and a metal-working torch. He was followed by the three prisoners she had seen in the moat. They all carried drills. Bindar had evidently not wanted them for execution after all. It all made sense now. *He wanted them for their safecracking skills.* Had no one put two plus two together? Evidently they had not or they didn't care. Bindar now had a team of safecracking techies, whereas before he only had one.

Niko lit his plasma torch. It radiated a strong blue flame. He applied it to the metal shell that was the last barrier to the treasure.

Bindar snapped at him. "You're too low."

Niko shut off his torch. "What do you mean?"

Bindar smiled like the Cheshire cat. "You should be drilling up here." He pointed toward where the wall met the ceiling. "It's the path of least resistance; they did not reinforce the sheathing up there like they did at ground level."

Niko took a stepladder and climbed up to where the wall met the ceiling. One of the prisoners from the swap handed him a sawzall. He turned it on and plunged the blade into the ceiling. It easily gave way and she could see through the rafters above. Next to them was the levitated jewel vault.

Niko poked through the opening in the ceiling and climbed further. He positioned himself on a joist over the door to the vault. "Torch!"

A swarthy American convict picked up the plasma torch. He handed it to Niko and guided the hose upward. Niko lit the nozzle and burned away the metal around the latch of the door. It yielded almost instantly.

Niko beamed with pride. "We're in!"

Bindar looked at Ashley. "Do not go anywhere." He locked the door to the patrol passage behind her. There was no way out.

The swarthy American convict leered at Ashley. He turned to Bindar. "What happened to your other girlfriend?"

Bindar stepped off the ladder and got in the convict's face. "She's dead. You so much as touch this one and I will cut your throat." He regained his footing on the ladder and stepped up.

She was his second girlfriend now? That was a creepy, disgusting thought. What did he mean by that? He had not made even a passing flirtation to her. It was braggadocio, she figured. He did want her. But for one reason only. She was his diamond handler.

The American convict backed off.

Bindar climbed through the ceiling. His plan was coming together. How could she foil it? *Diamonds are a girl's best friend.*

***

The Yeoman Warders huddled beneath the archway of the St. Thomas. The building was rectangular, long and wide with two corner turrets facing the inside. It afforded a perfect shelter to stay out of harm's way. Clive peered over the parapet at Potters Field. He had never seen so many police. On the waterfront, he noted a fleet of Marine Policing Unit (MPU) speedboats manned by tactical teams. In and around the cherry trees SAS Special Air Service (SAS) commandos prepped amphibious gear. A squad of army techs readied more drones. This gear was next-level. There were black combat octocopters: eight rotors apiece. Met constables worked crowd control around police cordons. But there were no crowds. The entire neighborhood was still deserted due to the evacuation orders.

John rushed in from Water Lane. "We have control of the Outer Walls. All Warder teams report they have secured Legge's Mount, Brass Mount, Byward and Develin Towers."

"Casualties?" Clive asked.

"No Warder casualties, sir," John answered.

The men were elated and voiced their approval in hushed tones so as not to give away their location.

Clive addressed the group. "We still have a long way to go. The enemy holds the high inner wall so you must remain behind cover from any potential sniper fire. A caged animal only becomes more dangerous. Remain at the ready for your orders in the next phase of our operation. Dismissed."

Clive peered across the Thames at the Met police command post. It was the quiet before the storm. The hostage exchange distraction and false attempt at diplomacy was now over. They were now organizing the impending assault. They would come in with full force. It was only a matter of time. He needed to get Ashley out as soon as possible.

John reached into his tunic and pulled out a piece of beef jerky. He proceeded to mimic the sound of a raven call. It was not the high-pitched caw-caw-caw of a crow but rather a lower pitched more guttural croak. He repeated it three times and then pulled from his pocket a castanet-like device. He squeezed it repeatedly. It sounded like the snapping of a bird's beak.

Herman descended rapidly toward John and landed on his outstretched arm. "There you are, good fellow." John ran his fingers through his jet black feathers.

He handed a bird treat to Herman. He refused to partake. John turned to Clive. "Something is wrong. He has a bit of indigestion."

"It's probably that luggage locator he swallowed."

"What?!"

"Ashley dropped it on the ground earlier. He swept down and ate it. I guess he thought it was a treat."

John examined the bird more closely. "Not good."

"Will he be alright?"

"He should be able to pass it. We'll have to see. In the meantime he's not eating."

Clive nodded. He had much bigger worries than the bird's appetite. He picked up the radio. "Met Police come in? This is Chief Yeoman Warder Bellamy..."

Danforth's voice crackled over the airwaves. "Clive your conduct is mutinous. You are in complete violation of your responsibilities at this point,"

"The Warders have the Outer Ward of the Tower. We have the enemy contained."

"You are obstructing constabulary business!"

"I am the constable of this castle for the moment, sir. And I will see it returned to Britain. In the meantime do not make any moves without my express knowledge. If you do anything to jeopardize the safety of one single person behind these walls I will make sure your name is known far and wide as responsible for the deaths of innocent civilians." He switched off the radio.

John sensed something was off. "You alright, Clive?"

"No. They have Ashley."

"She came back?"

Clive nodded. "What could she have been thinking? That somehow she would help me by staying in harm's way? She's so damned stubborn that one!"

John raised an eyebrow. "Reminds me of someone I know."

"Gather the men. Tell them to take defensive positions on the outer ramparts."

"I thought we're going inward?"

"Change of plans! I can't have the SAS commandos barging in here with Ashley's life on the line! We're going to have to hold the Outer Wall!"

"Right," John said. He walked off towards the huddled Beefeater crew to give them their orders.

Clive found himself in the unenviable position of defending His Majesty's castle from Britain's own soldiers. But if he were to ensure Ashley's safety he had no choice.

***

Ashley stood in the patrol passage listening to the dripping water. The swarthy convict kept leering at her. She did not want to remain here. So she climbed the ladder and followed Bindar through the hole in the ceiling.

The convict called after her. "Hey! Where are you going?"

But she was already on top of the rafters. She kicked the ladder down so he could not easily pursue her. She dropped down through the open hatch and landed on the floor of the display room.

A banner above the exhibit noted: *Kohinoor: Symbol of Conquest*, a nod to its many previous owners, including Mughal Emperors, Shahs of Iran, Emirs of Afghanistan and Sikh Maharajas. In a compromise to appease critics of UK custodianship the diamond exhibit was redone to present its history in a more balanced approach. There was not one display case but three, showcasing the different eras.

The first display contained an enameled armlet with a replica of the original uncut gem. The second exhibit presented the Kohinoor at it was on Queen Alexandra's coronation crown. It was a more refined cut, as it looked in 1902 when Alexandra wore it for her coronation. The third case featured the diamond on the Queen Mother's crown. On the rim was a Maltese cross and set into the crux was the actual Kohinoor. It looked different than it had this morning when the royal jeweler cleaned it. On the crown it looked more regal than ever.

"Three diamonds for the price of one!" Niko shouted. Did he not realize that two were replicas? Or was he joking? He took the plasma torch and cut holes into each display case.

Ashley marveled at the ignorance of the men who had come to pillage the jewel. She rose before them like a teacher and spoke slowly and clearly. "The first two displays show the diamond's earlier history in Britain. This armlet was worn by Duleep Singh in 1849 when he brought the diamond to Queen Victoria. It shows how the diamond looked with its Mughal cut. Many were disappointed with its appearance." She reached into the display and slipped the large rock out of the armlet easily. "You will notice it doesn't have many facets nor is it brilliant when held up to the light."

Bindar laughed. "That stone is not real."

"Right," Ashley replied. She set the stone down on the jeweler's bench at the back of the room. "The second display is how the Kohinoor looked after it was re-cut in 1852. This setting is on Queen Alexandra's coronation crown. She was the daughter-in-law of Queen Victoria." She picked up the crown and held it up for the group to see. "Notice how much shinier this diamond is. But it lost a lot of its volume in the process." She set the crown down on the bench next to the armlet.

Bindar stepped forward, taking the diamond in, but keeping his distance. He seemed slightly apprehensive. Reverential almost. "That stone is a replica, too."

"Yes." Ashley sauntered over to the third display. Niko was about to take the Queen Mother's crown out of the glass box.

Bindar lurched. "Don't touch it!" He waved Ashley forward. "Only she handles it."

Niko backed off and Ashley carefully reached down into the display to lift up the platinum crown. It was heavier than she anticipated. How uncomfortable to have this on one's head! It had first enchanted her back in 2002 when she and her mom watched the Queen Mother's funeral. The crown was placed atop the Queen's coffin for the funeral procession. Ashley and her mom watched intently as the crowned coffin made its way through the streets to Westminster Abbey. The choir sang and mourners wept as the funeral cortege carried the crowned casket to the cathedral. The altar was blanketed with camellias. Ashley had been so impressed with the transcendent occasion that it began her lifelong interest in diamonds.

In the treasury room, Bindar stood next to Ashley and regarded the Kohinoor with a sense of awe. Sedgewick gazed upon it with an expression of pure greed. The American convicts hovered as well.

Niko offered his own color commentary. "That's five hundred ninety one million worth of carbonized crystal right there."

Bindar scoffed. "You can't reduce it to a monetary amount. You're looking at living history."

Niko sneered. "I don't care about living history. I care about my cut. Which is much larger now that half the crew is dead."

Bindar fumed. "Why don't you should stand back and let the adults do the work now?" He turned to Ashley. "Take the diamond out of its setting."

"What?" Ashley asked. "Why?"

"Because a crown doesn't travel well." He pointed out the jeweler's bench at the rear of the vault.

Ashley took in the worktable. She had just stood there this morning. "I'm not a jeweler."

Bindar simpered. "You'll do. Get to it. We don't have much time."

Ashley delicately placed the crown on the bench. The morning's stint with Bernard came back to her. She reached for a pair of white cotton jeweler's gloves, placed them on her hands. She gripped a tempered steel implement with notches: a prong opener. She had seen him use it that morning to remove the diamond for cleaning. She wielded it just as he had and poked at the platinum prongs, bending them forward. Once that was done she took a curved scalpel blade and inserted it between the diamond and the bezel setting. She gently pushed at the diamond until there was some give. Then she took a wood handled tool called a lifter and placed its flat side against the stone. She moved it around and gently pushed the diamond on a piece of velvet.

Bindar chortled. "You are quite a pro."

"My mom dated a jeweler. He taught me a few things," she lied. If only. She placed the diamond inside a velvet pouch and attempted to hand it to Bindar. He backed away as if she were holding up a snake or an asp for him to hold.

"Oh, no, no, no. You are keeping that on you."

She shrugged and placed the velvet pouch in her pocket.

Bindar picked up his sat phone and dialed. "I have the package. Ready for extraction."

He led Ashley by the arm back toward the ladder.

Sedgewick blocked his way. "I have another buyer for the diamond."

***

Clive looked over the edge of the wall to Tower Wharf. Met counterterrorism commandos disembarked speedboats with carabiners, cleats and smoke grenades. Clive imagined they would not use the grenades until snipers cleared the wall. Basic siege warfare: the first escalade, or scaling of the wall is usually deterred by castle defenders. They had the upper hand to repel the invaders. The Beefeaters had a legacy of medieval tools at hand: boiling oil, crossbow bolts, flaming arrows, rocks and bricks. But the knights of yore never had to contend with sniper fire from neighboring skyscrapers. That was a variable which could easily turn the tide. So Clive's men would use smudge pots to cover their positions.

Clive visited the Beefeater positions on top of the Outer Wall. "Do not engage until ordered but hold your ground!" He wanted to avoid a clash if at all possible. But did his counterparts in the Met have the same attitude? He and the Beefeaters were likely regarded as deserters, mutinous former comrades who deserved no mercy. Typically deserters were shot. So it was no stretch to assume that SO15 would have no compunction about firing on them.

Several shots rang out on the wall. Clive ducked. "Take cover!"

Beefeaters held up shields. They were purely symbolic, as long range rifle shells could pierce straight through them.

A couple longbow archers independently fired arrows at the source of the gunfire flashes. They fell short of their targets.

Clive rushed them. "Hold your fire!" He realized this was going to be a bloodbath. Should he raise the white flag? He did not want to be responsible for the death of his men. At the same time he wanted to ensure the safety of his daughter.

Several Beefeater grenadiers placed ceremonial cannons between the merlons. They loaded live shells and tracked an assault speedboat as it made its way across the river. Warder Harrington crouched behind the loaded cannon. He awaited an order. This would be a direct hit. The Met assault boat would sink into the Thames. What good could possibly come of it? It would only escalate matters and inspire commandos who might be having second thoughts to carry out the attack on their fellow countrymen. Clive knew once they pulled the trigger it would be no holds barred war.

He turned to John. "Hold them off as long as you can without any bloodshed."

***

The patrol passage of the jewel vault looked like an open can of tuna fish, its steel sheathing was peeled back now, revealing the contents of empty jewel displays, lighting and unobstructed bullet proof glass that had protected its valuables. It was now completely looted. But that was not good enough. The thieves wanted more.

Bindar stood in front of Sedgewick, defiantly. Ashley thought of any number of American cowboy standoffs: Ike Clanton and Wyatt Earp, the Hatfields and the McCoys. She gripped the Kohinoor tightly in her fist, waiting to see the results of this impending duel, this British version of a shootout at the OK corral.

Sedgewick crossed his arms in defiance. "We go to the highest bidder."

Bindar smoldered. "Maybe you don't recall? I hired you. You work for me."

"I supplied you with the personnel who made it possible for you to get in here."

Bindar pointed out the Met uniforms. "Do you think you would have gotten in here without my connections at Scotland Yard? They opened the gates because they know me!" He pointed at the released convicts. "I got your men out of Belmarsh!"

"You did not negotiate in good faith. You undersold the diamond to your preferred bidder."

"My preferred bidder is in the country from which the diamond was stolen! Where is yours from?"

"I don't know. Doesn't matter. My bidder is ready to move six hundred million worth of bitcoin into hard crypto wallets upon delivery."

"Mine will pay in gold bullion!"

"We're not going to India," the welder replied. He, the convicts and the four mercenaries lined up behind Sedgewick.

"How do you plan to get out? My buyer has two teams on the way to exfiltrate us!"

"We have a PSV coming down the Thames right now."

Bindar seethed. "A submarine?"

"Mini-sub."

"I suppose it's all good then, mate. We'll go with your bidder."

Ashley was shocked. Bindar was not the type to back down easily. What was he up to?

Bindar pointed to an old safe in the back of the jewel vault. It was the vintage safe that Bernard had pointed out to her this morning. "There's one last thing to do before we go."

Sedgewick looked at the safe, his interest piqued. "What's in there?"

"That's going to be the Heresford Ruby. Easily worth two or three million. We can't leave without it." He pulled off the dial of the safe and aimed his drill into the core. The drill bit spun and plunged into the steel. He was punching through the lock.

Ashley had never heard of the Heresford ruby. What was he talking about? Then it came to her. This was the safe waiting for the Haz Mat team because it was booby trapped with vials of tear gas.

Bindar must have known this. He after all, was a Haz Mat guy. He had probably defused these types of safes before. He would know that it was very easy to puncture the tear gas vials when punching through the lock. He did not seem to care. He pushed on the drill with force. She backed up. He was using this vintage safe as a weapon.

A cloudy gas emanated from the hole in the safe. Sedgewick and several of the mercs were caught completely off guard. They began to cough and hack. She held her breath. Bindar appeared to be doing so as well. He whipped out a gas mask and put it over his head. Then he pulled his sidearm. His mutinous comrades could not react in turn. They were too busy crying, sneezing and grasping their throats. She turned away as she heard gunshots.

**

The moon hid behind a cloud. Suddenly the Tower and environs were completely dark. It gave a false sense of security. Clive stayed low, still hovering near the ceremonial cannon. He knew the snipers used thermal target sights and infrared illuminators. Darkness was not a problem for them. The smoke did obfuscate their positions though.

"Stay below the parapets!" Clive said.

The men stayed low. And one woman. Sheila Hansty army crawled toward Clive.

"Hansty what are you doing here?"

" I led the hostages through the subway tunnel to safety."

"You should have stayed with them behind police lines!"

"I could not do that, sir. I belong here my brethren."

Clive poked up over the parapet briefly. More commandos took positions to prepare for the first wave of invasion.

"The terrorists have Ashley. I'm trying to manage on my own rather than have SO15 come in here with guns blaring."

"I support you, Clive." She picked up a crossbow.

He peeked through an arrow slit.

SAS divers rigged zip lines. He spotted three SO15 sharpshooters perched in neighboring office buildings. Drone techs in VR helmets revved the engines of assault drones. More commandos boarded speedboats below Tower Bridge.

His Beefeater grenadiers continued to man the ceremonial cannon on the Outer Wall. Archers held longbows with arrows at the ready. Others held crossbows. More yeomen held spears and pikes. They were certainly an anachronism in this age of modern warfare.

The first commandos donned cleats and prepared to climb the Outer Wall. In the distance eight or nine drones buzzed toward their position. Laser beads scanned the perimeter, obviously night sights for the sharpshooters. For some reason though, the helicopter squadron had retreated. Scratch that, there was one helicopter incoming.

"Ready yourself for impact," he warned Sheila. "Fire only on my order."

The phone rang. Clive picked it up. "Yes?" he asked.

It was Danforth. "You win, Clive."

Clive took a breath of relief.

"You have a friend in a very high place."

Clive knew it must have been the King. He must have seen television footage of the standoff. The last thing in the world His Majesty wanted was to see the Yeoman Warders fired upon by military counter-terrorism forces. The optics were terrible.

"Tell him thank you."

Danforth's voice hissed through the radio. "But only for the moment. You had better get something done very soon or all the king's soldiers and all the king's men will come back again. And this time there will be no stopping them."

Clive looked over the wall. The commandos on Tower wharf retreated. The drones flew back across the Thames. Assault boats withdrew to the other side of the river.

He had to go into the belly of the beast now. This was his Earth to Mars window, his opportunity to get into the vault and defuse the situation on his own.

He rushed down the steps of the Wakefield Tower.

John chased him. "What are you doing?"

"I'm going after her."

"You don't even know where she is!"

"Oh yes I do. I'm sure she is in the jewel vault with them."

"I thought this was a terrorist vendetta?"

"No, definitely not. It's a heist. Bindar is going to use the pandemonium of the maximum police assault to make his escape. I have to get in there before that. It's my only chance to get Ashley out."

John signaled his assent with a salute. "We will try to hold them as long as we can."

"Do not follow me. I go in alone. No one else."

"Okay."

"Go back and man the battlements. You will be in command if something happens to me."

"I'm just the Ravenmaster!"

"A damned good one too."

Clive descended the Wakefield steps and emerged downstairs on to Water Lane. He hoofed it to the Bloody Tower archway.

Clive waved over Warders Shuffington and Haverly. They stood guard at the lowered portcullis beyond which lay Tower Green.

"Open her up."

Shuffington and Haverly nodded and worked the block and tackle. The heavy wrought-iron latticework gate rose slowly. Clive entered the inner sanctum of the castle, hugging the walls to stay out of sight of any mercs on the Inner Wall. There were none.

He passed the empty Raven aviaries, the entrance to the King's house, the Bell Tower which he had originally used to sound the alarm. He sidestepped the entrance to the Beauchamp Tower and found it unmanned. Were the mercs already preparing a bug out? And from where?

The scaffold site was empty, affirming his belief that this was not at all about the spectacle of execution or retribution. He marched by the Chapel of St. Peter Ad Vincula. Its dignity and façade were unimpeached by the treachery taking place. It was a beacon of calm in the midst of the storm.

He tread lightly over the stone of the parade ground towards the entrance to the Waterloo Barracks and jewel house. As he neared the entrance he drew the Glock he had repossessed from Sven. It had about half its rounds left.

He emerged from the shadows in front of the vestibule. No one manned the entrance. Where had they gone? He slipped inside, whirling right and left with gun drawn. No one.

He turned a corner and looked down the corridor. He tread lightly through the hall, past the regal portraits of past and present monarchs. He reached the second chamber and stood outside the open doors, waiting to see if he could hear any movement inside. He heard nothing. It was absolute silence. Was this a trap?

He burst through the door and entered the second chamber with the video projections of His Majesty's regalia. There was an animated coronation procession for the benefit of the kids. Then actual documentary footage from the 1953 coronation procession played. There were no mercs, no thieves.

The grand entrance to the Treasury Room, aka the jewel exhibit entrance beckoned. Its doors were closed. Bindar had to be in there. He would catch them off guard. Once inside he would tell him the only safe way out was under his escort. He would protect him from the police. He would see to it that he could escape unseen but only if he gave up Ashley. It was a fair trade. A logical exchange. His life for hers.

He put his hand on the door handle and pulled gently. The door gave way. It was not blocked or barricaded. He could see inside where the patrol portal of the closed vault had been pried open like a fatal car wreck sliced open by the jaws of life.

He could hear the trickle of water beneath his feet. Those security conduits were definitely not sealed. In all likelihood the moisture had triggered the vault to elevate.

He pushed forward through the jagged, wrenched door to the patrol portal and that's when he saw it.

Absolute carnage. Dead littered the floor. His heart skipped several beats as he thought Ashley might be one of them. He scanned the bodies. They were all males. He recognized several of the faces. They were the crew that had entered the fortress this morning with Bindar. He also smelled the unmistakable scent of dissipated tear gas.

What had happened here? It was some kind of infight, some kind of mutiny perhaps, a double cross amongst thieves. It appeared the tear gas had been used to incapacitate the victims, and then they were shot at point blank range, execution style. The dead clasped jewels and baubles, lesser items of importance than the Crown Jewels. The victor of the battle had not cared to pry them from the hands of the dead.

Clive glanced inside the inner vault. He immediately saw the jewels from the Kohinoor display were gone. Of course it was the Kohinoor.

His main takeaway: Bindar had Ashley and the Kohinoor and they were at large within the castle. For the moment. But where?

***

Tower Green had a creepy vibe—it was deserted and littered with detritus, not the prim, medieval village plaza it usually was. Bindar held Ashley's hand firmly and led her across the parade ground. She could see damage to the Bloody Tower in the distance. Herman the Raven circled above. She was never happier to see him.

Ashley ripped her hand from Bindar's grip. "There is no way in hell you will get out of here this way."

Bindar waved his pistol in the air. "Oh, we'll get out."

"My father has been holding the Met back. They have the place surrounded and will enter any minute."

"I know. Isn't it grand?"

He led her to the entrance of Beauchamp Tower. They ascended the circular staircase in the center of the turret. She wondered where he was taking her. She was comforted by the fact that she had an insurance policy: the Kohinoor. It would keep her alive. *Diamonds are a girl's best friend.*

They emerged on to the roof. Bindar peered over the parapets. You could see the vast police presence across the river. More cops congregated outside the perimeter of the moat.

She looked down at the Beefeaters assembled on the Outer Wall. They guarded it from the besiegers, in this case the Met police.

It was an uneasy standoff, an eerie calm, the two factions standing down for the moment. The Beefeaters were hopelessly outgunned and they had to know that. But nonetheless they stood their ground. Ashley knew they were following Clive's orders. He likely believed that an attack by the cops would put her in greater danger, so he sought to prevent it. Wasn't that insubordination? She had placed him in this position. This was her fault.

If she had not come back here none of this would be necessary. The Beefeaters would not have to risk life and limb, their careers, their pensions, anything else they had to protect these walls from the counter-terrorism force assembled to deal with the infiltrators. She could only think that maybe her presence here served a purpose. Perhaps she was just not aware of it? She resolved not to regret the past but to live in the moment.

Bindar picked up his MP5 and leveled it over the wall. Was he going to shoot someone? Maybe he wanted to end this détente? He wanted the Met to come in here with guns blazing? Perhaps he needed the chaos to create a cover to escape with her in tow? Yes. She figured he wanted all out war between the Beefeaters and the cops. It was all to his benefit at this point.

He placed his finger on the trigger.

She elbowed him. "No!!!"

But it was no use. He fired indiscriminately at several positions on police lines.

"It's not the Beefeaters!" she yelled over the parapets.

The sound of her voice was drowned by the sound of automatic weapons fire. She ducked down beneath the merlons.

The sleeping dragon that was the police and counter-terrorism and SAS forces was awakened. They did not care who had fired the weapon. There would be hell to pay this time.

***

Gunfire reverberated in and around the stone walls of the castle. Clive rushed out of the Waterloo Barracks and looked around to see what was happening. He could not immediately ascertain the source of the shots. But he could make out two men sprinting toward him in the dark. He pulled his sidearm and prepared himself for an assault. Until a friendly voice rang out in the night.

"Don't shoot!"

It was the voice of John the Ravenmaster. Heath appeared behind him.

Clive placed his weapon back in its holster. He marched over to John. "I told you not to follow me!"

"Sorry, Clive. But you weren't answering on the radio and police are incoming."

"Who fired the shots?"

John frowned. "Not us. They came from the Inner Wall."

Clive figured it must have been Bindar. He wanted to trigger the assault. He wanted Beefeaters killed by friendly fire. It only helped his cause.

Clive picked up his radio. "All Beefeaters stand down. Do not engage Met. Let them come in. Do you hear that Danforth? We are standing down. We did not fire the shots at police lines. Those were fired by the terrorists! Bindar is at large in the Tower and he has my daughter as his hostage. He wants you to kill as many Beefeaters as possible. Please exercise all caution as you enter the premises. Do you copy?"

There was silence on the other end of the radio.

Clive clicked on again. "All Beefeaters take defensive positions and assist the Met CTC in any way possible." He handed John the radio and walked off.

John crinkled his brow. "What about you?"

Clive looked over his shoulder. "I have to find her."

John searched the dark sky for signs of the raven. "If only we could see Herman in the dark. He never lets her out of his sight."

Clive waved them off. "If he's even alive after eating that chip."

Heath's ears perked up. "What chip?"

Clive stopped walking. "She had some electronic locator fall out of her backpack. He accidentally ate it."

Heath's eyes widened. "If only we had her phone."

Clive dug into his pocket. "I have it but the battery is dead."

Heath held up a portable charger. "No problem. May I see the phone?"

Clive pulled it out of his pocket. Heath plugged it into the spare battery and it came to life. He pulled a small bottle of baby powder from a kit on his belt and sprinkled it on the phone screen.

Clive was curious. "What are you doing?"

"Hacking her password." He tapped the places where the powder stuck to the screen. The phone opened. He found the air tag app.

Clive was impressed. "The local phone network is down."

"Actually this is separate. A Bluetooth signal from the phone to the device. Good up to one thousand meters."

Clive raised an eyebrow.

John piped in. "If you can locate Herman, Ashley will not be far away."

Heath did a little jig. "I've got a location!"

***

Bindar led Ashley up the "wall walk" toward the Wakefield Tower. Below them and above it was pure chaos. The police landed a helicopter on Tower Green and offloaded a team of armed counter-terrorism police. They looked just like Bindar so he acted like one of them: a police commando rescuing a hostage. In the spotlit sky she observed Herman following them. His presence was oddly comforting to her.

Bindar took her through a doorway into the turret of the Wake-field. They descended one floor below. The covered bridge to the St. Thomas loomed. But its portcullis gate was closed. Beneath it was one of Bindar's compatriots, impaled by the iron spikes. Ashley cast her eyes away from the grim sight.

Bindar did not seem too concerned with the loss of life. He tried to lift the heavy grating. It did not budge. "The damn thing is locked!"

"I thought you wanted to take the subway tunnel? I can lead you there." She was doing her best to ingratiate herself.

Bindar thought for a moment. "No. We're not doing that."

He led her back upstairs to the wall walk. He pointed to the rain downspout bolted on the Wakefield's turret. It led to the roof of the covered bridge.

He pointed. "Climb it."

She reached into her pocket and pulled out the stone. "If I fall, so does your diamond. Why don't you take it? That way you can be sure..."

He backed away from her. "I am not taking that. Climb the downspout."

She decided to push his buttons. "What are you so afraid of? It's only legend."

"I was a police officer for seventeen years. Too many legends are true: Full moons bring out the psychos. If you ever say 'It's a quiet shift' the shit hits the fan. If you make plans right after your shift, something major goes down. Lucky gear whatever it may be, a special pen, a rabbit's foot, a picture of your mother, can protect you. There is no way I, a male, am touching that diamond until it's safely in the hands of its rightful owners. Know this, if I go down, you go down.

In other words, that diamond keeps you alive. If you don't have it I have no need for you."

Ashley climbed up the downspout. He followed. They reached the roof of the covered bridge and traversed to the Outer Wall.

She could see the Beefeaters in the distance, they were clearing the chevaux de frise and other obstacles they had previously placed on the gunnels in order to deter the police. Several of them were helping commandos over the walls.

Ashley knew she would not be released in some sort of hostage exchange even if that were possible. Bindar was planning on taking her all the way to his destination. Once she handed over the diamond to his buyers, she would be useless. No leverage. Subject to the whims of her captor.

She pulled out the lipstick her father had given her that very morning. She had kept it inside the waistband of her leggings.

***

As the main gatehouse to the fortress, Byward Tower had seen many dignitaries and historical figures pass through its entrance to conduct business with the king. This evening the Beefeaters opened the heavy doors to a squad of SO15 armed police. The yeomen directed the commandos through the stone archway to the Outer Ward. Red tuniced Yeoman Warders conversed with black clad police commandos. It presented an odd sight, Clive thought.

He bolted down Water Lane. Winklough, Heath and Sheila followed. According to the air tag Herman was hovering above St. Thomas Tower. That could mean only one thing. Ashley was at Traitor's Gate. Bindar was planning to make his exit there.

Clive reached the staircase that led to the moat. He scrabbled down to the first landing. The water level was much higher due to the explosions. There was now an opening in the Wharf wall where there had been none before.

It was like old times. The Tower had taken a four hundred year time warp.

He heard footsteps below. A peek around the corner wall and he got a glimpse of Ashley. She descended the last few steps toward the water with Bindar gripping her arm.

Where were they going? Were they going to swim? Certainly not. He saw a boat approach from across the Thames, it was the typical Met marine policing unit (MPU). Could it be a rogue? A decoy? He was not sure but it was possible this was Bindar's means of escape.

He scanned the area. What was the best way to take Bindar out? He had to do this himself. There was no way he had time to brief the Met about the situation in the midst of the pandemonium. He could take a shot from here but if he missed it would be all over for Ashley.

Then he saw the arrow loops. John drew close behind him. He spun around. "Give me your weapon."

John handed over his SA-80 carbine. He also offered a crossbow and a quiver of bolts. "You might consider this one. After all, it's what the arrow loops were designed for."

Clive nodded and took both weapons. He blew past the steps to the water gate and darted inside the door to the southeast turret of St. Thomas Tower. He descended down the quarry stone stairs, directly adjacent to Traitor's Gate unseen by Bindar or Ashley.

He passed an arrow loop facing the Thames. He glanced out over the river. He could see the Met command post, brimming with activity. Heavily armed commandos boarded more MPUs and embarked for the Tower.

They were applying brute force where a surgical strike was needed. He continued down the stairs towards the arrow loop that overlooked Traitor's Gate. There was a faint trace of light glowing through it, as if intentionally providing a beacon to him.

**

Ashley and Bindar stood at the edge of the steps of the water gate. She thought about what Clive had said, that this was the main entry to the castle back in the day. Back then it was much safer for the royals to travel to palaces by boat than through the crowded, dirty streets of the city. It had transitioned to the so-called "Traitor's Gate" in the 1500s, named after the doomed prisoners who had been brought into the Tower via this entry. Queen Anne Boleyn, Sir Thomas More, Edward, Duke of Buckingham and others were taken through this portal.

Now she was here. Unlike Anne Boleyn she was not being taken into the Tower but out. She was the captive custodian of the famous Kohinoor diamond.

Bindar signaled an incoming police boat. They returned his flash semaphores. Ashley did not entertain the thought that she was being rescued. It was obvious that Bindar was using the police assault as a cover to escape. The police boat beelined for their position. Was there a woman on the boat, someone who could take her place as the safe custodian for the cursed diamond? She did not see one. That meant only one thing: Bindar planned to take her with him, wherever he was going.

It was now or never. She drew up alongside Bindar and depressed the actuator on the lipstick tube. She sprayed his face from ear to ear with mace. He shrieked in pain. Reached for his eyes with his free hand. But he did not drop his gun. She decided not to try and wrest it from him. Instead she ran for the stairway.

Bindar stomped towards her, his vision still impaired by the pepper spray.

He could not easily aim his weapon in his present blinded state. But he could shower bullets in an arc.

Bindar wiped his eyes with his sleeve. "Ashley!!! I want the diamond! Where are you?" He drew closer to her. She quietly backed away from him, away from the water, back up the stairs.

The fake police boat drew ever closer now. There were two men aboard, dressed in police uniforms. She stepped forward on to the first step of the stairs back up to the Outer Ward. Then she slipped.

***

Clive dove down the stairs deep into the basement. He turned right to find an embrasure that looked directly over Traitor's Gate. It was a triangular room, not in use at the moment nor open to the public. There were gardening implements stored there! What sacrilege! He would have someone's head for this. He dragged a wheelbarrow, two rakes, a spade and a pickaxe out into the stone catacomb. He returned and kneeled before the arrow loop and peered through the cross to get his bearings.

On the lowest step of the water gate he made out Bindar, who pointed his carbine towards Ashley. She was dashing up the steps to get away from him. Bindar was stumbling, weeping.

Clive placed the SA-80 in the slot and aimed for Bindar's chest. He was wearing a soft Kevlar vest and an assault team helmet. Clive thought about this. The Kevlar would protect its wearer from a bullet but would it prevent an arrow from piercing through? He could fire the arrow at 300 feet per second. Unlike a bullet, the arrow had more weight behind it. The fiber mesh of the Kevlar was designed to absorb the kinetic energy of a projectile by catching it like a ball hitting a net. It was not designed to protect against the slicing action of a knife or an arrow. This was not a sure thing. If Bindar had a harder armor beneath the Kevlar the arrow could be deflected. But his chest didn't appear bulky enough for both. Clive had to make a life or death decision. He had only one shot to deter Bindar. If he failed Bindar would either kill Ashley or escape on to the river with her.

A police boat docked at the water gate. The men on board did not have military posture and their uniforms were disheveled. Clive could tell they were not friendlies. They were here to exfiltrate Bindar.

He dropped the SA-80, picked up the crossbow and aimed it. It felt at home in the arrow loop.

***

Ashley writhed on the ground as Bindar approached her. She had twisted her ankle. While he was still likely foggy-eyed, she did not have the speed to escape the range of his gun. Her only chance was in her pocket.

"Here, take it! Take the diamond!" She pulled out the large round stone. Even in the darkness it caught the dim light of the sconce and refracted it into beautiful colors.

Bindar cringed and lowered his weapon. "No. You carry it. Let's go..."

He wiped his eyes with his sleeve and stomped to her. Grabbed her by the arm. She tried to resist but the injured ankle gave way. She had no leverage. He dragged her towards the waiting boat.

Something caught her eye in the dim light. It was a broad edged arrowhead, emerging from the arrow loop down at the dock. The arrow followed Bindar as he walked. That must be Clive, she thought. But was she too close to Bindar to allow a clean shot? Her ankle smarted. She could not run away this time. But there was something else.

She rolled the diamond on the ground like a marble. "I'm not carrying it anymore." Bindar looked on in horror as it spiraled towards the water's edge.

***

Around 200 BC the arrow loop was invented by Archimedes during the siege of Syracuse. He designed the cross slit for archers to fire in defense of city walls yet remain protected from incoming projectiles. Over one thousand years later Clive was making use of this aperture. He held firm on his bow, following Bindar as he scrambled for the rolling Kohinoor.

He yelled at the two fake cops on the boat. "Get it!"

They leapt on the dock and fumbled for the rolling stone too.

Clive aimed at Bindar and plink, released the arrow. A gentle whoosh echoed off the masonry. The bolt arrived on target. Bindar's chest spasmed with a loss of air. He fell on his stomach. The shaft of the arrow protruded through his shoulder blade. The body armor had not stopped it.

He quickly reloaded and plugged arrows into the two fake cops. They each dropped to the ground.

***

Ashley watched the large stone plink into the waters of the Thames just off the wharf. It did not faze her in the least. She sat, catching her breath. She was lit by a dim sconce on the side of the water entrance.

Clive bounded down the stairs. She turned and rushed into his waiting arms.

He held her tight. "Are you alright?"

She smiled. "I'll be fine. Diamonds are a girl's best friend."

"I don't care about the diamonds."

She gasped. "I do. In case you're wondering, the one that just dropped into the Thames is a replica. It's from Alexandra's coronation crown, not the real stone." She pulled *the* Kohinoor out of her pocket and offered it to him. Then thought twice and pulled it back. "On second thought, I think this should stay in female hands, given all of the omens of late."

The look of relief on Clive's face was immense. "Suit yourself."

She could see her reflection in his eyes. There was one thing of which she was very sure at this moment: he did love her.

John the Ravenmaster and a team of Beefeaters rushed down the water gate steps to secure the area.

Clive leaned over to look at her injured ankle. "You do know that she who holds the diamond rules the world, don't you?"

"I'd settle for Queen for a day. Perhaps lunch at Le Caprice? Tea and shopping at Harrods afterward?"

He nodded. A tear came to his eye.

She looked out on to the Thames wharf to see Herman the Raven circling above. She had never been more grateful or glad to see him.

Chapter Twenty

The Chapel of St. Peter Ad Vincula was a sea of red. The Yeoman Warders looked regal in their dress uniforms, and the red was interspersed with the funeral black of civilian attendees. Ashley, dressed in black, sat in the third pew and looked to the pulpit where the chaplain delivered the service.

"And now in honor of the deceased I'd like to read a poem by John Dryden:

Happy the Man Happy the man, and happy he alone,
He who can call today his own:
He who, secure within, can say,
Tomorrow do thy worst, for I have lived today.
Be fair or foul or rain or shine
The joys I have possessed, in spite of fate, are mine.
Not Heaven itself upon the past has power,
But what has been, has been, and I have had my hour."

There was a moment of silence in the solemn hall. The chaplain continued. "These are the words our dear friend, Yeoman Warder Frank Kincaid lived by. He was known in the Tower community as a man with a hearty laugh, a zest for life and a depth of kindness seldom known. He is a man who lived. And in dying he allowed others to live as well. Looking down from the heavens, I am sure he has no regrets. In closing, we have some people who would like to share brief anecdotes of Warder Kincaid. Our first speaker is Chief Yeoman Warder Clive Bellamy."

Clive rose from his seat in the pew next to Ashley. She beamed at the sight of him. He walked up the aisle to the pulpit and addressed the crowd. "Yeoman Warder Frank Kincaid was a man who loved pranks, football and the Tower in that order. He was well known for his generally harmless capers, like the time he placed vanilla ice cream in the mashed potato tray at the mess hall. It was the first and only time I had prime rib a la mode. There was the time he tended bar at the warder's pub and extolled the virtues of the best Russian potato vodka, which turned out to be water. There was the time he hosted a game of footy in the moat and challenged us to a drop kick contest which he handily won because it turned out his ball was filled with helium. But there was one thing Frank did not joke about. That was the tradition of this Tower. He held this place as sacred and gave his life to defend this institution and those visiting here. In closing, I'd like to read this devotion to a yeoman warder:

A Yeoman Warder I would see
Tunic Aflare from neck to knee
His halberd held straight and high
His collar ruff'ed, the ladies sigh
From his chest the medals jangle
Marking many a foe he had to wrangle
He's acted in defense
Of truth, what's right and common sense
Oh he would a Yeoman Warder be
I'd be honored to have him stand with me

Clive stepped down from the pulpit and people stood. He sat down next to Ashley. She held a handkerchief tightly and daubed tears off her cheeks. On Clive's left sat John the Ravenmaster, who nodded in approval. In the row behind him, Yeoman Warders Hansty, Harrington and Weebly and the other Beefeaters bowed their heads.

***

Mourners streamed out of the chapel and congregated on the Green. A construction scaffold abutted the portcullis under the Bloody Tower. Masons repaired several walls where bullets took chunks out of the Caen stone. The parade ground was empty and clean, there were no clues a battle had taken place here recently. The entrance to the Waterloo Barracks was boarded up with a sign that read:

Please excuse our dust

Otherwise it was a perfectly fine Fall day at the Tower. The execution site and its memorial sculpture had been freshly cleaned and polished. The windows of the King's house had been washed. The White Tower rose into the sky at level right angles. The raven aviary was occupied again by the Tower ravens, except for Herman, who flew freely, directly above the object of his heart's desire.

Ashley looked up and smiled. She, Clive, Yeoman Warder Sheila and John mingled in the center of the Green.

John narrowed his eyes. "He's going to miss you."

Ashley paused for dramatic effect. "Who said I'm leaving?"

John face widened into a broad smile. "Is it true, Clive?"

Clive nodded. "She's decided to finish her last few baccalaureate classes remotely and then enroll at University College London for her master's degree."

Sheila piped in enthusiastically. "Master's degree in what, may I ask?"

Ashley did not hesitate. "Medieval and Renaissance Studies."

John hugged her. "Congratulations!" He offered a fist bump which she returned with gusto.

Clive bowed to the group. "If you'll excuse me I'm going to change out of the State Dress for the wake."

John sidled over. "What are you doing Saturday, Clive? I heard you had the day off. I'm going out to Kent for a day of falconry. Maybe you'd like to join?"

Clive shook his head. "I promised Ashley she is Queen for the day. We're off to Harrods for shopping and then dining at Le Caprice."

Sheila put her arm around Ashley. "Have you been before? Oh, you absolutely must see the Tiffany diamonds in the jewelry department."

Ashley shook her head. "No thanks. I'm off the diamonds for quite a while."

Clive walked towards the casemates. John and Sheila joined several other warders swapping stories about Kincaid. In the distance Ashley made out someone she recognized. It was Heath, dressed in gold corduroy slacks and a tweed blazer. He walked briskly towards the construction exit beneath Bloody Tower.

She ran after him. "Heath? Wait!"

He turned around and blossomed. "Hello."

"I had no idea you were here!"

"I wanted to pay my respects. Your dad said I could come. Such a courageous spirit. May he rest in peace."

She put her hands in her pockets and sighed. "Indeed."

An icy wind blew off the Thames. Heath shivered. "I best be on my way then."

Ashley took his hand. "Wait. My father told me what you did. I'm sorry I haven't called. Life has been such a whirlwind."

"No apology necessary. I understand."

"When I heard the story I don't think I was ever so happy to hear that a young gentleman was searching through my phone."

"I didn't see anything private. Just worked the air tag app like your dad wanted me to."

"I'm so lucky you did."

Heath pointed towards the sky. Herman criss-crossed the Green. "It's really the raven that deserves all the credit."

"Yes but they never could have seen him by cover of night without you."

"It was nothing, really."

"It wasn't nothing. You risked your life and I thank you for it."

"Did they pump his stomach?"

"Whose stomach?"

"The raven's. To get the air tag out."

"He pooped it out on his own."

If Herman could blush he would have. Instead he merely fluttered above.

Heath shuffled his feet. "I suppose you'll be going back to Cali pretty soon, yeah? Get a bit of sunshine?"

"Actually I am going to stay here and do my masters degree."

His eyes lit up. "What? That's great!" He immediately toned down the enthusiasm. She could tell he realized he had displayed too much emotion. It endeared him to her.

She pressed her hands together. "Thank you."

"What about your dad? Is he okay?"

"Yes, he's fine. A bruise on his chest the size of a golf ball, but doctor says he's mending nicely."

"He looks fit as a fiddle to me. But I meant about his job? I heard there was an inquiry?"

"He has been cleared, with help from His Majesty. Given the circumstances and outcome the council agreed he took the best action possible."

"That's good. So very good," Heath said. "Well, I better be going. May I call on you sometime? If you're not studying too hard, that is."

"Anytime. You're in my phone. But you probably know that."

He laughed. "I told you I didn't invade your privacy!"

She snickered. "Saturday I'm queen."

"Excuse me?"

"I'm having a day with dad. We call it queen for a day. He's taking me shopping at Harrods, then we're having dinner at Le Caprice."

"Fancy!"

"I wonder if you might like to join us for the dinner? Dad wouldn't mind, I'm sure. It would probably make him more comfortable given the posh environment."

"It would be my honor."

"Be there at seven. Dad's treat, of course."

"I'm looking forward to it."

"You should wear what you're wearing right now. You look smart." She winked.

"Your wish is my command, majesty." He bowed. She chuckled. He walked off under the Bloody Tower portcullis and turned down Water Lane.

***

Clive emerged from his flat in a blue blazer and gray slacks with comfortable loafers. He was ready for the wake. He turned the corner and found himself confronted by a stuffed shirt type and DI Emma Winklough.

The stuffed shirt offered his hand. "Good evening, Clive. I'm Superintendent Ian Danforth."

Clive shook Danforth's clammy palm. "Yes, I figured." He could tell a bureaucrat from a mile away. He had worked with too many of them in the service.

"You remember DI Winklough..."

Clive nodded politely. "Came to pay your respects, did you? I'm afraid you missed the main event. But we're hosting a small reception at the yeoman warder's mess. Tea, cakes and a bit of sherry, if I'm not mistaken. Please, follow me." He knew Danforth was not there to pay his respects.

The superintendent cleared his throat. "Is there somewhere we can talk privately?"

Clive straightened his collar. "You mean now? I'm expected at the wake."

"It won't take long."

"Very well," Clive said. He led them to the yeoman warder's offices and unlocked the door.

He ushered them down the hall to a conference room. The walls were decorated with the royal coat of arms circa 1603. At the crest was a golden crowned lion on all fours atop a knight's helmet. Astride the helmet on hind legs were a crowned lion and a chained unicorn. At the bottom of the escutcheon the Latin phrase: *Dieu and mon droit.* God and my (birth) right.

Clive sat down at the head of the table. "What seems to be on your mind?"

Danforth pulled out a folder with a stack of papers. "Before re-opening tomorrow, you need to have each and every member of your team sign this. I will have a representative here to collect them. Anyone who does not sign this document will not be cleared to work on these premises going forward."

Clive perused the document. "Secrecy agreement?"

"That's right," Danforth replied. "Boilerplate language. What we all sign."

Clive read further. "No one can speak of what happened?"

"That's correct. The entire incident is hereby classified information."

"What about the hostages?"

"They have already signed."

"What about the media coverage?"

"We are dealing with that, Clive. But we want no talk of diamond theft, the jewel vault, commandos or anything else."

"What about the death of Warder Kincaid?"

"He suffered a heart attack unrelated to the circumstances."

"No. I won't sign it."

"Then you are done here at the Tower. If you go to the press about anything, it will be considered outside the bounds of your previous secrecy agreement signed when you became a yeoman warder and you will be prosecuted. You will be labeled a conspiracy theorist and mentally unstable."

Clive groaned and looked at Emma. "So you're back in the saddle?"

"Yes, Clive, I signed it too."

Danforth added to her answer. "She has been demoted one rank for insubordination, to Deputy Inspector, with the opportunity to have the demotion expunged from her record for good conduct," Clive could tell this guy just toed the company line all day long.

Clive offered a mocking salute. "Very well."

"You will also need to have your daughter sign."

"And she will face no further repercussions?"

"That's correct. I'm sure she will understand, given her enthusiasm for the subject of diamonds. We must maintain the mystique of the Kohinoor at all costs."

Clive scooped up the stack of NDAs and placed them in a manila envelope. Then he rose from the table.

Danforth waved him back. "I have spoken to the Constable of the Tower and given the sensitivity of this issue we will need you to remain on post every day for at least the next week until this blows over."

"Saturday is my day off. I will be taking it."

"As I said, we need you on hand to ensure that the official story is properly related to any and all Tower visitors who ask about the incident."

"No. Not Saturday. John the Ravenmaster can fill in."

"What, may I ask, is so important that you absolutely cannot work on Saturday?"

Clive offered a resolute gaze. "My daughter is queen for the day." He marched out of the room and did not look back. He closed the door and strode briskly down the corridor. The exit to Water Lane beckoned.

He ventured into the cool night air and buttoned the top of his jacket. He looked up at the foggy sky.

Ashley greeted him. "There you are! I was looking for you." She was all smiles, almost aglow.

"Sorry. Just had to talk to the Superintendent."

She took his arm and they walked down the cobblestones towards the warder's mess. The entry was decorated with posies and hand-tied bouquets of lilies, gladioli and chrysanthemums. White lights adorned the windows and doorway. A string trio played Pachelbel's *Canon in D*. The soothing music calmed his nerves.

Chapter Twenty-One

The Yeoman Warder briefing room was full. It had a few tapestries on the walls but otherwise nothing was distinctive about it. Clive stood in front of the assembled Beefeaters. They wore their State undress uniforms: navy blue trousers and long coats with red trim and blue flat-hats. They each held a copy of the secrecy agreement. Clive paced before the chalkboard.

"You may not be happy about the edict from the Home Office. I am not either. I can only say sometimes there is a price to be paid for living and working at a World Heritage Site. Sometimes there is a moment when one must suck it up for the sake of propriety and dignity. Sometimes one must refuse to air dirty laundry on the world's stage because doing so only emboldens random sociopaths to imitate the behavior. I thank you for signing the agreement and I will be there to collect them at the door."

He walked to the door and took the papers from the men and women as they exited. One of Danforth's men stood in the back of the room, ready to collect the documents.

***

Clive walked with military gait through the newly repaired portcullis. He held the keys to the Tower. On the cobbles of Water Lane he was joined by gray coated members of the Grenadier Guards in bearskin caps. They marched in military lockstep down Water Lane to Byward Tower. There the sentries presented arms. Clive saluted and used the ceremonial keys to open the two thick green oak entry doors. Ashley cheered with enthusiasm.

The Tower was officially open to the public. Clive walked over the bridge and saw the moat dry again. The levees that kept the Thames out were newly rebuilt and stood firm.

He reached the Middle Tower, the gateway or barbican entry to the fortress. There he spotted a BBC News crew filming a reporter with a microphone.

The reporter gesticulated as he spoke. "American billionaire and developer Robert Slater, a visitor to the Tower, attempted to evacuate through the dry moat but was tragically killed as flood waters breached its walls. The moat has now been restored to its former dry state."

Clive scoffed. It wasn't so much omission of the facts that bothered him. It was that the true heroes of this episode would never be known. He did not care about his own exploits but he wished the public could know what the Beefeaters had done to preserve the monument. How they had risked their lives in the service of a sacred historic legacy. The official story contained no legendary acts of heroism or anything else.

He walked to Tower Wharf. The area was cordoned off from the public. The Honourable Artillery Company prepared three 105mm ceremonial light guns for a 21 gun salute. It was to celebrate the reopening. Clive placed his ear plugs in and stood at attention. The battery commander gave the order: "Fire!"

Gunners released the first of 21 rounds. Clive saluted as they reloaded and fired again. One round every ten seconds over the Thames. After three and a half minutes it was over.

He walked back to Byward Tower and greeted the tourists as they came in. "Welcome to His Majesty's palace and fortress, the legendary Tower of London!" He pointed out several Beefeaters on podiums. "Queue up around one of our Yeoman Warders for some fascinating facts about the Tower and its lore!"

A kid approached him. "Hey mister, what happened here? I heard terrorists took over the place?"

Clive guffawed. "Just a movie company filming." The kid jeered and pushed past him.

Emma Winklough arrived with her daughter Roxanne.

Clive held out his hand for the little girl. "It's about time we got you that tour that your mum promised you!"

Roxanne giggled and grabbed at his hat.

Emma spoke in an amused but scolding tone. "He needs his hat, darling."

"What brings you here, Inspector?"

"Deputy Inspector," she reminded. "I wanted her to see the Tower, the reason why I didn't come home that night."

Roxanne shook her finger at Emma. "My mommy stayed out too late."

"Yes, she did!" Clive agreed. "Let me get someone to show you around."

Roxanne protested. "We want you to do the tour!"

He doffed his hat. "Well then you shall have me!" He led mother and daughter through the entry.

***

Clive followed the throngs to the Inner Ward past the Waterloo Barracks. The queue had already started for the entrance to the Waterloo Barracks and the jewel exhibit. It was always the jewels—they were the main attraction for visitors in the past and today was no different. Enthusiasm was in the air as the true aficionados had been deprived of precious moments with the baubles. People of all ethnicities and backgrounds were present. Diamonds captured the imagination of all.

Security was beefed up. Extra Scots guards were on duty at the parade ground, marching back and forth with automatic weapons on display. Undercover security operatives lurked, dressed as tourists. Clive walked to the entrance of Waterloo Barracks. The guards nodded and stood at attention as he passed.

Inside the exhibition was as it was. The introductory room displayed portraits of past and present monarchs. The second chamber presented video projections showing the regalia. There was an animated coronation procession for the benefit of the kids and then actual documentary footage from the 1953 Coronation. Elegant, regal classical music resounded on high end speakers.

At the end of the corridor the grand entrance to the Treasury beckoned. One would never know that the walls had been jaggedly carved up only weeks earlier. Clive nodded at security operatives and passed through the hallowed doors. Visitors ooh'ed and aah'ed at the gems and trinkets on display. New security and display technology was implemented, including fiber optics. The diamonds were protected by 2-inch-thick (51 mm) shatter-proof glass.

Clive approached his main area of interest, the exhibit for the Kohinoor. It was shown as before in three incarnations: the diamond uncut as it came to Queen Victoria, the diamond's cut form on the crown of Queen Alexandra, and the diamond's final resting place, on the Queen Mother's crown.

He studied the diamond, none the worse for wear. He pondered its curse. Certainly he believed the previous and even current holders of the diamond had experienced tragedy and death in their times. Was this tragedy the result of a metaphysical vexation or simply the plight of greed and its consequences? He was not sure. Regardless, he would ensure the diamond's safety as long as it was within the confines of his castle, on his watch.

End Note

"Any legal claim to the diamond would be liable to dispute by several governments. Would Iran, Afghanistan or Pakistan agree that India, based on the Mughal past that its present Hindu rulers reject, has the strongest claim? And should the diamond be returned to the central government at New Delhi, or to the state government of Punjab, or indeed to surviving descendants of the last Punjab king, Duleep Singh, who was comfortably settled in England under royal protection?

There is no simple answer. If the diamond returns to India, it might be triumphantly exhibited for a few months and then buried in government vaults. That was the fate of the equally spectacular jewels of the Nizam of Hyderabad that the Indian government acquired two decades ago....

As with so many art treasures acquired over millennia by the British Crown and various museums, their provenance can be disputed ad infinitum and their legal ownership is almost impossible to establish. But what seems to me decisive in the case of...the Koh-i-Noor is the principle of making them as freely available as possible to the maximum number of public visitors from across the world. That criterion dictates that the diamond should remain where it is in the Tower...."

Dr. Zareer Masani, author and historian

Article published in the *Daily Telegraph* 13 October 2022

Also by David Boito

Valley Fliers
Bee Conspiracy
Fatal Castle

Watch for more at www.davidboito.com.

About the Author

David Boito is a screenwriter and novelist. He studied film at UCLA, where he also participated in the creative-writing program led by acclaimed novelist Brian Moore. He has written screenplays for Warner Bros Television and Revolution Studios. Boito's first novel, *Valley Fliers*, was awarded the *Literary Titan* Silver Award. His second novel, *Bee Conspiracy*, is recommended by *Kirkus Reviews* as a "seriously fun ecothriller." *Fatal Castle* is his third novel.

Read more at www.davidboito.com.

www.ingramcontent.com/pod-product-compliance
Lightning Source LLC
Chambersburg PA
CBHW050247110726
47898CB00007B/2310